HIGH LIGHTS

KAREN PERADON

RED FEATHER PUBLISHING

Book Cover by 100 Covers

Designed by Red Feather Publishing

www.redfeather.com.au

ISBN for print: 978-0-9942845-5-6

CONTENTS

PROLOGUE

Another hectic day at the Wavy Lady hair salon had come to a close; three brides, sixteen perms, and another dozen trims. Sylvia had a full appointment book the next day, too. She knew exactly how the day would go. Every client was familiar. Every cut tried and tested. No one was daring or different in the sleepy suburb of Hardup in Perth.

A brown Ford Falcon drove past, and she waved at the local bank manager, Reg Barrow. It was exactly 5.10 pm as usual, having closed the doors of the bank for the day. She knew old Mrs Whitely would walk her Jack Russell dogs in precisely seventeen minutes as she did every day. Nothing exciting happened in this remote corner of the world. She got her kicks from the hairdressing missions the United Guild of Hairdressers sent her on. The framed photos on the wall reminded her of the exotic places she had visited. But the head of UGH, Wizard Blowave, known as Wiz, had been quiet for months.

"Alright, Sylv, the towels are all put away. I'll see you in the morning." Her second-in-command, Jez, turned the sign to 'closed' and pulled the door open to leave. "Remember, I'm having a half day tomorrow to get me wedding dress sorted?"

"No worries, dove. Have a good night."

Sylvia locked the door behind Jez and turned off the lights. Jez's boyfriend, Clive, had finally proposed over a schooner of beer and fish and chips. Jez was as happy as a nit in a wig. Outside the shop window, Jez got into Clive's car and gave him a kiss. Clive was no looker, but at least her friend had found someone. Sylvia wondered when her prince in shining hairspray would turn up. There were slim pickings in Hardup.

She looked around her salon. She had owned it for ten years now. Perhaps she could redecorate—a lick of paint, new capes, fresh towels? Maybe time for a change of premises? Or a second salon? None of the ideas scratched the gnawing hole inside her—her love for adventure, the empty chair at her kitchen table, the ringless finger, the untold love story. She made her way through the salon, straightening a chair, pushing in a trolley, wiping a mirror. She leaned into its reflection and inspected her face. Time to bleach her upper lip. She could do with a trim to her round bob, too. She cursed her hirsute Italian heritage, and stuck her tongue out at herself. Mid-sigh number three, the phone rang.

"Wavy Lady Hair Salon, Sylvia speaking, how may I…"

"It's me, Wiz."

"Wiz, I was just thinking about you." She pictured her boss. He was one of those annoying men who never seemed to age. And what a quirky character he was. He had tightly curled white hair which frizzed around his head, and he wore colorful, outrageously tight-fitting outfits. "Where have you been? It's been months…"

"Yes, dear. I'm away. Not going to make it back in time…"

The line crackled.

"You're cutting out."

"The Golden Scissors."

"The Golden Scissors?"

"Can't get back, dear."

There was more interference, and Wiz's voice drifted in and out. Sylvia adjusted the phone, wedging it closer to her ear. "What?"

"... information coming through."

"Information?"

"Intercepted... no reports... investigate."

"You're not making any sense, Wiz."

"New mission." She could just make him out. "No data incoming to UGH. No requests for special agents."

"Are you saying that no one has been sending in their reports?"

Wiz had founded UGH to connect hairdressers across the globe. The salon owners reported all comings and goings, sales, trends and even rumors to HAIRnet (High Access Information Repository). In return, Wiz published a quarterly newsletter, the *Hair'd Honcho*, and put on the extravagant Golden Scissors Awards in Las Vegas every two years. But the real value of UGH was in its band of special agents. When there were problems in the hairdressing world, Wiz dispatched the trained agents to help. Sylvia had been an agent for ten years. She had first helped the world-renowned hairdresser to the stars, Vitale Crassoon, solve a hair dye fiasco. Since then, she had been on many assignments. Once, she'd caught a hair thief who made wigs with his spoils. In New Zealand, she'd assisted two feuding hairdressers to part ways smoothly. In one thrilling mission, she'd parachuted onto a private island to find a priceless hair pin. She'd even trekked through a jungle to apprehend a barber who was illegally harvesting the sap from a special tree that reversed hair loss. But it had been ages since she had been on a case.

"I'll come up to head office."

Sylvia jumped at the chance to drive seven long, boring hours north to the town of Kalbarri, where Wiz lived and ran the guild.

"No, go to Vegas. Everyone will be there."

"Did you say Vegas?" Sylvia squeaked.

A strange beeping noise filled her ears.

"Wiz?"

"Going out of range... find out what you can at the Golden Scissors."

The line went dead. Things didn't sound good, yet a thrill went through her. A new mission, a trip to America and... she looked at her calendar... she'd still be back in time for Jez's wedding.

MONDAY

1

Sylvia stood underneath a giant pair of golden scissors suspended from the ceiling in the foyer of the Pharaoh's Palace hotel, Las Vegas. She was out of breath and sweaty from climbing the steps to the hotel entrance. They resembled the base of a pyramid of Giza and were almost as steep. A pair of stone sphinx flanked the entrance, and the foyer was tiled in an Egyptian pattern. She gazed wide-eyed at the huge blown-glass baubles hanging around the scissors with the names and faces of past winners painted on them. Her dead husband Solomon Scutlash, ten years gone, twinkled from several. She gave his bauble a small nod and wondered who would win the 1987 Golden Scissors Award.

Hundreds of colorful bodies clamored, chattered and curled through the vast lobby. The crowd pulsated towards the check-in desk as each person fought to get served. Clouds of permed hair were back-combed to breaking point, creating a haze above all the heads. Voices shrieked, others laughed, calling out greetings, all dressed in a blazing array of shiny neon shades. Suitcases, hairdressing cases and trunks were piled around the foyer. The porters raced backwards and forwards, laden with luggage as the guests headed to their rooms. Sylvia sucked in a deep breath through her nose. The metallic tang of hairspray mingled with a mix of perfumes and the faintest whiff of singed hair. She closed her eyes and smiled.

Remembering her mission, Sylvia gawked at the mass of hair specialists. How was she ever going to find out why UGH was losing customers? She didn't know where to start. She wished Jez was with her, but someone needed to look after the salon, and besides, Jez would never have left her fiancée two weeks before her wedding day. And where was Wiz, UGH's leader? He had created the Golden Scissor Awards and had judged every competition. He must be somewhere far, far away. She wished she had a partner like all the good TV shows—Miami Vice, Cagney and Lacey, Starsky and Hutch. But as usual, she was on her own.

"S'cuse me, ma'am, coming through."

A porter maneuvered a trolley packed with cases past her. He wore a uniform of dark purple pants and shirt with a small striped turban instead of a cap. He broke Sylvia out of her reverie. She pushed her glasses back up her nose and steeled herself for the fray.

Sylvia smoothed the side of her conservative black bob, hoping she was presentable, and joined the queue. In front of her, a short, neat elderly man snapped at someone bumping into him. As the throng inched onward, a dense crowd of people gathered around a woman. She wore a bright blue skirt suit with sharply padded shoulders that extended way beyond their normal allotted space. The woman seemed to know everyone. She gave them air-kisses and hugs. She yoo-hooed across the foyer, blew kisses to others, waving her hands animatedly.

Sylvia progressed and reached two enormous banners with flashy silver lettering. It was advertising a brand of hair product called Fritz. The woman in blue was manning the Fritz booth, which displayed the range of products. Sylvia had not come across it before.

"Mr Borlotti! So glad you came!" the woman greeted the man in front of Sylvia. "You see! I told you Fritz would be featured here this year. Have you tried those samples I left for you?"

"No, as I keep telling you, Miss Feathercombe, I'm happy with the products I've used for the last 40 years," the man said.

"Oh, Mr B, don't be such a stick in the mud! This is the best stuff, cross my heart and hope to die! I'll come and have a chat later!"

The man raised his chin, shook his head a little and moved on. The woman moved her gaze to Sylvia.

"Hi, welcome to Pharaoh's Palace and the Golden Scissors! I'm Clippy Feathercombe from Fritz Hair. How do you do?" She held out her hand, which Sylvia took. Clippy's electric blue suit reflected her bright eyes. She sported a mass of tightly permed yellow curls which were clipped back on either side with diamante hair slides.

"G'day. Nice to meet you." Sylvia shook her hand.

"You in the hairdressing biz? You must be. Ain't anyone in Pharaoh's Palace this weekend who isn't. Here, let me give you one of my product brochures for you to look at. We have an excellent range of hair product. Fritz Hitz Shampoo, Fritz Ritz Conditioner and Fritz Fitz Lacquer. We are so proud to be sponsoring the Golden Scissors this year."

"Sponsoring?" Sylvia echoed. UGH had always been the sponsor.

"Yep, we are so excited! Here..." Clippy aimed a silver bottle at Sylvia's nose with the word Fritz blazed across the label like a bolt of lightning.

Sylvia sniffed. It had a spicy, fresh aroma.

"Very nice."

"Where are you from? Can't place your accent."

Sylvia had barely time to speak, let alone show off her accent.

"Oh, I know! You must be from Australia. Am I right? That's the only place I've never been, but it's on my list for this year."

"Yes, I am!" Sylvia was taken aback by the tidal wave of commentary.

"So you won't be aware of our wonderful range of product? You'll find some samples in your welcome basket in your room, but let me give you some more information."

She thrust a brochure into Sylvia's hands.

"Any questions; please come and see me. Great to meet you!"

Before Sylvia could say anything, another guest who Clippy clearly knew elbowed past her. Clippy reached up on her toes and put a kiss on the enormous man's cheek. He caught her up and twirled her around, squeezing her tightly. Sylvia shoved the leaflet into her bag and shuffled past them.

At last, she checked-in and turned to the next challenge of getting in an elevator and finding her room. But she was saved by a familiar voice.

"Mon Dieu! Ma petite angel! Sylvie, ma cherie! Over here!"

Sylvia could hear but not see the owner of the distinct voice. Through the towers of bouffant and back-combed hair, a hand holding a comb shot up somewhere in the middle of the lounge area.

"Vitale!" she called.

Sylvia pushed through a crowd of Madonna lookalikes, and Vitale elbowed aside a couple of mullets in turquoise and pink shell suits. A man whose hairstyle looked like he had a bleached palm tree growing out of his head obscured him for a moment and then, there he was; Vitale Crassoon, in a white suit with heeled silver snake-skin boots. Before she could take in all his short stature, he drew her into his embrace, and he kissed one cheek, then the other repeatedly until she sneezed.

"Monsieur, your fringe is tickling me!"

Sylvia's old friend was a world-famous hairdresser from London.

He sported a classic 'flock of seagulls' cut. His sweeping fringe dropped across one eye and met his curled handlebar mustache. On either side of his head, his hair was piled into wings.

"Aha! You like? Humphrey did it." He did a little twirl.

"Hump is here?"

"Oui, bien sur! He's checking us in."

"I'm so glad to see you! I was afraid I'd know nobody here."

"It's been too long, ma cherie. Are you entering any of the categories?"

"Oh no!"

"Why not, Sylvia? You are a very skilled 'airdresseur!'"

"Why thank you, kind monsieur, but no, I'm on a mission for you know who." She lowered her voice. "UGH."

Vitale linked her arm and guided her to the other side of Cleopatra's Fountain, which nearly filled the ground floor of the hotel. Instead of water, milk sprayed out of the fountain around a bronze statue of Cleopatra. It gave off a slightly sickly smell.

"Really?! What is going on? I 'aven't heard from Wiz for months."

"Me neither, then he rang me last week. Said he couldn't make it to the Golden Scissors, and that there's been a breakdown in incoming data to HAIRnet."

An upper-class English voice interrupted them.

"What are you two doing squirreled away over here? Sylvia-Sue, my old possum! Give Humphrey a hug!"

"Hi Humpo, so good to see you!"

"Oh, look at your hair, honestly! Don't you read Tatter in little old Oz? Oh well, I suppose I should be grateful you <u>have</u> hair this time."

He tried to break a thread of it out of her thoroughly lacquered bob.

"The Jackie O is so yesterday, sweetheart, come and see Humphrey and I'll give you a makeover."

Sylvia slapped his hand away and huffed. "I haven't seen you for years and the first thing you do is criticize my hair?"

"Give me a cuddle then, darling."

Sylvia hugged her friend, delighted she wouldn't spend the week alone. Humphrey turned to Vitale.

"Vitale, how much stuff do you need? It's taken the porter three trips to our rooms. I practically spent all my gambling money on his tip," Humphrey moaned.

"What do you mean? I packed light zis trip! Anyway, I am not merely flying in and out! After I 'av won zis prize, I have many clients who are coming to see me."

He went on to list the celebrities, fashion designers and other famous people whose hairstyles he managed. Then Vitale's eyes scanned over Sylvia's shoulder. "Merde! Sylvia, I must go. Ramone Figurelles from Ramona Foama 'as arrived. Agh! Zat man!"

Vitale shook his head angrily.

"What about him?" Sylvia asked, glimpsing Vitale's latest rival.

"I will tell you later. Meet us in the Babylon bar at 6.30 pm for the cocktail party."

Vitale took Humphrey's elbow and marched him across the crowded foyer, using him as a shield from Ramone.

As Sylvia was turning to head to her room, she saw a room-sized pyramid at the other end of the lobby from the concierge desk. A couple dressed as Cleopatra and Caesar came out arm in arm. The woman smiled at her escort and held up at the ring on her finger. Sylvia went closer. She could smell a wedding a mile off and couldn't resist eying the bride's dress and her hair style. The Nile Aisle Chapel had a queue of couples waiting, all dressed Egyptian style. There was even one Elvis Caesar, or Caesar Elvis—Sylvia couldn't quite decide. But as they cheered the latest newlyweds, a man in a cream linen suit moved in, holding a police badge up.

"You're under arrest," he said to the groom.

The bride squealed, and the groom unhitched his new missus and bolted for the entrance. Two uniformed police officers went to chase, but the linen suited man was quick off the mark. He grabbed a laurel wreath off a waiting groom's head and frisbeed it across the foyer. The solid plastic wreath hit the felon on the back of the head and he fell forward, skidding face down to a halt at the feet of the man with a palm tree hairdo. The hairdressers squealed and stood watching while the plain-clothed policeman, who was really quite hunky, grabbed the man and arrested him for polygamy and embezzlement. Sylvia was enthralled. It was like being on a TV show with a handsome cop and high drama.

She headed to the elevators, daydreaming about being paired up with a charming man like that detective, solving the crimes of the hairdressing world.

2

Sylvia took the plush elevator up to the 18th floor. She disembarked and looked left, right, then left along the endless corridors. She pushed up her slipping glasses and saw the sign pointing to her room number. Other guests bustled back and forth along the endless corridor with few distinct features, just door after door after door. She found her room at last and let herself in. This room was typical of the many hotels she'd stayed in—except for the large windows, which presented her with a view of Las Vegas. She looked forward to seeing the city lit up at night.

The porter had delivered her suitcase, and she heaved it onto the counter next to the welcome gift filled with Fritz hair products. Sylvia untied the gold ribbon and unwrapped the basket. There were two miniature bottles, one of shampoo and one conditioner, plus a small jar of gel and a little can of hairspray. The Fritz lettering glittered across the labels. Sylvia unscrewed the lid of shampoo and gingerly swept it under her nose again. It smelled fresh, a pleasant under-note of... what was it? A familiar aroma which she couldn't quite grasp.

Sylvia settled into her room with her hairdressing tool case set up on the dressing table. She unlocked the secret drawer with a scissor blade. It always gave her a thrill to hear it click open. She put her passport inside for safekeeping and retrieved the fax Wiz had sent her after their brief phone call. She cleaned her glasses and read:

My Dear Sylvia,

I'm sorry I've been out of touch. I'm on important business in a very remote location and unable to attend the Golden Scissors this year.

A serious issue has come to my attention.

THERE HAVE BEEN NO REQUESTS FOR SPECIAL AGENTS FOR OVER SIX MONTHS

I repeat: NO REQUESTS FOR SPECIAL AGENTS FOR OVER SIX MONTHS

Missions have always come in weekly. Who is untangling the issues of the hairdressing industry? Who is smoothing out the problems in the salons?

In addition, when I last checked in with HAIRnet, there had been no data incoming since early this year. My secretary reports she has received no post or faxes.

Without the sales data, trends, I cannot compile and send out the newsletter my patrons rely on. Nor can I complete my market research for the development of my new product, which will benefit the hairdressing industry.

Are hairdressers leaving the guild? Have they stopped sending in their reports? Your mission is to discover if members are leaving the union, and if so, why.

Anyone who is anyone in hairdressing attends the Golden Scissors, and so is the ideal place to get to the root of it.

Yours unwaveringly,

Wiz

As head of the United Guild of Hairdressers, Wiz should be monitoring incoming information regularly. Where on earth had he been all that time? This was serious. There was no other organization like it. The United Guild connected hairdressers all over the world. Wiz was their guru, the glue who gave them advice and information. Not only that, he put on the Golden Scissors Awards every two years and, most importantly, sent out special agents to comb out any mysteries or problems in the hairdressing industry.

There were as many members of UGH as there were hairs on a head. A select few, like Sylvia, were initiated as special agents. Going on these missions was her lifeblood. There were only so many blue rinses and local gossip she could stomach. Not only was the very web of UGH in danger, so was the only thrill in Sylvia's life. If no one was communicating with Wiz, then how was he able to serve them, and how would he know if they needed her help?

Sylvia took a deep breath. The Golden Scissors took place over a week. She had seven days to talk to over five hundred hairdressers and work out what was going on. Noticing the time, she put the fax away and headed into her bathroom to get ready.

Sylvia stood in front of the mirror just like she did every single day in the salon. Instead of studying someone else's reflection, now she inspected her own face. She had a few faint lines between her eyes, a slight crease around her neck. Where had the last ten years gone? Into the Wavy Lady Hair Salon, that's where. She'd hired and then lost so many staff members to marriage and motherhood, but here she was thirty years old, stuck on the shelf like the holey worn-out towels in her storeroom. The few dates or love interests that dotted her past had come to nothing. Maybe it came down to either marriage or business. Maybe she wasn't meant to have both. She sighed and took off her glasses. Now she looked better; in soft-focus. Maybe that's what she needed to do; not look so closely and ignore the flaws she saw in herself and others. But that was what made her good at her job—cutting hair and investigating for UGH.

In the shower, Sylvia let the water wash over her head. She reached for her own bottle of shampoo but withdrew her hand. Should she try Fritz? Dare she? Her own hair caused her enough problems as it was—thick and wiry and only behaved under the firm control of the most potent hairspray and a strong tong. She opted for her usual brand and gave her arms a workout, washing out the old hair product and combing out the knots.

Once out of the shower, Sylvia dried, styled, straightened, styled, combed and sprayed. She smoothed down a few stray hairs that still escaped. Was her hairstyle really that bad? She fought with her thick black hair every morning to contain it in the round bob. She wasn't sure what else to do with it. Give her another person's head of hair and she could work wonders, but her own mop was a different story. Maybe she should let Humphrey at it, but his avant-garde style scared her. She learned in Tatter (which Aussie's did read, thank you very much) that his latest fad was adding extensions, not just a few, but hundreds, creating a bunch of crimped strands that weighed as much as a large cat. One woman had threatened to sue him for damage to her neck as she carried around a heavy topknot.

Sylvia told herself she was quite content with her look, even if it was 40 years out of date. But maybe it was worth stopping by the hotel salon on the way to the cocktail party and allow herself some time in the seat for a change. Besides, the salon would be the first place to begin her inquiries. She could kill two barbers with one cut!

The in-built clock in the headboard clicked over the hour. She'd better get a move on if she was to meet Vitale and Humphrey at 6.30 pm. She wiggled into a black knitted turtle-neck dress. It was suitably invisible for sleuthing against the neon-hued tutu skirts everyone wore these days. As an UGH agent, she disliked drawing attention to herself. She reapplied a frosty pink lipstick to add just a dash of color. Another squirt of hairspray and she was done. It was time to get UGH back on track and then have some fun with her friends.

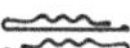

Sylvia walked wide-eyed through the world-within-a-world of the hotel. She took in the sumptuous decorations; great lofty ceilings, oversized lounges, the faces of Cleopatra and Tutankhmoun decorating walls, and golden motifs everywhere. You could survive in here for months before needing to go out into the city below. The choice of shops and recreations was mindblowing.

The Pharaoh's Palace Hotel had twenty floors. A sumptuous lobby had a large seating area around Cleopatra's fountain and at the opposite end of the large hall, the Nile Aisle chapel. The casino and slot machines lived on the entire first floor. The second level housed the grand Dynasty Ballroom, along with two cavernous function rooms and smaller conference rooms. Above that were sixteen levels of bedrooms. Sylvia's room was on the 18th floor, and above her was a shopping mall, a gym, a beauty salon and, of course, the current center of the universe; the hairdressers called Salon Sphinx. Guests could enjoy all recreations on the top three floors. On floor 20, one could dine at an abundance of restaurants and drink at several bars. The roof of the hotel was a giant gilded pyramid, where one facet was open. There was a swimming pool, spa and bar with 'golden, commanding views', the brochure had bragged. Plus, there were six enormous penthouse suites that could allegedly house a large family of camels and their owners.

Sylvia stood outside Salon Sphinx and looked inside the glittering hair palace. It was the biggest salon she had ever seen. Seven stylists were hard at work along the four banks of booths that ran down the floor of the salon, not dissimilar to a bank of slot machines. Fruit motifs, jewels, and, of course, 777s decorated the mirror frames and, in the counters, were actual slot machines. Along most of the back wall, patrons occupied five of the six wash basins, wearing capes covered in dollar signs. It seemed Sylvia wasn't the only one wanting a haircut. She looked up to see the UGH motto Nihil Mali Capillos—Do Hair Not Harm—above the door. She stepped inside behind a crowd of people waiting to talk to the manager. While she waited, she took it all in. One couple talked about Wiz not judging and who would take his place on the panel of three. Another pair argued over who might get through to the finals. The brash Clippy Feathercombe also took up space. She was having another animated conversation with Mr Borlotti, who sat in a chair reading a piece of paper. He grumbled something and thrust the page back at Clippy.

Sylvia waited for the manager to finish booking a hotel guest for an appointment later in the week. She tuned into the conversation happening beside her.

"Look Mr B, it's a good deal. Just give me a go."

"Listen lady, I've told you a million times, I'm not interested. There are plenty more knots in the beehive. The hotel's full of opportunities. You don't need my little barbershop to make you successful."

"It's not just one little shop, though, is it?"

"Yeah, yeah, yeah, so I own a few shops. You still don't need my business. Now get outta here." He turned away from Clippy. "Hey, Bonnie! You got that coffee on?"

"Be with you in a sec, Giuseppe," the manager called out.

Clippy turned. Her mouth quivered, then set in a straight line as she noticed Sylvia watching her. She gave Sylvia a dazzling smile.

"Oh, howdy again. Crazy in here, ain't it? Well, I've gotta get ready for the show. Enjoy your evening!" Clippy swept out and Mr Borlotti picked up his newspaper and gave it a flick.

"Hi there," a bright voice said. The manager was waiting to serve her.

"G'day. I don't usually get my hair done by anyone else, but I was hoping you could squeeze me in for a makeover..." Sylvia grabbed the end of a lock of her hair. "I've been told the Jackie O look is long gone."

Bonnie smiled. "I'm sorry ma'am. I'm booked out all week. Let me see where there's an opening free after that."

"No worries, dove. I'm only here for the week. I'm sure I can find someone else to help me."

"Pretty certain you will in this place. Good luck!"

"By the way, I see you're an UGH member." Sylvia gestured to the motto. "I've been asked to check on members by head office. Everything going OK? Managing to send the reports in?"

"That's very kind of you. Yes, I'm faxing in my report each month."

Sylvia smiled and thanked her. As she turned to leave, she caught her reflection in the mirror. Humphrey was right. She looked ridiculous in contrast to the waves and shaves, the highlights and bleached tips that surrounded her. She needed a cocktail to cheer her up.

3

Humphrey shrieked when Sylvia arrived. The cocktail bar was thick with guests dressed in neon colors, lace gloves, bangles and back-combed hair. Pink, violet and turquoise lights along the floor, bar top and shelves behind the bar clashed, making Sylvia feel tipsy before she'd even had a sip.

"Sylvia, where have you been? You just missed the most entertaining showdown in hairbiz!"

At that moment, Vitale arrived back from the washroom. He quivered with rage. His cheeks a ferocious pink against the blond point of hair that covered most of his face. The acidic lighting extenuated his bright red, blistered lips.

"'Umphry Le Bonne, you could 'av backed me up. That leetle piece of dandruff... how dare he insult me?" Vitale murmured like a ventriloquist.

"What happened?" Sylvia said, stifling a laugh.

"Ramone happened," said Humphrey. "He and his stooges came into the bar and bought Vitale a cocktail."

"That was nice of him."

"Except the cocktail was a Flaming Flicklicker."

Sylvia looked puzzled.

"The barman lights the cocktail. It's a bit showy, flames coming out of the glass, rah, rah, rah!" Humphrey flickered his fingers above the glass. "Except the barman lit it and then extinguished the flames before he served it. When Vitale took a sip, it practically singed his lips to the side of the glass."

"Zat cheating leetle dicksqueak. I will not stand for this! 'Ow was I supposed to know it would be so hot?" Vitale winced as he tried to shout. "The great Vitale will not be outsmarted!" he mumbled and stormed out of the bar, leaving Sylvia and Humphrey chuckling guiltily.

"We shouldn't laugh. That was a pretty low trick. We'd better keep an eye on the monsieur."

"He can look after himself. I don't want to be a man-babysitter, sweetie. Humphrey wants to play this week."

"Play?"

"The casinos, possum. Las Vegas time is make us money time!"

Sylvia tipped her head to one side and frowned at him.

"You know the casinos are usually the only ones to profit from gambling, don't you?"

She sipped the lurid blue cocktail that was so sweet it made her tongue curl into a lollipop. She unstuck her cheeks from her teeth.

"I've got the Midas touch, baby. I can feel it in my waters and my waters are never wrong."

"I've got enough to do with solving this mystery to be distracted by gambling. You're still reporting to UGH, aren't you?"

"Yeah, yeah, of course."

"Every month?"

"Of course, possum." He waved his hand in the air. "Anyway, back to my plan. They say Australia is the lucky country, so you can be my mascot. Let's hit the tables tomorrow after the first round."

"I don't know, Humphrey. I should really…"

"Great, it's settled then."

People finished their drinks and were now leaving the bar en masse.

"The show's starting. Let's go."

They followed the crowd to the Dynasty Ballroom, where the competition would take place. When Sylvia and Humphrey joined Vitale, he had applied a thick slather of moisturizer to his lips, making them shine from under his mustache.

"Are you OK, Monsieur?"

"Non, ieei keei at iicile!"

Sylvia and Humphrey looked at him sideways.

"I think he said he will kill that imbecile," Sylvia suggested.

Vitale nodded in agreement. She could see she would have to help her two friends as well this week. They seemed incapable of keeping themselves out of trouble.

The excited mass of hairdressers was loud and the atmosphere flamboyant, everyone merry from the free cocktails and champagne. Reflecting the lights as it spun on its podium, the most coveted trophy took pride of place in the middle of the stage. The huge solid-gold statue of open scissors glittered next to a display of the Fritz products. Sylvia was already getting sick of seeing the brand emblazoned everywhere.

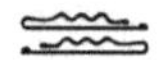

Music burst from the speakers. An orchestra sounded DUM, DUM! Then trumpets screeched. Sparklers erupted along the front of the stage. DUM DUM the intro went with more trumpets. The curtain shot up to reveal a glittering, towering drag queen. DUM, DUM! pumped sassily out of the speakers. She stepped forward in a diamante encrusted golden frock with a long trail which swooped from side to side as she sashayed to the front of the stage. She teasingly dragged her taloned fingers across the trophy. DUM, DUM went the music and elephant-like trumpets sounded. Her hair, sprayed gold, was piled and curled up into a huge beehive. Dum, dum. The music quietened, and she opened her mouth and sang:

"Goldenfingers!"

She glared at the crowd and twirled her hands around her head.

"Hairdresser, curl presser with a golden touch

An emboldened touch

Such precious fingers

Beckons you to enter his hair salon

Puts the cape on

Golden scissors will puncture the air

Runs his fingers through your hair

For the golden client will know when he's preened her

You can never stay away

from Mr Goldenfingers

Pretty hair be aware of this master cutter

Slices hair like butter

Golden scissors will puncture the air

Runs his fingers through your hair

Once under his grip, you'll never escape

The one and only cape

Of Mr Goldenfingers!

Pretty hair be aware of this master cutter

Makes your heart flutter

He loves only hair

Only hair

Only hair

If you enter, beware

He loves hair

Only hair

Golden haaaaaaaaaaaaaaaairrrrrrrr!"

She belted out the last few notes and ended in a dramatic bow to thunderous applause. The curtain dropped. Everyone whooped and whistled, yelling for more, more!

A man's voice boomed out of the sound system.

"Well, good evening, Hair Pressers and Style Expressers! I'm your host MC Brian Charmly. Welcome to the first evening of the 1987 Golden Scissors Competition!" He elongated the last syllable. "Let's give another round of applause to our amazing resident cabaret act... Ava Rice! Isn't she magnificent?"

The crowd of fluffed up hairdressing folk cheered and clapped. Brian continued.

"Anybody, whether they are royalty, or a movie star, a politician, a mother, a food handler, or even a chimney sweep, desires to look their absolute best in public. Every day these people visit their favorite hairdresser at their favorite salon. They sit in the chair for an hour or more with someone they trust, someone who makes them look better, feel better. Someone who can match the image they have of themselves in their head to the one they see in the mirror. And that someone is you, my fine people!" The crowd cheered. "As you work your magic, your client feels safe. You are their confidante. And amid the swirling salon of blow dryers, the chatter and the gush of taps, they will cheerfully impart their life story, their darkest secrets, their deepest longings to you, their new best friend. Who doesn't value loyal, trustworthy, talented and downright magical folks like you?"

The puffed-up coiffures beat their feet on the ground and clapped.

"So now let me introduce you to our judges... Aaaaaaal Fa'Rou!

Over to you!"

A handsome man bounded on the stage. The crowd hushed. Al Fa'Rou was one of the founding members of UGH who Sylvia had met when she was first initiated. He was tall and lithesome with an enormous afro that held itself in a perfect sphere. He wore an electric blue velvet dinner jacket and black jeans. The music faded.

"It pleases my body and soul to see your bright faces," Al said into the microphone. "To gaze across the ocean of hope and hair, to feel the beat of your hungry hearts, to taste the thrill of the competition in the air... Yes, it brings me such sweet joy! We have a vast array of heart-stopping events lined up for you this week, and of course, the finals and award ceremony. On Sunday night, we will declare the winner of this coveted trophy, the Golden Scissors!"

Sylvia joined in the cheers and applause. Al quietened the audience with one hand.

"Let me bring on stage my co-host, someone you all know and love... Emmy-Lou Bangs. Put your hands together!"

Emmy-Lou skipped on stage. She wore a tight pair of stone-washed jeans that flared out below the knee with tassels. Her long blond hair was crimped like a washboard. The crowd clapped and whistled as Emmy-Lou cowboy-hopped across the stage to Al. He held the microphone to her.

"Wah hoo! Thanking you Al. So good to be here again! Howdy y'all! How y'all going?"

The crowd erupted again.

"How are you, Emmy-Lou? Tell us what you've been up to," Al crooned into the mic.

"Wayell, as y'all know, I decided to pursue ma songwriting career. Ah've had maself a busy ole year, scooting up 'n down this fine country of ours, touring with ma band. We've just loved performing in all the hairdressing salons. Now y'all from all over the rest of the world... ah'm comin' to visit ya next year."

"You can pluck my strings any time!" someone shouted out.

Emmy-Lou laughed and waved her hand at the comment.

"Emmy, before we go on, I'd like to first of all thank our sponsors for this year's Golden Scissors."

"Uh, huh. Have you tried the Fritz products, Al? They are ace! In fact, let's ask our friendly rep on stage to tell us more about it. I'd like y'all to give a warm welcome to Clippy Feathercombe!"

Clippy came on stage with an off the shoulder layered lace, neon pink dress with shiny matching stilettos. She strutted over to Emmy and Al.

"She's all over the place, this woman!" Sylvia said to Humphrey.

Clippy leaned into the microphone. "I am so thrilled to be here this year to introduce everyone to this choice new range..."

Clippy held up a bottle of shampoo and repeated the same pitch Sylvia had heard that morning. "So check out the complimentary samples in your rooms. Come sign up with me for all the benefits my company is offering you. Get your mitts on some Fritz!!"

"Thank you, Clippy. I bet y'all can't wait to try it if you haven't already!" Emmy-Lou said.

Al nodded. "Emmy-Lou, would you like to tell our eager crowd of hair teasers all about our new fellow judge?"

The audience shuffled. Word had already got out that Wiz was not attending this year's awards. Sylvia had heard murmurings and there was high anxiety about who would replace him to judge the heats.

"Sure. Are you folks ready to meet this year's special judge?"

The crowd yelled "Yes!"

"Ah cayn't hear ya!" Emmy-Lou put her hand to her ear, and the audience ramped up the volume.

"Well, alrighty then! Of course, we miss our respected Statesman Wizard Blowave."

The floor threw out a few hear-hears.

"Don't you worry now, he'll be back next year as fresh as ever."

Hoorays followed.

"But for the 1987 Golden Scissor Awards we would like to welcome... another pillar of the hair AND BEAUTY AND FITNESS industry..."

The crowd took an in-breath and recoiled. The fitness industry? The beauty industry? They had had a wobbly history with the hair industry. Complete hair removal did not sit well with many hairdressers. An unhappy ripple went through the audience.

Al resumed the introduction. "A hugely respected giant of our closely connected friends in the gym, spa and cosmetics sector, the one, the only, the not-to-be-messed-with... Geeeeeeeeeeeeeeeeeene BUSTLE!"

4

From the left wing, the stage tilted and creaked as one silver sneaker stepped out from behind the curtain, followed by the other. Bright orange narrow shins supported enormous bulging thighs. The bum was caught in impossibly tight shorts before the body flared out like an inverted pyramid into a rippling tangle of bronzed muscles, barely contained by an open tracksuit top. His head looked too small for the shoulders, especially since there was not a single hair on his head. The crowd was unified in a silent breath before Al clapped into the microphone and the crowd reluctantly followed. Emily-Lou stretched onto her tiptoes to kiss Gene on his smooth cheek, and Gene took Al's hand in a firm shake.

The once gregarious hairdressing crowd was now so silent you could hear a hairpin drop. Al looked to the wings and gestured to an invisible stage manager. The music blared again, drowning the silence.

"Let's give him a round of applause, beautiful people!"

Obligingly, they clapped a semi-decent welcome. Gene nodded, his large flat forehead morphing into a shiny bald head. He drew his lips up into a pout and threw his balled fists in the air. His biceps nearly ripped the sleeves of his tracksuit. He turned his body slightly one way, then the other, and looked lovingly at his muscles. A couple of people whistled.

"We're thrilled you could join us, Gene. Would you like to say a few words to our audience?"

"Thank you, thank you. Boy, what a crowd, you're too kind, really!" He smiled to show a row of perfectly straight white teeth. "It's a dream come true for me, Al. I've watched the hairdressing industry from the sidelines for many years and, as you all know, I'm not a hairdresser."

More murmurs from the floor, but one man clapped loudly. Sylvia could see it was another body-building fan at the front of the stage.

"But I had a vision when I started out. I had a wish that the hair and beauty industry would unite. It's a dream come true that Bust-a-Butt Gyms and Spas have opened in this hotel, and an honor I've been invited here this week to judge this prestigious competition. I hope it will be the beginning of a long and fruitful union."

The reception for Gene was so damp, it's a wonder anyone's perms stayed fluffed. Though the one man near the front of the stage seemed to be a fan.

"Thank you, Gene," Al stepped in. "I know we're all eager to get acquainted and show you our stylin' ways this week. Now friends, let's get this partay started with our very own Emmy-Lou and the Toning Tongs!"

Everyone was immediately back on board and screamed as the trophy was wheeled off and Emmy-Lou reappeared with her guitar. The backdrop curtain lifted with another spray of sparkles. The rest of her band were at the ready and a drum rhythm set off the first song.

All the hairdressers, stylists, barbers, artistic directors, product consultants, owners, managers and apprentices let their hair down and crowded onto the dance-floor at the foot of the stage. Sylvia viewed the throng in dismay. How was she going to speak to all these people in one week? The thought exhausted her. Her eyelids drooped. But the answer was in here somewhere, and she forced her eyes open again.

"Zis is no fun without champagne, but my lips are too sore to hold against a glass. Pah, I'm going to bed," Vitale moaned.

"And I can't keep my eyes open. I'm going up too," Sylvia yawned.

They waved at Humphrey, who was jigging on the dance-floor. He laughed and swung a girl around him. Al was also shaking his butt. Ramone high-fived Gene as they discoed. Clippy was being commandeered by the body-builder Sylvia had seen her with earlier. The bodies of hundreds of crimped and pimped pulsed in time with Emmy-Lou's songs.

Out in the deserted foyer, Sylvia and Vitale could hear the faint thump of music as they waited for the elevator.

"So, what's the story between you and Ramone?" Sylvia asked.

"'E is a bully and a cheat!"

"How do you know?"

"In 1979, I won my first Golden Scissors. Two years later, I won again and just beat Ramone. In 1983, zat bastard played dirty and beat me. Ach!" Vitale clutched his stomach. "Zee humiliation! He short-circuited my hairdryer, and I nearly killed zee poor model."

"What?!"

"Oui, but I could not prove it was him. But I know it..." He thumped his heart. "in here. I was too busy to compete in the following one and dat pipstick somehow won. This means he will be the only other person to win three times in a row. He will attain your dear 'usband's record and be the reigning champion. And I tell you, Sylvia, he will do whatever it takes, anything, to do it."

"He'll never beat you, Monsieur. We'll make sure of it. I certainly don't want to see his ugly mug all over the magazines."

The winner of the Golden Scissors enjoyed two years of free publicity. They were in demand for fashion shows, interviews and for tending the locks of the rich and famous.

The elevator doors opened, and a man stepped out.

"Sylvia!"

"Jerry!" Sylvia turned to Vitale and introduced him. "This is my Australian sales rep for Latherlongs. It's my favorite range of salon shampoo, conditioners and styling products. He's been supplying the Wavy Lady for years."

"Pleasure," Vitale bowed.

Jerry was stocky and favored denim on denim. He wore his shirt tucked into stone-washed jeans and a Rob Lowe mullet. His fringe flicked to one side with frosted tips.

"G'day love. Didn't know you were coming this year. How ya going, chook?" Jerry said.

"It was a last-minute thing. Good to see you."

"I will leave you to talk. Bonsoir, ma cherie. I would kiss your hand, but..." he waved at his blistered lips. Sylvia smiled and pecked him on the cheek.

"Goodnight, Monsieur. Sleep well. And don't worry. You'll win the Golden Scissors. Come hot or high water, you will!" He disappeared as the doors closed. She turned to Jerry.

"Can you believe this place?" he gushed. "They're giving out free grog, the buffet is out of this world. Why haven't I come before? Latherlongs would go down a treat!"

"I think you missed your chance. I see Fritz is sponsoring the awards this year. Looks like there's a bit of competition for Latherlongs."

Jerry's smile dropped. He held his gold-ringed fingers palm up. "I saw that. Who's that chick? Clippy Feathersomething? That she-monster is running ringlets around us, Sylv. She's pushing all the other brands out of the market. Even L'Haireal is losing ground. No one has ever had the opportunity to sponsor the Scissors before. UGH always puts up the cash, and then, BOOM!" he yelled, making Sylvia jump. "This newbie arrives on the scene out of nowhere, plastering her goddamn leaflets everywhere, shoveling free samples like they're snow in Canada and getting in everyone's face like a bloody Halloween ghoul!"

"She's good at her job, that's for sure. What are you going to do?"

"I'm going to throttle her bloody neck, that's what I'm going to do."

Sylvia looked at him wide-eyed.

"Agh, I don't know, Sylv. Talk to people, give discounts, beg!" He threw his hands in the air.

"Hey, have you heard anything about clients backing away from UGH on your travels?" she asked.

Jerry shook his head. "No, no one's said anything. Why?"

"Apparently membership is down. Let me know if you hear anything."

"Sure, sure."

There was a beat of silence, then Jerry said, "Have you used it?"

"Used what?"

"That Spitz Jitz Gitz stuff."

"Fritz? Oh no, not ye…, I mean no, Jerry," Sylvia spluttered.

"I hope you aren't thinking of dropping Latherlongs."

"Of course not, Jerry! Your stuff is the best. Besides, Fritz isn't even available in little old Aus."

Jerry humphed. "You're right, you're right, Sylvia. Us Aussies have got to stick together. Remember that, Sylvia. No good comes from a monopoly. Trust me, I never won at that game."

The elevator arrived.

"Aren't you jet-lagged? I'm off to bed," Sylvia yawned.

"Nah, not me. I'm used to getting around. I'm gonna join the party.

See you around, Sylv. Stay true blue!"

In the solitude of the elevator, Sylvia exhaled. She was sure Jerry was exaggerating. No new brand had the power to push everyone else out. Jerry was just fearful of losing out on sales. But that did give her an idea. If Clippy had been visiting all the salons, she might be able to shed some light on the missing data. She resolved to have a chat with Clippy the next day. Questions rolled through her mind. How was she going to untangle the mystery of the missing data? Would Ramone bully Vitale again? How much money would Humphrey lose in the casino? And should she go against her supplier's wishes and try Fritz?

TUESDAY

5

It was deadly quiet in the dining room at breakfast after the big opening night. Sylvia was awake before the birds farted thanks to jet lag, and she tucked into the enormous breakfast buffet on offer. She revisited for a second course of bacon, mushrooms and eggs.

"Good morning! Don't eat the scrambled eggs, they're as tough as a dead man's gizzard."

Sylvia raised her head from the bain-marie filled with fried bacon to identify the voice.

"I didn't catch your name yesterday," Clippy said with a lip-sticked smile spread across her face.

"Sylvia, Sylvia Scutlash."

"Great to meet you! Did you try the Fritz shampoo and conditioner yet?"

"No, no, not yet."

Not only had she not tried it, but her guilt for even thinking of betraying Jerry had made her throw them in the bin.

"Well, you must. It will do wonders for your hair. And I can tell you need help, no offense." Clippy gave a dazzling smile. "I heard you asking Bonnie for an appointment yesterday, see. Imagine if a simple wash and condition transformed your hair?"

"That would be something."

"I would love to get my product into the Aussie market. You got time for a chat?"

"Yeah, I wanted to talk to you, anyway."

Sylvia led her to her table. The waiter poured them coffee. Before Sylvia could ask her anything, Clippy launched into her spiel and talked and talked and talked.

"So, what do you think?" Clippy had finally come to an end.

"I think you'd make a bloody good hairdresser. You could talk the chin hairs off a chinchilla!"

"Oh you!" Clippy tapped Sylvia on the shoulder. "I make a way better saleswoman than a hairdresser, let me tell you. I can't cut a straight line along a folded page. Now, are you up for it, Sylvia? Please say yes to being my Australian sales rep! You can still run your salon and sell this gear as a side hustle."

Sylvia thought of Jerry. "I would, but I'm really happy with my current supplier, Jerry. Have you met him?"

"I think so. Cute guy, short? Palaver longs, or something?"

"Yes, Latherlongs. He's afraid you're trying to squeeze him out of the market."

"Well, I'll take that as a compliment if he thinks I can take over the world! No, I just believe in my product. I mean, we can't be the best if there's no one inferior to us, can we?" She smiled.

Sylvia bristled. "Well, I'm happy with what I've got, thank you."

"Oh, I totally get you, babe. But just so you know, my company offers a suite of perks like…"

Before she could continue, a French voice interrupted them.

"Sylvia! *Mon Dieu*, I can barely talk wiz zeez hot lips."

"Monsieur Crassoon! So awesome to see you again!" Clippy gushed. She got up and allowed Vitale to take her seat. "I'll leave these papers with you, Sylvia. Have a look over the contract. I'm desperate to have you on board. Good luck today, monsieur. I'll be rooting for ya!"

She headed off for her next victim; the poor man she was talking to in the salon before the cocktail party. The waiter poured Vitale a coffee, but he pushed it away and tentatively licked his red lips.

"A glass of cold milk, *s'il vous pla"t.*"

"You look like the Rolling Stone's logo, Monsieur!"

"Sylvia! You insult me! Just as I was about to say how *jolie* you look zis morning."

"I'm sorry, Vitale. That was a shocker what that man did to you. Where's Humphrey?"

Vitale shrugged. "He didn't answer when I knocked on 'is door zis morning."

"Ah, here he is!" she said, noticing Humphrey as he hesitated at the door. He strode to their table once he saw them.

"Morning Humpo! How come you were up so early?"

Humphrey ran his fingers through his hair. He looked depleted.

"*Mon Dieu*! Zee naughty boy did not go to bed! Ay? Where 'av you been?" Vitale winked.

Humphrey gave a guilty smile. "That's for me to know and you to find out." He blinked a few times while Sylvia and Vitale scrutinized him.

"It's the first round today! You needed a good night's sleep!" Sylvia scolded.

"Who do I have to ask for a coffee around here?"

"Av mine," Vitale said, nudging the saucer towards Humphrey.

Sylvia leaned in and cocked her head to Clippy sitting two tables over.

"Do either of you know Clippy Feathercombe? She seems to know everyone here."

They all looked. Her sales pitch seemed to fall on deaf ears as the man pushed some typed pages towards her and she pushed them back.

"Yes, of course we do. She spent the whole of last summer in London schmoozing all the salons with her new product," Humphrey replied, looking happy the conversation had moved away from him.

"Yes, Fritz. Is it good?"

"It's wonderful if you like the soft, flowing look. Monsieur uses it more than me," Humphrey said.

Sylvia decided she should probably fish the shampoo and conditioner samples out of the bin and give them a go.

"Oh, and their newsletter is fabulous. It's just as useful as the *Hair'd Honcho*," Humphrey continued, as he stole a mushroom from her plate.

"Hey, get your own brekkie! They send a newsletter?"

"Yeah. What's it called? Um, *Lighten Up*."

"Huh. I'll have to get a copy and see what it's like. I'm surprised Wiz isn't sponsoring this year. It's one thing to not be here, but to bring in a sponsor...? Especially if these people produce a rival magazine."

Sylvia mopped up the last bit of egg on her plate. She blew out her lips and patted her tummy. "That'll last me. Right. I've got to go do some sleuthing. Vitale, you're still sending stats through to UGH, right?"

Vitale nodded. "Bien sur! Nothing's changed."

"Hmph, I thought so. Weird. Right, you two need to pull yourselves together for the competition. I'll see you in the arena later. Good luck."

She gave each a kiss on the cheek and went to find Al Fa'Rou. As she scoured the hotel, she debated whether she should take up Clippy's offer. Would this new brand really transform her hair as promised?

And then, in turn, her clients? It appeared to be a no-brainer, if the price was right. But something didn't sit well in her stomach. Maybe the eggs *were* dodgy! No, she wouldn't betray Jerry. Loyalty was one of her highest values.

6

Sylvia squinted into the blazing sunshine as she emerged onto the pool terrace. She spied the effortless strokes of Al Fa'Rou gliding through the water and stood waiting at the end for him to finish his lap. Though Al was not a hairdresser, he helped train UGH agents, including Sylvia. The training process was grueling, but nothing compared to the final hurdle. Having all her hair shaved off and the UGH logo tattooed on her skull by Al had been the worst of it. Al had seen and marked the bare scalp of every UGH agent in the world.

As he reached the end, his skin shone under the droplets of water. His afro, usually full and round, was now slicked down, and Sylvia saw his equine face as if for the first time. He was an exquisite man, and it did not surprise her that his other specialty was hypnotism. His voice sounded like a bass note from a honey-wood guitar.

"Sylvia, spirit of the wood, keeper of the forest, guardian of the trees whose name falls like silver droplets and coats my words in shining brush strokes. It's good to see you, sister."

"Good to see you too, you smooth talker!"

"Pass me my towel."

He propelled himself effortlessly out of the pool, as if made of champagne bubbles. The water cascaded off his skin and hair, which he shook. She chucked the towel at him. They linked arms and sidled to the edge of the rooftop. The view of Las Vegas spread before them, ceasing abruptly against the dusky plains of yellow scrub in the distance.

"How's life? What exotic places have you been to since I last saw you, Al?"

"Too many to narrate, so I'll tell you my most recent. I went to visit the king of Voracito."

"Voracito?"

"An island in the Indian Ocean. The king needed my skills to charm his first and favorite wife. It is a sorry tale."

"I like your stories, please tell."

Al directed them to a couple of sun-loungers.

"It was not customary, but after marrying his wife, the king took another wife, then three, then six. The women of the island were so beautiful and he was so powerful and rich (and having so much fun) that he took another four. The king reveled in the attention of his wives, but instead of being satiated and content, he wanted more. By the time he had fifteen wives, the troubles started. His wives talked, you see. They were friends, allies. They got themselves educated and wanted equal rights. The women were young and lively and were not satisfied with the one man between them. So they decided they would each take another husband, or maybe two or three. Then those husbands took more wives, and lovers, too. The king was too busy with his island and all his wives to stop what was going on under his nose. Soon, the entire population of the island had many lovers. It was a delicious amount of fun for a while, but soon the king and his wives bore children, so many children he couldn't even remember their names. And what's more, the women all over the island started having babies, lots of babies. Often, they were not sure who the baby's father was, and the men fought over the paternity, or against it. There were many mouths to feed and arguments to sort out. There was not enough food or money to go around. The king was not rich enough to feed everyone and after a while, the people were in poverty. They were forced to leave the island, for they had even eaten all the fish in the sea. Eventually the king was there all by himself, on a barren desolate island with little food, no company and definitely no frolicking between the sheets."

"That's a terrible story!"

"Indeed. Such is the weakness of men. And women."

"Did you manage to get his first wife back?"

"Of course, no one is immune to my golden tongue!"

"Well, I guess that's a happy ending."

"Until he asked me to speak to all the other wives as well."

"Oh dear."

Sylvia stared into the horizon. "Why can't people be happy with what they've got? I'd be happy with just one husband," she said quietly.

"All that is gold does not glitter," said Al enigmatically.

They both watched as the sun pulsated in the morning sky.

"When did you last see Wiz? He's been a bugger to get hold of recently," Sylvia said.

"As you just heard, I too have been incommunicado for a while. I spoke to the old boy once or twice. The dreams he is pursuing are... far-reaching."

"Do these dreams involve the guild? 'Cos it feels like he's taking his eyes off the hairline."

"UGH is always close to Wiz's heart. But it's growing like a yeti's beard in winter. I think perhaps he is finding it hard to handle."

"Is that why he brought Gene on board? What do you know about him? I mean, he's not even a hairdresser!"

Al shot her a look; half amused, half stern.

"And neither am I. A team cannot be too pointed at one end. You need other tools in your kit."

"What kind of tool is Gene, then?"

"Beauty & Fitness is like a cousin to hairdressing, on a parallel course, where one day they promise to meet on a far horizon."

"But why him? Who is he? Is he an initiate?"

"So many questions! No, he is not an initiate. He doesn't know the hairdressers' code. He's an outsider."

"So how come he's judging the Golden Scissors?"

"Fresh eyes, an open mind, a clear history."

"You mean past judges have had 'favorites' or may have been swayed?"

"There have been rumors, complaints. After all, your noble husband, God rest his soul, won three years in a row. He was the only one to have achieved such a feat."

"That's because he was brilliant, not bent!" Sylvia bristled. A flare of indignation rose, reddening her cheeks. "Well, he was bent," she realized her Freudian slip about her gay husband. "But Sol is still the best hairdresser the world saw, even though he's been gone for over ten years. He won those scissors fair and square."

"My dear, he was a superb scissorist, please, I don't mean to suggest ..." He left the suggestion open. "This year there is the chance that another may reach the heights of your dearly departed husband."

"Ramone? Yes, he's going for the trifecta though he'd be hard pushed to beat Monsieur Crassoon. Is that why there is an outsider on the panel this year?"

"That may have been Wiz's reasoning."

"But Al, you have been a judge for most of those years. Surely you would have known about any corruption?"

"I didn't say there *was* corruption. I said there were rumors. The Golden Scissors is the most prestigious award, one every hairdresser aspires to. We have to make sure everyone can see the playing ground is even."

Sylvia sighed. Al always had a habit of talking in riddles.

"Wiz trusts this guy?"

"We must assume so. Wiz is working on another project. He'll be back."

"Right."

"My dear, I must leave. It's time to get ready for the competition today." He kissed her on each cheek. "Catch you later!"

He left Sylvia at the poolside. She felt a kind of discomfort. She didn't know if it was Al's story, or if it was because Wiz seemed to have dropped off the edge of the world.

7

The Dynasty Ballroom had been transformed into a huge hairdressing arena with tiered seating on three sides. A stage took up the fourth side, the trophy of the Golden Scissors at its center. Every hairdresser worth their wax aspired to win this award. It was the pinnacle of a career but by no means an easy feat. The judges were rigorous, the qualifying vigorous, and only the *crème de la crème* made it as far as the Pharaoh's Palace arena. There were several prizes for different categories: cutting, styling, chatting and even sweeping for the juniors. But the Golden Scissors Award went to the most skilled and innovative hairdresser who was combs and tongs above the rest.

Sylvia slipped into the Green Room where the competitors prepared and waited before the heat. All the competing hairdressers had their team; coaches, assistants, or friends there to support them. Hairdressing was an art, and each artist had their own process. Vitale paced on his heeled boots, praying, or maybe swearing, in French. Humphrey puffed on an aromatic cigarette. The man Sylvia had seen in the salon the day before spoke in Italian and slapped a young, weedy guy called Marco around his cheeks with violent affection. Ramone was getting a rubdown from one of his team. Vince Crow was singing an opera at the top of his lungs. Jimmy

Baggs sat cross-legged, meditating. Gloria Frank perched on a stool, motionless under mirrored sunglasses. Sylvia tried not to stare at so much hairdressing royalty present in one room. These coiffeurs graced the cover of magazines with their rich and famous clients.

"Let the games begin!" Ramone said to the room. "Good luck everyone, you're gonna need it!"

A few of the contestants smiled. Most of them ignored him. He clicked his neck and jogged on the spot, punching the air like a boxer.

A commentator knocked on the microphone. Sylvia gave both Vitale and Humphrey a good-luck hug and took a seat in the auditorium. She hoicked her glasses back up her nose and dragged her focus to the arena, now lined with hairdresser dummies.

"Goooood morning, Hair Preeners and Brylcreemers! This is Brian Charmly, your MC and host for the week. Welcome," he breathed into the microphone in a low voice, "to the opening round..." He paused. "Of the Golden Scissooooooooors!"

Everyone applauded and cheered, pumped for the days to come.

"Please put your hands and hearts together for our eminent, our beloved, our incredible judging panel, Emmy-Lou Bangs, Al Fa'Rou and Gene Bustle!"

Again, the spectators did their part as the judges took their positions.

"This morning's heat, 'The Big Cut,' separates the whiskers from the coif by executing a simple, yet deceptively tricky hairstyle. Our worthy hairdressers have but one hour to create the perfect bob. This simple haircut leaves no room for error, ladies and gents. Just one hair out of place will see them eliminated. Judges, do you have your rulers at the ready?"

Al waved his golden ruler in the air, Gene flexing his between his hands, and Emmy-Lou twirling hers like it was the handle of a lasso.

"Faaaantabulous! Now let's welcome our first contestants!"

Music pumped from the speakers.

"Here they come, ladies and gentlemen. Put your hands and combs together for this morning's competitors!"

The forty hopefuls jogged onto the floor, and each positioned themselves behind a dummy. They limbered up as the audience cheered. Vitale looked sprightly and confident. He had pioneered the resurgence of the bob. In fact, it was the first cut he trained his apprentices to master. Humphrey looked the part in skintight leather pants and a Hawaiian shirt with a fringe of safety pins. Ramone, dressed in a shell suit with a thick gold medallion, cricked his neck again. Other well-known stylists such as Gloria 'the Pilot' Frank, Jimmy Baggs and Sparkle Jones stood shoulder to shoulder with the upcoming youngsters, including Marco, Milly Fulbright and Gonzalo §.

The music faded. The judges sat down. Brian spoke in a low voice.

"Hairdressers at the ready. Your time starts... NOW!"

Two sparklers shot out of each end of the arena. The crowd cheered.

Vitale held his special, custom-made scissors and comb aloft, closed his eyes, and took a deep breath. He looked across at Ramone, tilted his head to one side, and swung his scissors into action.

"Sit back and enjoy, ladies and gents. Let's go down to the floor to find out what our competitors' game plan is today. Al, over to you."

Al began at the end of one row. He interrupted each hairdresser to give their name and the type of bob they were executing. Vitale was cutting his model's wig straight to the chin, creating an exact 90° angle to the bangs. A classic, but not an easy task. It was the style he had maintained for the editor of *Tittle Tattle* for years, and she was a perfectionist. He wielded his scissors with precision and flair. Ramone, who was opposite Vitale, had started by standing with legs astride and combing his own hair. He shook his curled mullet off his shoulders, then spun his scissors around his finger and started cutting. The audience loved it.

"Jiminy clippers, that man is such a showoff," Sylvia huffed to herself.

Humphrey could not resist a shaggy bob with razored layers, his comb and scissors a blur, probably like his vision, Sylvia thought. She chewed a thumbnail as she watched.

"Hey, Sylv!" Jerry tapped her on her shoulder from behind.

"Hi Jerry. Wouldn't like to be the judge this year."

"Nah, me neither. Hey, has Clippy hit you up yet?"

"Yes, she collared me at breakfast. She knows how to sell, that's for sure!"

"It's OK, I've got a plan." He winked at her as if she was supposed to read his mind.

"Good, good." She wobbled her head at him in confusion. He kept winking as if he had a hair in his eye. "Uh, Jerry, stop winking, would you? Listen, have you heard of anyone unhappy with UGH lately? You reckon hairdressers are still using the guild to solve mysteries and stuff?"

"They don't talk to me about that business. But now you mention it... There was a hairdresser in Melbourne complaining that she'd sent UGH a request for an agent and never heard back."

"Really?"

"That's what I heard. Anyway, gotta go. I want to catch Clippy. I'll see you later." He gave her another wink and moved off.

The hour's end was fast approaching. The judges walked up and down, tilting their heads and studying the different techniques. Ramone's shoulder-length bob was taking shape. He picked up his spray bottle and gave the dummy head a good squirt at arm's length.

A final vigorous spray left a cloud of droplets shooting across the divide to Vitale. Ramone spun around to the audience and gyrated. He moon-walked up and down the arena to the squeals of both men and women, who seemed to view him as a hunk. Sylvia could not bear to look at him anymore and returned her gaze to Vitale. But something was off. Vitale had stopped cutting and his face had gone bright red. His eyes watered. Sylvia shifted forward in her seat. Vitale was having trouble breathing.

"Two more minutes to go. Make your final adjustments!" Brian announced.

Vitale rubbed his eyes, squinting and coughing. To Sylvia's horror, he felt blindly for his glass of water and knocked his dummy over. The neatly cut style, just minutes away from being finished, now hung off the dummy's head over the counter, the hair in a tangle over its face.

"We've had an incident!" the commentator shouted in glee. "Monsieur Crassoon has lost his model. Looks like he's struggling down there!"

Sylvia jumped up, craning to see what was happening. The audience gasped and murmured.

Ramone was now crouched on his knees, laser-focused on the final touches to his model's do.

Vitale was still flailing around. He fumbled on his worktop and found his glass of water. He threw the water into his eyes, gasping and coughing.

"What's happened to him?" Sylvia and others around her asked.

"He can't see!" someone exclaimed.

"Must have sprayed some hairspray in his eyes," another suggested.

But Sylvia knew Vitale only used hairspray at the very last moment.

Vitale rubbed his eyes. Emmy-Lou ran over and passed him a tissue. Red in the face, his skin wet with snot and water, he righted his dummy, but the precise bob of seconds ago was now a scraggly mess.

"Ten seconds, folks! Nine..."

Everyone counted down with Brian. Sylvia couldn't bear it. If Vitale, the greatest hairdresser in the world, didn't make it through the first round, his reputation would be in shreds. Vitale gave the dummy a shake, allowing the hair to fall back into place.

"Eight..."

He combed each section, tears still gushing down his face.

"Seven, six..."

He made one last-minute cut as he coughed and gasped.

"Five..."

He scrambled for his hairspray on the counter, his eyes streaming.

"Four..."

He put his thumb on the aerosol and pressed, shooting a mist directly into his chest.

"Three..."

Vitale grappled with the can and twisted it around.

"Two..."

He sprayed the head with hairspray but noticed one stray hair longer than the rest.

"One..."

He made the tiny snip.

"Zero! Put down your scissors and combs and step away. Time is up!"

The hairdressers stepped away from their dummies' heads. The crowd went crazy. Vitale bent over with his hands on his knees, heaving in lungfuls of air.

Emmy-Lou, Al and Gene walked up and down the aisle between the two banks of twenty workstations. They twisted the dummies around, measuring the lengths and taking notes. Emmy-Lou described the ins and outs of a good bob to Gene. Finally, as the hairdressers held their breath, except Vitale, who tried to catch his, the judges finished their rounds. They handed a list to the commentator's booth.

"OK, folks! Let's give our contestants a big hand. Didn't they all do well! And now, I'm pleased to announce the results. Going through to the next round are… Gloria Frank, Billy Torch, Ramone, Jimmy Baggs, Sparkle Jones, Vitale Crassoon…"

Sylvia blew out a breath of relief as Brian read out the rest of the twenty winners to cheers and applause. Humphrey's name was not called out. She knew it was a risk doing a shaggy bob when such stringent measurements were required, especially with no sleep, but that was Hump for you.

The audience dispersed. Sylvia headed down to congratulate Vitale, commiserate with Humphrey, and find out what on earth had happened. Humphrey had grabbed the blinded Vitale by the elbow and escorted him off the arena. Sylvia elbowed her way into the Green Room. The winners' teams slapped high-fives and celebrated. Others offered commiserating back slaps. The old guy, Giuseppe, didn't look happy. He had a firm hand hooked behind Marco's neck and hauled him out of the room.

As Sylvia arrived, Vitale was trying to shout. But every time he opened his mouth, his lips split, and he called out in anguish. Humphrey mimed a glass being tipped to his mouth. Sylvia grabbed a bottle of champagne from an ice bucket and poured a frothing glass. Humphrey put the glass in Vitale's hand and guided it to his mouth. Vitale sculled the glass and waved his hand for a refill. Sylvia obliged.

"What happened, V?" Sylvia asked.

Barely opening his mouth, Vitale growled, "Ramone…"

"Did you see anything, Hump?"

"It was after he sprayed his water bottle. I reckon he put something in it."

"Ch, chee-yee," Vitale mumbled.

"What Monsieur?"

Vitale rubbed his eyes and forced one open.

"I zink it was chili."

Sylvia gasped. "Chili spray?"

Humphrey punched his hand. "Why, that smarmy, cheating, little..."

"Can you go up and settle him down in his room?" Sylvia asked Humphrey. "I'll get some milk to wash his eyes out."

She was relieved to get away from the Frenchman's wails of agony. She knew there was a place where she could get milk quickly—Cleopatra's Milk Fountain.

8

Sylvia punched the elevator call button repeatedly until it arrived. The doors slid open onto the foyer. She thumped her head; she'd forgotten to bring a container for the milk. She looked around. A scattering of lounges, high wing-back armchairs and low coffee tables populated the area. As she approached a table with an empty glass, a neighboring table was occupied; a sneakered foot dangled from the end of a muscled orange calf.

"He won't, Mr Bustle. I've tried every angle."

It was the unforgettable shrill of Clippy Feathercombe.

"Try again."

"I have!"

"Well, honey, not. Hard. Enough!" Gene punctuated his words by punching his fist into his palm.

"Gene, go steady on her!" It was the voice of the second bodybuilder.

"It's OK, Wes." Clippy patted his knee and smiled.

"If anyone can win him over, Clippy can. Just give her a break!" Wes said.

"What's his goddamn problem, anyway?" Gene said.

"He's a mulish old mullet," said Clippy. "He says he's not getting into a triangle."

Gene growled. "Well, tell him he can get into a body-sized rectangle if he's not gonna join! I'm a fair man, Clippy, but your job description was clear. I told you to use every means you could. If you can't get this deal, you're fired."

"But Mr Bustle..." Clippy's voice cracked and her eyes flooded with tears.

"Dammit, woman, don't turn on the waterworks! Typical broad."

An elbow poked out beyond the chair as Gene rubbed his forehead. "Look, meet me in the Tutan-Khasino in half an hour and we'll make a plan. I'll give you some coaching to make this thing work. OK?"

Clippy sniffed. "Thank you, Mr Bustle."

"Wesley, get me a table in the casino. Open a tab at the bar."

Gene's meaty hands clutched the arms of the chair, ready to hoist his massive frame out. Sylvia scooted to the other side of the fountain and watched Gene head to the elevator. Fascinated, Sylvia inched nearer to their table.

"Can you talk to him, Wezzie?" Clippy asked in a baby voice. "He's being such a gwouch about it. Why's he so set on getting Giuseppe on board, anyway?"

"It's his business goals. He gets awful upset if he doesn't make them. Besides, that barbershop is in his building on Fifth with the flagship Bust-A-Butt. He needs the guy to stock the goods. Listen babe, don't you worry. He just gets a bit over-enthusiastic."

"So, you'll help me out?" Clippy squeaked.

"Of course, baby-girl. Let's go."

They stood, and Wesley put a protective arm around her. They left, and once out of sight, Sylvia filled a glass with milk from the fountain and headed back to Vitale's room. The elevator paused at the second floor where the competition took place. The doors opened.

"Stupid boy! Why didn't you try harder? I come all this way for you..."

It was Mr Borlotti and his nephew.

"For me? You're the one who thinks this comp is so special. You're the one who wants the glory," Marco said.

"After all I've done for you..."

The pair turned and looked as Sylvia waited for them to get in.

"Going up?" she asked.

They shook their heads, and Sylvia pressed the close-door button. But just when there was a small gap between them, Marco slid in, leaving his uncle behind. He punched the buttons with his fist, then raked his hands through his hair. He looked like a coiled spring, clenching and unclenching his fists by his side. Sylvia stood unmoving in the corner of the elevator, trying not to make eye contact through the mirrored walls.

"Old people, eh?" Marco said at last, as if he just realized he wasn't alone.

Sylvia gave a polite smile and she was relieved to arrive with a ding at Vitale's floor.

"Where have you been, Sylvia? His lordship has been whining like a turbo-charged hairdryer!"

"Sorry, dove. Here, Monsieur, tip your head back."

Sylvia washed Vitale's eyes out and the stinging subsided. She placed a cool, damp flannel over them.

"Champagne, in zee bucket!" he commanded.

Humphrey positioned an ice-bucket with a bottle of fizz next to his bed. Vitale blindly waved his hand around and felt the bottle.

"Non! Not in a bottle! Fill zee bloody bucket with champagne. None of zis ice business. Seul champagne!"

They poured three bottles into the empty ice-bucket and gave him a straw, closing the door on his sighing and slurping. They both blew their lips out.

"OK! Play time, possum!"

Humphrey jiggled from one foot to the other.

"Play time?"

"The casino! Come on, let's hit the high lights!"

"OK. I've got to ask around, anyway; see if anyone can shed some light on this guild situation."

"You do you, honey, but I'm gonna crack some dice!"

9

Humphrey led her towards the casino through acres of slot machines. The whir, beeps and tinny music gave a mechanical energy to the place, while the immobile humans who played them resembled sleeping robots. A sudden clatter of a payout would jolt them back to life as they redoubled their efforts. The sumptuous carpets, fancy chairs and gilded fittings looked like Aladdin's Cave. It was filled with milling bodies looking for treasure. Las Vegas, the playground for adults, both fascinated and repelled Sylvia.

A blue rinse sat next to a comb-over, dreadlocks shoulder to shoulder with a high ponytail. Across from her were two tumbling perms, and several people—who really needed a good cut and color—lining the rows of hundreds of machines. An entire family was huddled around one. Cowboys, businessmen, scruffy truck drivers, the retired, Indians, Japanese, Russians and one agitated male hairdresser—Sylvia was as mesmerized by people playing as the gamblers were with the slot machines. Humphrey kept jogging ahead, then coming back to pull Sylvia onward to the gambling hall of blackjack, roulette and poker.

"Come on, Sylvia!"

"Keep your hair on, Hump! What's the hurry?"

"I've got a tremendous feeling about today, my friend! Today is the day that Humphrey Egbert Jemanko Lebonne will become a wealthy man!"

"Wow, Egbert Jemanko, that's one fancy name!"

"My mother's legacy. She was descended from an Indonesian princess."

They entered the Tutan-Khasino through a pair of heavy wooden doors studded with coins. Two security guards stood at each side, dressed in nothing but a skirt, a striped head-cloth and a broad ornate collar. The vast windowless room was full of game tables, chatter, and intense poker-faces. It stretched as far as the eye could see. Croupiers wearing long white gowns and Cleopatra wigs guarded their patch of land like queens, keeping a cool command of their territory. Some serfs were loyal and remained, while other nomads roamed the world looking for opportunity and riches.

Humphrey exchanged his money for a pile of chips.

"Game on," he declared.

They approached a roulette table and squeezed into the game.

"Black or red?" he asked her.

"Oh, red... no black... red, red," Sylvia stammered.

"OK. Pick a number."

She called a number, crossed her fingers, and sent a silent prayer. The croupier spun the wheel. It clattered luxuriously, slowing, counting down, tick, tick, tick, tick. Sylvia held her breath. Humphrey clutched the edge of the table. Black, red, black, red... black... red.

"Yes! Sylvia! What a charm, you Aussie genius!"

Humphrey hugged her and poured his pile of chips into his bag. His eyes widened and shone.

"Beginner's luck, Hump," she said modestly, but she was delighted. She couldn't help but feel somehow special.

"Let's go again! What color?" he said.

"Red, again!"

"Inside or outside?"

"Inside."

"Numbers?"

"4, 5, 6."

"Place your bets, ladies and gentlemen," the croupier called.

Humphrey placed his chips as Sylvia suggested. The roulette dial spun round and round and round. Sylvia held her breath. She wanted to look away, but she couldn't take her eyes off it. It slowed and clicked past the numbers agonizingly to red 3, 4, 5 and stopped just in time. Humphrey leaped on to Sylvia, laughing like a hysterical five-year-old. He gathered his chips and looked at her expectantly.

"OK Hump, that's me done, dove. Your turn to choose. I can't stand the suspense!"

"Come on, Sylvie-Sue! You're my lucky charm."

His big brown eyes gazed at her with intent. He nodded his head manically.

"OK, last time."

It was kind of fun, the risk, expectation and the win. Humphrey rubbed his hands together.

"Call it!"

"Um, black, outside."

He pushed a towering pile of chips onto the spot.

"Humphrey! That's too much!"

The croupier spun the dial. Sylvia prayed. Humphrey held her hand. The clickety clack set off. All eyes were on Humphrey and Sylvia. It slowed, slowed and clicked on to red.

"Shit," he muttered.

"Oh heavens!" A wave of dread worked its way over her scalp.

"Come on, it's time to go, Hump."

She touched his arm, but he flinched away.

"I'm sorry," she said, though she was not so much sorry but cross at him for forcing her. The high from moments before sank into a chilly pit of swirling feelings—anger, guilt, loss.

"Why did you pick black? We've won on red every time!"

"I... I said I'm sorry. How could I know?"

"For the love of God, Sylvia! I've lost all my money!"

"I didn't make you bet it all!"

"You could have stopped me!"

"I tried..."

"Well, not hard enough. Now what am I going to do?"

"I have no idea. You work it out, you spoilt little prince."

She pushed him out of the way and marched off. How dare he blame her. She felt used and dirty. All she wanted was to get out of this gilded nightmare. She skirted around the blackjack tables and had the doors in her line of vision. Then, out of the corner of her eye, she saw a flash of platinum curls that could only belong to Clippy Feathercombe. Sylvia had only been there one night, and she'd seen Clippy at every turn.

"Sylvia!"

Clippy trotted over to her.

"Hiya! I'm so glad Vitale got through. Yay! Hey, come and join Gene, Wesley and me for a Crazy Kahuna cocktail. I've never tasted anything so good."

Clippy had recovered her pep after the conversation Sylvia had heard earlier. The baby voice was back to one of a professional saleswoman.

"I... er..."

"Oh, don't say no! Me and the boys are on a winning streak."

Clippy hooked her arm through Sylvia's and pulled her along.

"Have you played blackjack? Gene is such a champion at it. I don't know how he wins every damn time. It's just so thrilling."

"No, I..."

As they approached the blackjack table, Marco Borlotti arrived. Gene and Wesley shook hands and then the three headed off together.

"Oh guys!" Clippy called after them, but they couldn't hear her. "Rude boys! They're probably getting more drinks. They'll be back soon. Now, I was wanting to tell you about the Fritz leave-in mousse..."

Clippy gushed on. Sylvia listened but watched over her shoulder as Humphrey stalked to a new table.

"And then you can apply the sheen cream. Our developer is amazing. He's working on..."

Raised voices reverberated across the room. Humphrey rushed from table to table, barging in and annoying the gamblers.

"... So you see why this product really beats all the others. And as well as that, the added keratin gives..."

Humphrey gestured wildly and yelled at a croupier.

"... have been working on this formula..." Clippy droned on.

He poked his finger at the croupier, calling the game rigged. She shook her head at Humphrey, pressing the button under the table for assistance.

"So, you gonna sign up? You won't regret it."

Security moved in on Humphrey from the outskirts of the room.

"...The beauty is every sale you make; you get a cut. And if you sign up some of your hairdresser friends to sell it, you can make enough money to stop cutting hair and start cutting sick! Plus, you can buy it today and take it back with you. I have plenty of stock in Bonnie's storeroom."

"Er, yes, yes."

Sylvia pushed Clippy aside. Humphrey jutted his chin towards a croupier, tossing his head from side to side. Sylvia winced. Three burly bare-chested bouncers talked into walkie-talkies and had nearly reached the furor.

"Great! Just put your autograph here, Sylvia."

Sylvia absentmindedly scrawled her name and stuffed the paper into her bag.

"OK thanks, Clippy. Got to go."

"I'm so excited!" Clippy delved into her handbag and pulled out a magazine. "Here's a copy of the latest mag…"

But Sylvia had left. She fast-walked towards Humphrey. The security guards were nearly there. If Humphrey got chucked out of the hotel, it would be a disaster. She would have to handle Vitale and his demands on her own. Sylvia ran towards them, almost being knocked over by a man leaping in the air after winning. She dodged a waitress with a tray of champagne, then a decrepit lady on a walking frame, and reached Humphrey seconds before security closed in. She grabbed his flailing arms and pinned them to his side.

"We are leaving right now, young man," she said firmly.

Humphrey opened his mouth to protest.

"Right now!" she repeated.

"But!"

"Walk!"

Security reached the table and hesitated.

"We're leaving," Sylvia told them with a brisk smile.

The croupier gestured at the men to hold back.

"Come on, let's go and get a drink."

Humphrey shook his head in resignation.

"But Sylv, she…"

"Zip it. Let's go."

Neither spoke in the elevator to the rooftop bar. Sylvia ordered them both a whiskey on the rocks. She took a sip and sucked air in through her teeth as the fiery liquid went down. Humphrey downed his in one go and gestured the barman for another.

"What happened down there?"

"I got shafted."

He was still angry.

"You mean you lost."

Humphrey stared at his glass.

"Come on, dove. You can't get angry at losing in a casino. It comes with the territory."

"That's what my father used to say to my mother. She lost half his fortune over a blackjack table. She had it bad—the gambling bug. The bastard pulled the plug on her, left her high and dry when I was ten. Never saw her again."

"Oh Hump!" She put her hand on his. Sylvia knew the pain of losing a parent.

"Why didn't he help her?"

"Pride, greed, shame... who knows?"

A trio of guests from the competition came into the bar, chattering animatedly. One was singing, twirling the female of the party around, his shoulders jigging up and down in glee. He threw a wad of cash onto the bar.

"Drinks all around!"

He glanced at Sylvia and Humphrey and nodded his head.

"Make it a double for my friend here! You win some, you win some!"

He winked at Humphrey and cha-cha'd to his friends.

"Let's get out of here," Humphrey said.

"How much did you lose today?" Sylvia asked gently.

"Ah... not much." His voice wavered.

"When you say not much...?"

"I've got to go."

He pushed the stool away and strode out of the bar.

"Hump!" she called after him. He ignored her, his head down.

"Flicking hell!" she muttered and went to follow him.

The man who had won led a conga line of hotel guests around the room. They crossed Sylvia's path, oblivious to her attempts to squeeze past. Just as she found a gap, a pair of hands grabbed onto her waist, and she was taken up by the line. Humphrey's back disappeared into the sliding doors. She finally broke free and ran to the elevator, but he was gone. The one next to it pinged, and the doors slid open.

"Sylvia!"

"Hi Jerry, how's it going?"

"Great, let me get you a drink and have a yarn."

Sylvia hesitated for a moment and watched as Humphrey's elevator dinged through the floors.

"OK, you're on."

She walked with him back to the bar. As she slumped on to the barstool, she sighed.

"Everything alright?" Jerry asked as he waved the barman over.

"Yeah, I'm just a bit worried about Humphrey. Seems he has a thing for gambling."

"Oh, just leave him be. He'll be right. "

They chinked glasses and took a sip.

"You know that Clippy chick?"

Sylvia nodded.

"She's actually a lovely sheila," Jerry said.

"Wow! You've changed your tune."

"Yeah, I decided I'd sleep with the enemy, ya know, metaphorically speaking. That was my plan. Infiltrate. But then, it turned out... not so metaphorical!"

Sylvia blinked for a moment, then clocked on.

"I thought she was dating that big guy?"

"Who? Oh, that Wesley dude? Nah, he'd like to date her, but no. She's not attached."

"Jiminy Clippers! That's good. Does that mean you're jumping ship from Latherlongs?"

"Have you tried Fritz, Sylv? It's bloody amazing. I mean, why wouldn't I? Clippy takes care of the Americas, me the Antipodes, and we, uh, meeta in da middle, you know what I mean?!" Jerry clasped his two hands together and laughed. "It's a match made in heaven."

"Congratulations, Jerry. I'm happy for you," Sylvia said, though she prayed Clippy was uniting with him for the right reasons. She wouldn't put anything past that one to make a sale.

"Thanks. Hey, isn't it about time *you* got yourself a fella?"

Jerry and Sylvia had known each other for a long time. She didn't mind his directness as much as the possibility she'd end up a lonely old spinster.

"Maybe, Jerry, maybe. It's finding the right person, though. Someone who is on the same wavelength. Someone who is smart, funny, handsome. No one fits the bill in Hardup."

"Maybe you need to cast the old hairnet further afield. Like me!" He winked and slugged back his drink. "Talking of which, I'm going to find Clippy right now."

"OK, have fun, Jerry."

He grinned, winked again, and left with a spring in his step. He's a fast worker, Sylvia thought. She wondered if she *should* look for love in other places.

10

It was early in the evening. Sylvia figured there was still time to investigate the missing data. On the airplane over, she had set out her plan of attack. She would interview the hairdressers she knew and then fan out to their contacts. She'd got all she could out of Al for now. It was time to track down Emmy-Lou. And she knew exactly where she would find her.

The Khartoum Karaoke bar was heaving. The ceiling was hung with light fittings that looked like microphones, and a musical note motif in gold and silver festooned the walls. Some of the day's contestants clustered around the karaoke console, arguing over which song to sing. Emmy-Lou held the crowded bar mesmerized with her rendition of Dolly Parton's 'A Gamble Either Way'. A few eyes were dabbed as thunderous applause met Emmy-Lou's bows.

Sylvia ordered a tomato juice and headed over to Emmy, who was now signing her autograph on napkins.

"Emmy-Lou!" Sylvia called.

Emmy-Lou looked up and seeing Sylvia, she broke into a smile.

"Hey there, Sylvia! Good to see ya!"

They hugged and Emmy-Lou beckoned her over to a booth as three caterwauling hairdressers took to the stage for Bananarama's 'I Heard a Rumour'.

"How ya going, honey?" Emmy-Lou shouted over the out-of-tune and out-of-sync singing.

"I'm good. The salon's going well. Hey, I wanted to ask you when you last saw Wiz?"

"Why, I haven't seen him for a couple of years. There's not been any agents initiated for a while."

"Did you know HAIRnet has been compromised?"

"I didn't. As you know, I'm retiring from cuttin' and styling' for my music career. Not got my scissors to the grindstone these days."

"But you're still judging the Golden Scissors?"

"Of course, it's my favorite event of the year. As long as I get invited... and they let me play!"

"What about UGH?"

"Still a member. I get to hear and see all sorts when I'm touring. I'm just not on the hairline anymore."

"So, no idea why reporting has stopped?"

"Maybe hairdressers are just too busy to send them off every month. I noticed he missed a couple of *Hair'd Honcho* issues last year. If Wiz ain't there collecting the data, what's the harm?"

Sylvia bristled. She believed the guild was integral to the industry. There was nothing better than entering a salon with Nihil Mali Capillos above the door. It felt like coming home, that she had a connection with the owner.

"UGH is an institution. We're not merely separate hairs on a head, Emmy. Wiz is the head that holds us all together. Keeps us together. Without the guild, we'll just be wisps blowing in the wind."

"You're right. But times are a'changing, honey. Have you heard of the new phones you can carry around with you? Gene's got one. Maybe UGH is stuck in the past?"

Before Sylvia could reply, a body hurtled past their booth and landed with a slide into a high table and bar stools. At that moment, the Bananarama wannabees came to an end. The body stood up and wobbled. The man who Sylvia now recognized as Marco raised his ringed pointer finger and jabbed it in the air.

"What did you do that for?" he yelled.

Sylvia and Emmy-Lou peered their heads around the booth to where an old, short, neat-looking man stood at the other end of the bar. It was Marco's uncle, Giuseppe.

"You promised me you were clean," Giuseppe said. "You're just a con man like your father. I got conned into looking after you, and this is how you repay me? How could you get knocked out in the first round, you idiot?"

"Did you really believe I could've pulled it off? You're more of a thick head than I thought!"

"You tricked me? Just to get to Las Vegas? To spend money with these ridiculous people? This event is a circus for freaks. I can see how you fit right in!"

"Coming from someone who claims to be some perfect goddamn citizen! You're a boring, square, bitter old man. You disgust me."

"Get your lazy ass out of this goddamn sleazehall and straighten up," Giuseppe growled. "We're leaving this hellhole."

"We only have one shot at this crapshoot called life. I'm gonna make the most of it. I'm not gonna end up a bitter, twisted and stubborn old ass like you."

Marco swayed. He shook his head, a sneer on his face, and spat at the floor.

"We're leaving. NOW!" the old man yelled.

"You ain't the boss of me, gramps. We're in Vegas and we're staying in Vegas. I'm gonna have some fun. Maybe you should try that yourself," Marco slurred.

"Don't you ever forget what I did for you, Marco. Don't you ever forget I *am* the boss of you. Get… out… now, go on, get outta here or I'll…"

"What? What? You'll disown me, change your will?" Marco wiped the spit and blood from his face. He wobbled again but steadied and took a step towards the old man.

"All you ever did was bully me, punish me for your lowlife brother, my scumbag father. I quit. I'm done with you. Done with your sermonizing. Done with your pushing. Done with all of it. I wish you would curl up and die in that hovel you call a barbershop."

Marco stumbled forward and pushed his uncle sideways, lurching out of the bar. Giuseppe steadied himself against a table.

"I'm leaving tomorrow, and I don't want to see you at my shops ever again. You're fired!" he spat. He dropped his head into his hands.

Everyone stared at him. Emmy-Lou slid out of the booth, and Sylvia scrambled after her.

"You alright, Mr Borlotti?" Emmy-Lou put her hand gently on his arm.

Giuseppe looked at his polished shoes for a moment. "A man should be able to have choices, but to choose between a receding hairline and alopecia is not called choice."

"And you sure can't choose your family," Emmy-Lou sighed.

He raised his eyes, which threatened tears. "Well, we'll just see about that."

He plodded out of the bar, shaking his head.

Outside the bar, Clippy, Gene and Wesley had listened to the row along with all the patrons inside. Giuseppe stopped.

"Mr Borlotti!" Gene gushed. "Great to see you outside NYC!"

"Just get out of my way." Giuseppe gave Gene a long, hard stare.

Gene calmly returned his eye contact before stepping inside the bar.

Inside the Khartoum Karaoke bar, the patrons murmured in gossipy tones, but Gene's arrival diverted their attention.

"My favorite people! Hello! I just had an incredible run in the casino." He clunked his brick-sized phone on the counter of the bar. "The drinks are on me!" he crowed.

The uneasy crowd received him with a cheer. A new song clicked on and someone took to the stage.

Clippy held back as they closed around Gene. She glanced towards Giuseppe's receding back, peeled away and jogged out of the bar. A couple of hairdressers rushed up to Emmy-Lou and asked her to sing with them.

"I'd love to! See you, Sylvia! Let's catch up again!"

Sylvia sat in the booth on her own. She wiped the condensation from her glass and wondered how she was going to solve the mystery. The people around Gene burst into laughter at a joke he had told them. Sylvia's eyes drooped. She was still jet-lagged. She downed the last of her tomato juice and decided it was time for bed.

As she waited by the elevator, yawning, Wesley joined her. He wore teeny tight gym shorts and leather gloves that weightlifters used. He was as bronze-tanned as his boss. She and Wesley stepped in together, along with three other guests. They each had their turn at pressing the correct button for their floor. Sylvia alighted and scrabbled around in her bag for her room key. She squinted at the bland corridor, trying to get her frazzled brain to remember where her room was.

11

Back in the blissful quiet of her room, Sylvia kicked off her shoes and dumped her handbag on the bed. There had been quite enough drama already, and it was only the second night. She was worried about Humphrey, but didn't want to go knocking at his door. He was a big boy, after all.

Sylvia lay on her bed and thought about the case. Maybe Emmy-Lou was right. Was the guild even relevant to hairdressers anymore? Al had said membership was growing, but Wiz had missed publishing the magazine twice and seemed to have his finger off the scissors. Everyone she had asked was still reporting and making requests for agents. So where was the communication breakdown? Her mind circled without relief.

Exhausted as she was, she needed the soothing noise of her favorite pastime—television. At home, she kept her TV on in the salon most of the time, but to have one in her bedroom was a luxury. She picked up the remote control—an extravagance she hadn't invested in at home—and pressed the buttons. She clicked through the channels; a Western, advertisements, an old black and white. She kept clicking, gasped at the horrifying Freddie Krueger and jammed her thumb on the button. MTV blared heavy rock and Sylvia skimmed on. A pair of naked bodies flashed on the screen, heaving and grunting, pushed up against a wall.

"Oh my!" Sylvia gasped. She pushed on the buttons on the remote frantically, but the scene played out. Sweaty flesh and unknown contours scorched onto her eyes. The nuns who raised Sylvia in a Catholic orphanage loomed in her mind, tight-lipped and finger-shaking.

"Jiminy Clippers, off! Turn off!" she squealed.

Two buttons on the remote had jammed together, and the scene jumped back and replayed again. Heavy breathing, fingers trailed through a mouth.

"Oh no, not again."

Sylvia untangled herself from the sheets and launched at the TV. There was no obvious off button. Kim Basinger and Mickey Rourke rewound and mashed themselves together again. And again. And again. She put her head under her pillow and tried to drown out the grunting and Bryan Ferry singing about a slave to love.

Sylvia's cheeks burned. She approached the TV again, squinting her eyes to block out the carnal lust replaying, but she couldn't find a button anywhere on the set. The power cord disappeared into the wall. She poked at the remote to no avail and threw it on the floor, where it smashed apart. Sylvia swore under her breath and picked up the phone. She waited in the bathroom until she heard a knock at the door. A young beefy porter whose name tag said 'Brad' came in.

"How can I help you, ma'am? Something wrong with your television?"

"I'm sorry to call you up like this but, I can't turn the flicking thing off. It's stuck on... on..."

"Ah, 9 1/2 Weeks, cracking movie." Brad stood in front of the TV. His head reeled, and he straightened his back. "Oh yeah, this is everyone's favorite scene." He chuckled, then blew through his lips as the scene climaxed.

"Can you please turn it off!" Sylvia squeaked through the hands on her face.

Brad cleared his throat and quickly adjusted his pants. He strode to the offending screen and snaked his hand to the back of the TV. The gyrating actors disappeared into a white dot and silence filled the room.

"Thank you," Sylvia sighed with a groan, not unlike the ecstasy just seen on the screen.

"My pleasure, ma'am." He winked at Sylvia and let himself out.

WEDNESDAY

12

I t wasn't the scream that awoke Sylvia at 4.52 am but her stomach getting ready for lunch time tomorrow. Her body still refused to accept it was fifteen hours in the wrong direction on the clock. It was the shriek that pierced through the floors of the hotel from above eight minutes later. Sylvia tumbled out of bed, feeling around for her glasses. She shrugged on her dressing gown and poked her head out of her room. One or two others were doing the same.

"Was that a scream?" said a young woman in a camisole.

"I thought so," said Sylvia.

"Where from?" The camisole wearer's tousled bed buddy chimed in.

"Sounded like it came from above." A slightly built latecomer next door to Sylvia said as he stepped out.

The small group headed to the lift and made their way to the nineteenth floor directly above them. As the lift doors slid opened, a woman had her hands over eyes and sobbed outside Salon Sphinx. It was Bonnie, the salon manager.

"What's the matter?" asked Sylvia as she and the other girl went to comfort her.

The two men gasped.

"Dead..." one said.

"... body," the other man said.

Sylvia looked and let out a yelp.

The body of a man lolled in a washbasin chair at the back of the salon, tucked in the right-hand corner. A box of Fritz products was open and strewn across the floor.

"What's happened here?" Sylvia asked Bonnie.

"I walk in here and... he's there."

"That's the man who was in here earlier. Giuseppe?"

"Yes." Bonnie collapsed in a cascade of tears.

"OK, let's get you a seat and some water."

Sylvia shuffled the hysterical woman out of the salon and propped her up in one of the large chairs outside. All the other shops, including the beauty salon, were closed. The lights were dim. A few more people drifted up, along with a porter and the hotel night manager. They were familiar with drunk guests and bankrupt guests, but not dead ones. The manager sent the porter off to call the police and an ambulance. Sylvia glanced in through the open door. She turned to Bonnie.

"Why is he in your salon? Did you leave him there?"

"No!" she hiccuped with indignation. "I locked up around 10.00 pm."

"And how come you're back here so early?"

"This week is crazy. I have so much to do. I'm short-staffed and these Golden Scissor people are so demanding."

"Does anyone else have keys to the salon?"

"Just me, management and Clippy."

"Clippy Feathercombe? Why?"

"She's got her product in the storeroom. She needed access morning, noon and damn night."

While the night manager sent curious, alarmed guests back to bed,

Sylvia slipped into the salon to get a closer look. She glanced around the room. All seemed to be in order, no sign of a struggle except some of the Fritz product scattered over the floor. There was a whiff of something fruity in the air over the smell of urine that the poor old man had released. Giuseppe lolled in the furthermost washbasin chair, wearing one of Bonnie's gowns secured with a loose knot. Only the half pair of scissors stabbed into his heart stopped it from falling away. His pale face was cocked back into the basin, his mouth slightly open. His hair was damp. She touched his wrist—still warm. Sylvia scanned the floor and saw a pen. An empty cup on a saucer sat on the trolley next to the washbasin.

"Has anyone called the police?" someone asked in the gathering crowd of hotel guests.

"They sure have. Let me through, please. Detective Danny Good." The man flashed his police badge. "Let me through. Stand back please, people."

Sylvia turned to see the owner of the voice. Her features involuntarily changed from shock to awe as a hunky dreamboat made his way in through the parting crowd.

"Nobody touch anything. Ma'am, can I ask you to step out of the crime scene, please?"

It was the hunky wreath-wielding cop from the foyer at check-in. He looked even better up close.

"Oh yes, can I? Um, I'm Sylvia Scutlash, ambassador of the United Guild of Hairdressers. I'm here to help. Nice to meet you," she gushed.

She held out a hand and remembered she was wearing her baby blue fluffy dressing gown. A hot flash of embarrassment prickled her hairline. She caught sight of herself in the mirror. Her hair was scrunched up to the left, with whiskers protruding in every direction where she had tossed and turned on her pillow.

Detective Good's soft, cool hand grabbed hers. He shook it confidently. She took in his cream linen suit, which he wore over a dusky pink t-shirt. He had dark hair immaculately smoothed back into a ponytail. His brown eyes matched his bronze-tanned skin, his full sculpted lips flanked by the most kissable cheeks. He definitely didn't look like he'd just got out of bed. Even his linen pants were not creased.

"I'm going to have to ask you to leave now, ma'am."

His handshake pushed her back into the crowd behind a cop who was erecting a tape barrier. She tried to protest, but the burly policemen positioned themselves in front of the shop. She stood in the crowd, watching. Danny Good scoured the room and crouched down. He picked up the ballpoint pen with tweezers and pulled a bag from his pocket. He handed the bag to his assistant.

One of the officers herded the hotel guests away from the window, where another pulled down the blinds.

"OK, back to bed people, or the bar. This is a crime scene. Off you go!"

The policemen ushered them away. Sylvia went back to her room. The images of a dead man and a drop-dead gorgeous man were seared on to her brain.

13

S ylvia tried but couldn't sleep. After an hour, she dragged herself out of bed to find coffee.

The restaurant was already full of guests. Clippy sat with Gene Bustle and the other body builder, Wesley, deep in conversation. Ramone and his crew were boisterous. Ramone wore a big smile on his face as he chucked bread rolls at his friends. Jerry sat alone but kept glancing over at Clippy. Vitale and Humphrey waved her over. Vitale's eyes were red-rimmed and swollen, much like his lips the day before, which were now crusty and scabbed. Humphrey also looked terrible. He narrowed his eyes at her with a small shake of his head. She took the hint and didn't mention the casino.

"Mon Dieu, Sylvia, you look like you have seen a zombie!" Vitale waved over the waitress with the coffeepot.

She tutted at him. "Well, thanks so much for your kind words! At least I don't look like a zombie!"

Vitale waved her comment away and smoothed his mustache.

"Anyway, I *have* seen a dead body." She plinked three large sugar cubes into her cup and slugged back the coffee. "Haven't you heard the news?"

"Mais non, what news?"

"There's been a murder!"

"What? *Qui*? Who?"

"Giuseppe Borlotti, a barber from Brooklyn."

"How do you know it's murder?"

"A blade of scissors in the heart kind of gave it away. I was one of the first on the scene."

Humphrey winced. "You saw that? How grisly!"

"Zis is terrible!"

Sylvia's stomach churned. "I know. Do you know him?"

"I met him a few times over the years," Vitale said. "He owns zees old barbershops in New York. He is a little traditional. Has—had—no flare, zero!"

"Short back and sides, Yawnsville, Arizona!" Humphrey chimed in. "I mean, who just wants all their hair cut off these days? I'm sorry, but he had no imagination. It's the kind of old-school place my father would go to." Humphrey shuddered.

"Humphrey! Have some respect for the dead. It was horrible to see a pair of scissors used that way. Might put me off cutting hair for life."

Vitale put his fingers to his temples. "Please don't put zis image in my head."

Humphrey patted her hand. "I wonder why somebody wanted him dead?"

"Surely 'boring' is no motive? His nephew got eliminated from round one yesterday. Why didn't he enter himself? Was he ever a contestant in the Golden Scissors?" Sylvia asked.

"Non, he never competed himself, but he insists his current prodigy enters. 'E says it is character building."

Humphrey groaned. "Yep, just the kind of thing my father used to say."

"Poor Marco," Sylvia said.

"Serves him right for being a precocious punk. Thinks he's the Scarface of the hairdressing world," Humphrey said in a Tony Montana accent. "They were having a right set-to after he got kicked out of the first round yesterday."

"And in the karaoke bar," Sylvia said. She yawned. The effects of the first caffeine hit had already worn off. She slumped her head on the table again. The waitress approached with the coffeepot and Sylvia nodded her resting head, her cheek squishing into her arm.

"Fill her up!" she murmured. Sylvia raised her head far enough to down the coffee before crashing down again.

"Ugh, jet lag or a dead body, I don't know what's worse," she moaned. She slouched further down her chair.

"I hope I never have to find out," said Humphrey. "Hey, who's that?"

Humphrey nudged Sylvia. She looked up to see three men entering the restaurant. They were a different breed from the neon-hued guests sitting at the tables.

"Oh my! That's Detective Danny Dream... I mean Good." She dropped her face back into her arms. "Don't let him see me!"

The detective moved through the restaurant, flanked by his two sidekicks.

"He's scanning the room!" Humphrey whispered.

"He's looking our way," Vitale added.

Sylvia groaned. "I'm not here."

"He's approaching!"

"Don't let him see me!" she hissed.

"He's pointing," Humphrey commentated.

"Pretend you're in a deep conversation!" she growled.

"Too late," Humphrey murmured from the side of his mouth.

Sylvia dared not look up. She had one idea; pretend to be asleep.

"Hey there, sorry to interrupt, guys. I'm Detective Good, Las Vegas police department. Is this Mrs Scutlash?"

He cricked his head to find her face. Humphrey and Vitale nodded.

"I need to speak to her. Do you mind if I join?"

"Bien sur, please take a seat, monsieur. Terrible business!"

Humphrey poked Sylvia, who made a semi-snore but otherwise didn't move. He elbowed her harder. She mumbled in her pretend sleep. Humphrey cupped his hand to her ear and yelled, "Sylvia, wakey, wakey!"

She shot up with a loud snort and looked straight into the slightly crinkled eyes of Detective Dreamboat. He smiled. Humphrey nudged her again. She threw an icy look at him, but he was mouthing 'mascara' and running his fingers under his eyes. She gave Vitale and Humphrey a hairy eyeball as she attempted to smooth her hair and rub the black shadows from under her eyes. Danny took the remaining seat. His sidekicks stood, making the other guests in the room stare.

"G'day," she swallowed.

"Sorry to, um, disturb you, ma'am, but as you were one of the first on the scene, we need to interview you and take a thorough statement."

Sylvia nodded, her creased cheeks blushing as Humphrey and Vitale looked on in glee. Danny gave a dazzling smile, and whatever was still solid in Sylvia turned to mush.

"Can you meet me in the Bonanza Beefhouse at 1.00 pm today?"

She nodded.

"It's on the 20th floor," Danny added.

He rose from the table and straightened his linen jacket. "I suggest you get some sleep before then. Freshen up a bit." He winked at Vitale and Humphrey, nodded to his men, and wove through the tables out of the dining room.

As soon as he was out of earshot, Humphrey slapped his hands and rubbed them together.

"So, an interview at the Bonanza Beefhouse? Sounds more like a date to me."

"Don't be ridiculous; this is strictly business."

"Plus, he wants you to freshen up!" Vitale laughed.

"And since when does a detective inspector carry out an investigation in a hotel restaurant?" Humphrey argued.

"Well, this is Las Vegas." She held her hands up to both their faces. "The rules are different here. Anyway, I can't get caught up in this murder hoohah. I've got to find out what's happening or is not happening with UGH."

She sculled her third coffee.

"OK, now I need food." She patted her rumbling tummy and looked to the buffet where near Clippy with Gene and Wesley's table. "Who is this Gene guy?" She nodded her head towards Gene.

Humphrey and Vitale shrugged their shoulders.

"How would we know? He's not in the hairdressing business."

"There's barely a hair left on that body. Do you think he waxes or shaves?" Humphrey pondered.

"Good question. I'll put it on my list because he's going to be the next person I talk to, if I can get a word in."

She managed to drive herself into the upright position and head towards the buffet, passing the table where Gene sat with Clippy and Wesley. She sidled along the breakfast bar, considering what to eat. Clippy was crying and chewed the inside of her bottom lip. Gene was talking.

"...a favor. We got to roll with the punches and capitalize. Wesley go find Marco. See where he's at."

Wesley grunted. Clippy sniffed and pulled a tissue out of her cleavage.

"Better this way anyway," Wesley said, squeezing her hand and bringing it to his lips.

Clippy allowed a small smile.

"Just keep to the bare facts, and we'll all be home and dry." Gene patted her other hand with a broad smile. "The only way is up, am I right?"

A shriek tore across the restaurant, interrupting the conversation. Sylvia looked towards the source of the scream, frowning. Vitale had leaped in the air, a cascade of French shooting out of his mouth as a waiter, holding a steaming jug of coffee, apologized profusely. Sylvia glanced around the dining room. Ramone smirked and his companions laughed into their hands. An almost imperceptible nod passed between Ramone and the waiter. She abandoned her post and rushed over to poor Vitale. The burning coffee had stained his white suit a muddy brown, and the material clung viciously to his crotch.

Humphrey blew air through his nostrils. "Ramone strikes again."

"What the flicking hell is wrong with that guy?"

"'Ee is jealous! 'Ee knows I am zee greatest hairdresser!" Vitale squeaked.

Humphrey dabbed at Vitale's crotch with a napkin.

"Aaah aaah! Stop it!"

Vitale batted Humphrey's hands away and used the back of the chairs to help him thread his way through the dining room, stiff-legged, teeth-gritted.

Humphrey turned to Sylvia.

"Do me a favor? Can you go and grab some hairspray from Bonnie for Monsieur? I have to help fix him up. I don't have time before the comp starts now."

14

Bright yellow tape sectioned off Salon Sphinx, guarded by a policeman.

"When will the salon be open?" Sylvia asked him.

"When forensics are done, could be today, could be tomorrow, could be never," he said.

"So, where's Bonnie based now?"

The policeman raised his nose across the foyer. Sylvia turned and saw that a hive of hairdressers buzzed in and out of the beauty salon opposite. Sylvia elbowed her way to the desk. A woman with pumped up lips, high cheekbones and extremely perky boobs held a phone between her ear and neck. She had a nail file wedged in her ponytail and was writing in the appointment diary. At the same time, a man asked her for a hairdryer, and a porter was trying to find a spare place to put a pile of towels.

"Hi there, I'm looking for Bonnie," Sylvia said once the woman had dispensed with the queue.

The beauty therapist gave her a withering look. Her name badge told Sylvia her name was Peggy.

"Everyone is looking for Bonnie and nobody is looking for a manicure. Ugh, I hate Golden Scissors week."

Sylvia was used to grumpy women. Her clients at the Wavy Lady would frequently arrive stressed, overworked and generally downtrodden. It was as much her job to do their hair as it was to make them feel more positive about life, to make them feel heard in her tiny corner of their world—the hair salon. In fact, Sylvia relished the most prickly of clients. It allowed her to sharpen her G.O.S.I.P skills—Gathering Of Secret Information Procedure, which she learnt in her agent training. To see the most cantankerous woman leave her salon with a smile on her face gave Sylvia as much pleasure as a successful cut and blow dry.

"Actually, I also wanted to book in for a manicure. Do you have a spot now?"

Peggy huffed and disdainfully ran a neon pink talon down a page of the booking diary.

"As it happens, yes I do. Then if Bonnie decides to grace us with her very busy presence, you can talk to her."

Peggy showed Sylvia to a small table. The only one left free from hair product, towels, a wash basket of gowns and several hairdressers practicing on dummy heads.

"Choose a color," Peggy ordered.

The array of nail colors was startling. The brand Mitz offered everything from misty blue to watermelon pink to baby violet. Sylvia chose pearly purple.

As Peggy filed and shaped, a woman wearing yellow spandex leggings entered the salon. Her oversized white baseball-style jacket was adorned with brightly colored geometric patches.

"Sandra Tress, the one and only. This is all I need," Peg moaned.

"Hey Peg!" Sandra called out.

"Can't you see? I'm busy," Peggy shouted.

Sandra chewed her gum with sucking noises. "Yeah, yeah, yeah, keep your hair on. I just wanna know if you seen Bonnie?"

"You see?" Peggy said to Sylvia. Then she yelled, "Bonnie gonna give me a pay rise for being her secretary? No, she ain't cos she's not got two dimes to her name. Geez, hang around long enough; she'll turn up."

"You seen Ramone then?" the other woman screeched.

"What am I? A telephone exchange?"

"Well, I hear you plug a few holes!"

Sylvia wasn't sure why the two women had to raise their voices so much, but then everything in America was bigger than Australia, bar the spiders.

Peggy threw down the nail file and like a dagger it caught in the tabletop, a millimeter from Sylvia's arm. Peggy stood up and squared Sandra off.

"You wanna say that again?"

"Ladies, ladies!" Ramone oozed into the salon. He winked at Peggy, then snaked an arm around Sandra's waist.

"Lucky your date turned up, or I'd plug one or two of your holes, Sandy McHandy!" Peggy said.

Sandra smirked and huffed through her nose.

"I've set up the meeting with Mr B. Come on," Ramone said, as they turned to leave the salon.

Peggy sat back down and settled her feathers like a hen.

"Friend of yours?" Sylvia asked as Peggy lifted her hand off the cushion.

"Hmm. Sandra Tress, Ramone's model. She's a snake, that woman."

"Ah, thought I'd seen her around."

"She ain't just got a head for hair, either."

"What do you mean?"

"She's got a head for figures and a backside for bouncing back."

Sylvia wasn't sure what Peggy meant. Five deliveries and three hairdressers bringing supplies interrupted any more flow of conversation. More people came in asking for Bonnie. Others used the beauty salon to practice and run mini-workshops.

"I can see why you're fed up!" Sylvia said.

"Right? This should all be happening at Salon Sphinx. Why did someone have to go and die in there?" Peggy moaned.

"Who do you reckon did it?"

Peggy leaned in and for once spoke in a whisper, a loud one, but at least she made the effort.

"I was closing up shop on Tuesday night and that Fritz woman and the dead guy were going in there."

"Tuesday night? What time?"

"I close up around 10.00 pm. Must have been about that." Peggy shrugged. "Now I got half her product in my storeroom. Quicker they clean up the crime scene, the better."

"Do you think she did it?" Sylvia asked in alarm.

"Who knows? People are still wandering around up here at that time. Would've needed to be short and sharp."

"Well, it was certainly that. Did you tell the police?"

"Detective Dan the Man? Yep, I told him."

"Dan the Man?"

"Yeah, wouldn't mind polishing his nails!"

Sylvia burst out laughing. Peggy patted the back of her hand to announce the job was done. Sylvia admired her nails. She rarely treated herself since her hands were constantly in and out of the washbasin. "Ooh, they look great!"

"Of course they do. Here, take my nail care kit so you can touch it up if it chips. There's your color, some nail files, a mini bottle of nail varnish remover and cotton pads."

"Thanks so much, dove! Oh, I nearly forgot. Any chance I can grab some hairspray?"

Peggy sighed and retrieved a can. Sylvia thanked her.

There was still had time to spare before round two began. She needed to push the murder out of her mind and focus on the investigation. She decided to head to the pool on the rooftop, where she knew the hairdressers would congregate before the competition.

15

The pool was thick with bodies, splashing and cavorting with no thought of ruining hair dos, Sylvia noticed with disdain. There was one person who was not joining in the frivolities. Gloria Frank sat on a barstool and gazed across the vista of Las Vegas through her impenetrable mirrored glasses. She savagely sucked a cigarette that was jammed in the end of a holder made from steel and ebony. The sides of her mouth disappeared under sharp cheek bones as she inhaled and then puffed out to release the smoke.

"Hi there, mind if I join?" Sylvia asked.

Gloria blew a strong dart of smoke out of her lips and looked at the empty stool next to her as a way of assent. Sylvia introduced herself. Gloria was silent, intent on her smoking.

"Beautiful spot, hey?" Sylvia admired the skyline.

"Beauty is a human concept that attempts to color our existence."

Sylvia frowned. "Yet something we hold dear in the hairdressing world."

"It means nothing. Existence means nothing. I am merely playing in this futile life until it is my time to die."

Sylvia blinked several times and wondered how this woman ever got or kept any clients.

"Oh well, I guess it's a fun way to pass the time."

"What is fun? I am a professional, Ms Scutlash. I find it satisfying to witness amateurs purely as a backdrop to sharpen my skills. Happiness, or fun, as you call it, is impossible."

Sylvia took a deep breath.

"Interesting. So, when I am having a good time with my friends, I swear I'm experiencing happiness."

"Then you have had a childhood of misery and suffering. It is a comparison, a measure."

It was like a stab to her heart. Sylvia had indeed had an unhappy childhood.

"Er, right."

"This 'fun' you speak of is an illusion."

Gloria was certainly sucking any joy out of this conversation. Sylvia changed tack.

"You're based in Germany, right?"

"It is the location I arrived in. I do not let it define me. I am not German, but I am... alive. You could define me by the mechanics of this body, I suppose. The fact is, I am."

"But you were born in Germany?"

"That is correct."

"And your salon is there?"

"My salons." She emphasized the plural. "I have twenty. But numbers are a human construct. I do not define myself by numbers."

"Winning isn't important to you? The trophy, the exposure, the cheque?"

Gloria turned the corners of her mouth down as if it was too irksome to even offer an answer. Sylvia was now curious why this unenthusiastic woman even bothered turning up. She was already clearly successful, yet acted uninterested in the trappings of that success.

"Then why did you bother entering?"

"I had other business in Vegas. I kill two birds with one scissor." She now turned her lips up slightly. Was she making a joke? Sylvia gave up making sense of her and got to the point.

"Are you still in the guild? Getting the *Hair'd Honcho* and reporting?"

"I have never reported. This data is worthless when we will all soon die."

Sylvia laughed through her nose. "Well, not too soon, I hope!"

Gloria answered with a tiny lift of one shoulder.

"Ooookay. Best of luck!"

Gloria grabbed onto Sylvia's arm as she rose to leave. "Luck is immaterial. Control is material. I have control, never luck."

"Ah yes, totally. Good to chat."

Sylvia slowly removed her forearm and backed away. The other hairdressers were too engrossed in their fun, and Sylvia could see it would be pointless to interrupt. Perhaps people just didn't care for UGH anymore. Perhaps they were sorting out their own problems. She called the elevator and headed to the hotel reception to find some hairdressers who had been active UGH members. It stopped at the next floor and pinged, receiving Clippy and Wesley into the small space. Clippy's face was wet with tears. Her usual glossy sheen was blotchy, and she dabbed at her eyes with a tissue.

"Oh, hi Sylvia! Excuse my mess. It's just so sad." Tears sprung from her eyes again. Wesley snaked a protective arm around her.

"He had no right to talk to you like that," he said.

"He's just doing his job," Clippy sniffed. "Just had my interview with the detective," she explained to Sylvia. "I was the last person to see Mr Borlotti alive, apparently. I just can't believe someone would kill him. Detective Good said it's not looking good for me."

"Yeah, well, wait till I talk to the police. I'll tell them my girl was with me all night." Wesley gave her a squeeze. She looked up at him with a weak smile and blinked for a moment.

"Well, there were lots of us together last night. I can barely remember who," Clippy said as she rifled through her handbag.

"I'm sure it will all come out in the wash," Sylvia said. "I'm talking to the police later today. Whoever did it will be caught."

"I hope so," Clippy found a bright pink lipstick in her purse. She looked into the mirrored wall and slicked it on, finishing with a pop noise from her lips. They alighted at the Dynasty Ballroom floor. Sylvia shivered. If Clippy was really a clear suspect, Danny would have arrested her. Sylvia doubted Clippy was capable of murder, but why would she leave Mr Borlotti in the salon after her demo? Perhaps she was hiding something.

The elevator carried her the two floors back to the ground floor. There was one competitor Sylvia was keen to talk to. She had followed Sorrento Starbright for years and had once helped him out with a spot of bother with a case of missing hairbrushes. Turned out the local toy manufacturer was stealing them for their porcupine toys. He was best known for making middle-aged women look twenty years younger. Since the majority of Sylvia's clients were slightly older than that, she was keen to learn some of his tricks. She knew he was a loyal UGH member.

Sylvia asked the concierge to call Sorrento Starbright's room to see if he was free for a chat. He agreed to see her. She hoped the conversation with him would be a little lighter than with Gloria. She tapped on his door.

"Sylvia, hello, hello. Come in."

Sorrento's large frame filled the door. He had his shirt sleeves rolled up and beads of sweat on his forehead.

"I hope I'm not disturbing you?" she said.

"I'm practicing my taper fade. Not my forte, unfortunately. It tends to be more popular for my male clients, which I don't have many of."

"Ah, yes, a tricky cut for those of us more used to working on women," Sylvia said.

"Thanks for seeing me, Sorrento. You know I'm a big admirer of your work. I was wondering if you have time to give a lesser hairdresser some advice?"

They discussed the pros and cons of a lightly layered bob versus a shaggy curly cut. How they framed the face, offering a distraction from the fine lines and ravages of age.

"So, I have given you some of my trade secrets. Do you have any tips for this blasted taper fade with only a razor and scissors?"

"As you know, I'm not a barber," Sylvia said. "But I do have a trick or two up my sleeve. I'd use a fresh blade and put salt in your water bottle."

"Interesting. I guess that increases the separation."

"I don't know the science behind it, but it works a treat."

"Thanks!"

"No worries, always happy to help. I might suggest it for the 'tips and flicks' section of the *Hair'd Honcho*. Are you still reporting to UGH, by the way?"

"Of course, regular as clockwork."

"And the last time you reported was…?"

"Last week. Why are you asking?"

"Wiz asked me to, er, check everyone is happy with the service. Customer satisfaction is Wiz's highest priority!"

She gave a bright smile. The last thing Sylvia needed was anyone thinking there was a problem with UGH.

"Where is Wiz this year?"

"Away on business. An awful shame he's missing the Scissors."

"What's the world coming to, eh? First no Wiz, then a random judge…"

"Then a murder. Did you know Giuseppe?"

"Our paths crossed over the years. Now, he could execute a taper fade with his eyes closed."

"Who would want him dead?"

"He was a nosy parker, probably found out about some dark secret."

"Hmm, name me a hairdresser who doesn't carry some dark secrets!"

"But we don't tell them." Sorrento shook his head with his forefinger to his mouth.

"Do you think he was threatening to expose someone?"

Sorrento shrugged. "That's my theory. Now, in a few minutes, I need to be in the arena." He brandished his scissors. Sylvia took the hint.

"Well, I'll leave you to prepare. It's been great to meet you. Good luck today!"

Sorrento confirmed it. All the hairdressers she had spoken to were reporting to UGH, and no one said they had left. Which meant the data was not getting through. So why was UGH's HAIRnet in a blackout?

16

Sylvia arrived at the arena in the Dynasty Ballroom just as a Jazzercise demo was finishing up. A skinny woman who was shrink-wrapped in lycra shimmied her shoulders and yelped to the music.

"Oh yeah, baby," she called into her headset. "Shake that toosh and one, two, three, left step right and shimmy. Hairdressers gotta be bright eyed and bushy-tailed. On your feet all day. Let's do the Stylist Strut. You got it, cats. Raise those knees. Let's feel the beat. A chop to the right, a chop to the left, right, left, right, left. Woooohah!"

The track ended, and she turned and clapped at the sweaty class. They looked less than energetic in droopy leg warmers and leotards, which were painfully etched in recesses that should never be etched. Onlookers, grateful to be looking on, applauded in appreciation.

Ramone was in the class. He jogged over to the instructor and draped his arm around her, whispering something in her ear. She giggled and gave his hairy chest a playful push. He gave her bottom a firm pat, swung around to face her and winked. He raised his left hand to shoot his fingers at her like a gun before trotting off to prepare in the Green Room.

The other contestants were arriving, and Vitale rocked up with his case. He had changed his coffee-stained clothes and now wore a loose pair of white linen pants. Ramone swaggered up to him. He looked Vitale up and down, settling on his crotch.

"Hey hot stuff!" Ramone teased. "How do you take your coffee? Short and curly?" he guffawed.

Vitale scowled as he strutted off. Sylvia joined him.

"Zat filthy piece of excrement!"

"Just ignore him, Monsieur. Stay in your lane."

They went into the Green Room and she gave him the hairspray.

"Wishing you the best of luck in this *heat*!" Ramone called over, laughing. He licked his forefinger and held it up with a hissing sound.

Vitale walked over to him, his mustache shaking. Sylvia stepped between them and looked into Vitale's eyes.

"Don't let him psych you out!"

Vitale nodded. She kissed him on both cheeks, spun him around and wished him luck.

In the auditorium, people drifted in and took their seats. The sweet but slightly astringent aroma of Fritz filled the air, and the arena was heavily decorated in banners advertising Fritz products. The usual buzz was subdued by the now leaked news of the murder. As Sylvia took her seat. Two rows down Sandra dangled her patent heeled ankle boots over the seat in front of her and held a small notebook, her bright yellow jacket a beacon. She stream of people approached her.

Humphrey appeared and sat down next to Sylvia.

"How is Vitale... down there?" she whispered, pointing to her lower waist.

"Sore. He's got a bag of ice strapped to his meat and two veg under those loose trousers."

"Ramone is trying to throw him off. Will he be OK this morning?

"He has to be."

"Have you heard? The hotel is in lock-down. No one is allowed to leave until their alibi is confirmed," he said.

"Makes sense. Pretty creepy there's a murderer among us. Who would want to kill an elderly barber, anyway?"

"He might have been as boring as a bowl cut, but I hear he was a pretty influential player here in America."

"How come?"

"Well, he owned a good stack of barbershops on some prime real estate in New York. He had the market tied up, and any competition that set up nearby didn't last long. The guy was a control freak. None of his managers could buy a new towel without his say-so."

"Who gets the shops now he's gone?"

Humphrey shrugged.

"I'll try to get some info out of the detective in our interview."

"Date, you mean?"

"Humphrey, it is not a date. Now about yesterday..."

"What do you suppose that chick's up to?" He tipped his chin at Sandra. "She's on Ramone's team,"

Sylvia pursed her lips at him. "Don't change the subject, young man. Your little hiccup in the casino...? Promise me you won't gamble anymore."

"I'm OK, Sylv. I know I acted like a dipstick. It won't happen again. Scout's honor."

He looked at her solemnly. Sylvia squinted her eyes at him, but before she could say anything else, he jumped up and leaped over the seats towards the girl. Sylvia watched him take his wallet out and press a wad of notes into her hand. She jotted something down in her notebook and Humphrey returned.

"Won't happen again? You just placed a bet!"

"Hush, possum. It's research. Listen, she's taking bets and says

Ramone is the favorite. He's a sure thing."

"That's nonsense! Vitale is by far the better hairdresser."

"*Exactement*, my little genius!"

"You mean something's not right?"

"As sure as there's a comb in my back pocket, something's not right."

A team of stagehands wheeled two long, mirrored counters into the center of the arena. The second round also used mannequin heads for models. They all wore long black wigs and were secured onto the counters. Their frozen expressions reminded her of the lifeless Giuseppe, his dead eyes staring at a spot on the ceiling. They made Sylvia feel sick. She looked away and saw Sandra Tress still taking surreptitious bets. The lights went out, and the audience hushed. Music blared from the speakers and the multi-colored lights flashed across the arena.

"Welcome back, Hair Sprayers and Style Slayers! We are so excited to be here for round two of the Gooooolden Scissors!" MC Brian's disembodied voice boomed out of the sound system. "But first, I have a shocking announcement. Last night, a heinous crime took place in our very own Salon Sphinx. It is with great sadness that Giuseppe Borlotti was brutally murdered. Let us come together for a minute's silence for this great barber whom I'm sure many of you knew."

The audience was subdued for a full minute, no mean feat for several hundred hairdressers.

"Thank you, ladies and gents. Detective Danny Good is in charge of the investigation. He has asked to address the hotel guests here this morning."

Danny walked onto the stage and gave a contained yet cool wave. Sylvia's insides swirled.

"Thanks, thank you. Good morning everyone. I apologize for

interrupting your competition. As you heard, the Pharaoh's Palace Hotel is now a crime scene. We are looking for a murderer, so you'll forgive me for saying that at this stage, everyone is a suspect."

A wave of indignation swept through the seating.

"I know, I'm sorry, but until we've collected all your alibis, I can't let anyone leave, guests or staff."

The audience moaned, and Danny left the stage.

"Ladies and gents, what better place to be marooned but the Pharaoh's Palace!" Brian chirped. "Please enjoy all the fine hotel facilities."

He listed the restaurants, bars and attractions at length.

"So you see, there's no need to be sad or mad. In fact, our beneficent management has gifted you some generous discount vouchers, including \$20 of free chips... and I don't mean the dipping in sauce kind!" There was a murmur of excitement.

"I feel confident that the Las Vegas police force will find the culprit of this terrible crime. Now, let us move onward. Purlease pound your palms together for our honorable judging panel... Mr Gene Bustle, Miss Emmy-Lou Bangs and Mr Al Fa'Rou!"

The crowd gave an over-enthusiastic welcome.

"Today we are down to twenty contestants whose challenge it is to... Say, Emmy-Lou, can you tell us a little about today's challenge?"

Emmy-Lou took the microphone off the stand. "Sho' thing, Brian! This round is a test of skill and speed. We ain't gonna be watching one haircut this afternoon, but three! First, they will demonstrate a pixie cut, then a mullet and finally a men's taper fade. We'll be judging the fastest and most accurate haircuts."

"Thank you, Emmy-Lou. It's gonna be a haaairy ride! Let's give our contestants a big cheer as we welcome them into the arena!"

The twenty hopefuls entered a little more subdued than usual, wearing black armbands.

"Let the games begin!" Brian boomed.

Each hairdresser opened up their box of tools on the mirrored counter. Vitale, whose eyesight was now back to normal, positioned himself well away from his rival. Ramone took out a comb and groomed himself.

"That guy is so full of hot air, I could use him as a hairdryer," Sylvia mumbled.

Vitale took a breath. He put his hand into his box and pulled out his scissors. His face dropped.

"What now?" Sylvia said.

She gasped as he held just one half of his special scissors in the air.

17

Vitale rummaged around in his case, pulling out combs and clips, but no more scissors.

"Oh, great Gods of Fluff! One of our favorite hairdressers is already in trouble! It seems Vitale Crassoon has not checked his kit and has broken scissors. This will set him back. There's not a second to lose in today's speed tests!"

"Jiminy clippers, Hump!"

Sylvia and Humphrey stood up, looking aghast. They both knew they were the only scissors Vitale would use, his favorite gold-plated, lucky scissors.

"This could throw him off his game."

"This could throw him off the whole comp."

"I hope he has a spare set, as every good hairdresser does," Brian breathed ominously into the microphone.

"He only uses his custom-made scissors. This is terrible!" Humphrey groaned.

Vitale's mustache quivered, and Sylvia knew that this was not a good sign.

"Fifth commandment of hairdressing, 'always help a hairdresser in need'," Sylvia said.

Humphrey nodded. They pushed past the knees of the people in the row. But they were too far from the end. Humphrey scissored his legs over seats and heads until he reached the front and leap-frogged over the barrier. He rushed to the Green Room. Sylvia caught up breathless as Humphrey rifled through his own case and pulled out his best scissors. He gave them a quick run over the sharpening stone. Sylvia watched the arena. The judges talked to Vitale, and he shook his head.

"Hurry, Hump. They are about to disqualify him."

Humphrey gave the scissors a quick wipe and fast-walked into the arena. He held the scissors aloft, and the crowd clapped.

"All is not lost, ladies and gents. The hero of the day is Humphrey Lebonne," Brian shouted.

"Adda boy, Hump!" Sylvia called.

Vitale looked gratefully at Humphrey. He gave a curt bow, grabbed the scissors, and dashed back to his post. Sylvia let out a deep breath. She turned to close Humphrey's case and saw there was someone else in the room. Marco sat in Ramone's area in a salon swivel chair, chewing his nails and staring at the floor.

"Hey," Sylvia said kindly. "You OK?"

Marco looked up slowly, glassy eyed.

"I'm really sorry about your uncle."

Marco shrugged, wobbled his head slightly and swung away from her on the chair.

Humphrey came in, and Sylvia nodded towards Marco. They left the room.

"Is he alright?" Humphrey asked.

"I don't think so. Why is he in Ramone's area?"

Humphrey pulled a face that said, 'I don't know.'

"That was a close shave. This has got to stop. Ramone is pulling

Monsieur apart hair by hair. You stay down here in case anyone has any other tricks under their gown."

"Leave it with me. Ain't no little punk gonna mess with the king."

They nodded at each other.

As Sylvia made her way back to her seat, she clocked Danny at the edge of the arena talking to his off-sider, who nodded vigorously. Her insides went gooey, but her joy receded when they gestured to Vitale. Danny approached the judges, looking serious and pointing. Al Fa'Rou shook his head back at Danny. They spoke heatedly for a few minutes. Gene joined the conversation. He towered over Danny. Danny stood his ground, but Gene blocked the gate to the arena. Sylvia tried to lipread, but Danny backed off with his men and they stood nearby, watching Vitale intently.

It wasn't long before the contestants were putting down their scissors. Vitale was one of the first to finish. He and the thirteen other hairdressers stood back while the judges strutted along the line. They read out the names of the three worst cuts of the six slowest hairdressers.

The remaining seventeen received a new dummy, and the clock started for the mullet cut. Elbows and scissors whisked around the dummies' heads. The countdown saw a line of flowing mullets finished and the judges took their time to assess. Three more left the arena. Fourteen new models were set up for the taper fade to be executed without clippers. There was a knack for fading to avoid the taper being uneven or too high. It was a barber's specialty. Ramone put his left hand in the air and spun his scissors before diving into the cut. To the layman's eye, each resulting hairstyle looked identical, like a row of cloned soldiers, but to the judges each was different. Though Gene let the others take the lead, he engaged the contestants in conversation, leaving each with a pat on the back.

Sylvia glanced at Danny, who was giving instructions to his men. They hovered at the edge of the arena as if held on an elastic band, ready to be released. At last, the judges announced the ten going through to the next round.

Everyone whooped and whistled. Ramone thumped his chest with his hand and kissed his fingers to the audience. Vitale clicked his heels and gave a small nod. Gloria Frank, Jimmy Baggs, Sorrento Starbright, Vince Crow, Sparkle Jones, Carrie Straw, and Gonzalo § all packed up their kits and exited triumphantly.

Sylvia rushed to the gate of the arena to meet Vitale, but Detective Good had beaten her to it. As she waited for the people to clear the path, Danny's men led Vitale firmly by the elbow to the exit. By the time she got there, Humphrey was shaking his head and yelling after the cops.

"He said Vitale is a prime suspect in the murder investigation. They have seized the half scissors. They think it might be the other half of the ones that stabbed Giuseppe."

"That's ridiculous! You were with him that night, Hump! Didn't you tell them he has an alibi?"

Humphrey stared at his feet.

"Humphrey?"

"We got separated."

"What do you mean?"

"I had to, um, try to get my money back."

"What are you talking about?"

"I went to the casino, OK?" he said defensively.

"Humphrey! You lost everything yesterday. Are you crazy?"

"I couldn't sleep. Vitale snores like a pair of clippers on speed. I could hear him from my room next door."

Sylvia squeezed her lips tightly and blew through her nose.

"Flicking highlights, Humphrey!"

He opened his mouth to speak, but no words emerged. She paced backwards and forwards while Humphrey squirmed. The Golden Scissors seemed to be jinxed. She was getting sidetracked from her investigation, but there was no way she'd let Vitale be disgraced or Humphrey mired in gambling debts.

"Well, we know it wasn't him, so they'll find the scissors are the wrong ones and let him go," she surmised.

Humphrey nodded. "But why did he only have half a pair of scissors in his kit?" he asked.

"Good question. Something's not adding up here."

They both glanced at Ramone, who was doing a celebratory moonwalk around the arena.

18

S ylvia had one hour to prepare for lunch… interview, she reminded herself. In her first two encounters with the handsome detective, she had looked like a washed out wig in the wind. This time, she was determined to look her best. She selected a cocktail dress, a black velvet fitted number with huge silk bows in different colors around the neckline. She redid her makeup with a slick of bright pink lipstick. Everything looked good except her hair. She had twenty minutes to get it in order. The sample bottles of Fritz were lined up in the bathroom. She didn't have time to wash her hair. But she hoped with a spray of water and an application of the styling product, she would look as presentable as one could in a hotel full of hairdressers.

Sylvia squirted the Fritz spray around her head and combed it through. She shook her head from side to side, admiring the result; her hair unusually soft and flowing. There was something comforting about the scent. Maybe she was right to get it for the salon. She retrieved Clippy's paperwork and smoothed it out. The contract text was so small, even with her glasses and a flashlight she couldn't make it out. She put the paperwork in her bag and resolved to ask the front desk to photocopy and enlarge it.

Sylvia arrived on the 20th floor just on 1.00 pm. Her tummy

rumbled, and she wondered just what kind of beef bonanza was on the menu. She walked across the foyer to a huge wooden sign cut out in the shape of a cow. The cow had a cowboy hat on and a large cask full of gold coins on its back. But there wasn't the usual Maitre d' waiting at the door. No hum of diners, no clattering of dishes coming from within. In fact, no smell of food at all. She looked around her, perplexed. There was the sound of men's voices coming from inside the room, and she peered around the door.

"Hey Dan, just off the phone from forensics," a man in uniform was saying. "The initial report puts time of death at around twenty-three hundred hours. Rigor mortis just setting in. Also, the angle of the murder weapon indicates the perpetrator could be left-handed. No prints."

Sylvia stepped through the door. All the chairs and tables were stacked up at one end, bar one being used as a desk with three chairs standing lonely in the middle of the vast room. The restaurant had been converted into an incident room. The view from the bank of windows of Las Vegas and the desert beyond was spectacular. And so was the view of the person sitting at the table. Danny Good tilted back on his chair, smoothing his sleek hair back off his face. Sylvia looked down at her outfit. She was completely overdressed. She hesitated, thinking a dash back to her room would not be impossible.

"Ah! Mrs Scutlash, come in, take a seat."

"G'day!" Sylvia said, swallowing.

Sylvia made the long walk to the table. The two officers were busy shuffling files. His officer slapped one on the table. They took in her attire. Sylvia held her head high and pulled the chair out. She sat down, crossed her legs and said, "It's *Ms* Scutlash."

"Damn feminists," one officer muttered.

"My husband died some years ago, actually," she replied, glaring at the man.

"Settle down, Smith. Let's show some respect to feminists *and* widows, OK?"

"You…" She looked pointedly at Danny, "can call me Sylvia."

"Thank you, Sylvia. Please ignore my Fred Flintstone colleague. Can I just say I'm very surprised you haven't been snapped up by anyone else?"

"Or I haven't snapped up anyone else myself?"

Danny dazzled Sylvia with a smile that, despite her indignation, melted her insides. He nodded.

"Anyway, thanks for your time. You told me this morning you were first on the scene after salon manager, Bonnie."

"Yes, but before we get on to that, what have you done with the Monsieur?

"The Monsieur?"

"Yes, Vitale Crassoon. You know he's the most famous hairdresser in the world. He would not take kindly to being manhandled like that."

"He didn't," one of the policemen said, rolling his eyes.

"Sure was a noisy one. Lucky we didn't understand a damn word he said," the other added.

"Where is he? I hope you haven't arrested him. You don't honestly think that the Monsieur is capable of such a crime?"

"My job isn't to make opinions but to find evidence. I don't know him from a bar of shampoo!" Danny laughed at his joke and repeated it to his officer. Sylvia widened her eyes at him.

"Look, Sylvia." Danny leaned towards her. She gazed at the hint of stubble grazing his chin. "I shouldn't tell you this, but he's been released. Your friend had an alibi."

"He did?"

"His neighbor in the room next door attested to hearing him snore for a good portion of the night. He tried to bribe me to lock Monsieur Crassoon up for torture."

Sylvia relaxed and smiled. Knowing Vitale was safe was one less thing for her to worry about.

"Now, back to your movements. Talk me through what happened."

"I heard the scream at four am. I opened my door, and some other guests on my floor had heard it too. We went up and saw poor Bonnie sobbing outside the salon. It gave her a big shock finding her friend dead in her salon. I hope you don't think it was her?"

"Again, I can't divulge our processes, suspects, or evidence. Can you tell me your whereabouts last night between midnight and 4 am?"

"I was in my room asleep."

"Is there anyone who can corroborate that? A sleepless neighbor, perhaps?"

"As we've established, I am a single lady. I hope you're not suggesting..."

"No, of course not, but a beautiful young woman must not be short of offers."

Sylvia blushed. Was he flirting with her? She hoped so. She hoped not.

"That's very sweet of you, Detective Good, but I'm still on the lookout for Mr Right."

Detective Good gazed at Sylvia. She got caught in his chocolate eyes. The officer coughed. Danny's attention came back to the room. Sylvia blinked.

"So Ms Scutlash, Sylvia, you can't prove you were in your room last night at midnight?"

Before she could answer, a waiter entered the restaurant with a tray of sandwiches and coffees. He set the tray on the table.

"At last, I'm starving," Fred Flintstone said.

The waiter, Brad, recognized Sylvia.

"Oh, hello ma'am. Did you sleep alright after I, um, helped you out?"

He winked at Sylvia, who felt a deep blush rising from her bellybutton to her neck and onto her cheeks.

"Oh, we were just discussing Ms Scutlash's 'movements' last night. Do you have anything to say, Sylvia?"

She swallowed and licked her lips. "Er, well..."

Danny leaned back in his chair and his officers snickered.

"Ms Scutlash was watching an interesting movie." The waiter, who clearly doubled as a night porter, cleared his throat.

"Ah yes, I had forgotten!" She smiled sweetly, though beads of sweat prickled her neck. "The movie jammed, and this kind man helped me to disconnect the TV."

"I've always admired the service at this hotel, above and beyond. I hope you gave him a very big tip."

"I beg your pardon?" Sylvia only just caught on to Danny's insinuation. "He just turned my TV off for me, for heaven's sake! I would never, ever..." Sylvia huffed.

"I'm sorry ma'am... sir, I was merely helping our guest to, as she says, turn *off* 9 1/2 Weeks."

"I wasn't watching it though... I didn't mean to..."

Danny's shoulders bounced up and down.

"Well, now you know I'm not the murderer, so I'll leave you with your investigation. Goodbye."

She snapped out of her chair and stood up.

"One other thing," Danny said.

Sylvia glared at him. "What?"

"Are you right or left-handed?"

"Right, Detective. Right-handed, right-minded and right in the head!"

She spun and flounced out of the room. As she reached the elevator, Brad joined her. She hit the call button repeatedly.

"Sorry about that. I just explained to the police what happened. Didn't mean to embarrass you."

Sylvia huffed a half-hearted noise of forgiveness.

"Anyway, I gotta thank you," he said.

Sylvia frowned at him as they stepped through the doors of the lift.

"I got to meet Mr Bustle in the elevator afterwards. I'm a big fan. Been watching his body-building videos for years. See, feel that."

The waiter flexed a bicep at Sylvia. She gave it a squeeze.

"Very, um, solid, well done." She wasn't sure what one said about a thoroughly pumped muscle.

"And I got his autograph!"

He showed her a docket from his pad with Gene's signature scrawled across it. Her floor dinged.

"Wonderful, I'm so happy for you. Thanks for getting rid of that terrible movie. Bye!"

"See you around and thank you! Let me know if I can help you in any way..." He waved at her as the doors closed.

Sylvia clomped back to her room mumbling about getting out of this ridiculous get-up. With relief, she leaned against the cool mirror in her bathroom and let out a big breath. She cringed at the thought of Danny and his sexist officers having a good laugh at her expense. Why was she trying to impress him, anyway? She was here to do a job.

19

Sylvia was not about to let herself get distracted by a dishy detective. She looked through the program. In between the rounds, the Golden Scissors hosted demonstrations, workshops, talks and small events for niche groups. The Top Knots were having afternoon cocktails by the pool. This group of hairdressers was particularly skilled at updos. They were also the go-to for red carpet events, balls and charity dinners. If anyone knew any gossip about anything amiss, it was them. Sylvia changed back into her black turtleneck dress. She checked her hair, which still looked surprisingly soft, and reapplied her lipstick.

The roof terrace buzzed with the Top Knots' chatter. A group of rah-rah skirted girls and camp men bitched about a movie star they had all crossed combs with. A stylist demonstrated how to master a chignon (not that anyone wore those these days, Sylvia thought). The server held a tray out for Sylvia, offering a towering cocktail that resembled a pimped-up fruit salad. She took a seat at a high table with two others, and they raised their glasses to each other amiably.

"This is the life, isn't it?" Sylvia said.

"Sure is, honey," the man said. "Johnny Bonkers, nice to meet you. And no, that's not my porn star name. People always ask. I can show you my birth certificate if you like."

"Oh, goodness, it's a great name. Bonkers by name...?

The man guffawed. "I love this gal, Sally. Bonkers by nature, yes, you got me."

"Sally Tifferton," the woman said, nudging her partner and rolling her eyes in mock jest.

"Sylvia Scutlash."

They chinked glasses.

"Where do you guys hail from?" Sylvia asked.

"New York, New York," they trilled.

"I'd love to go there."

"It's a crazy place—Yonkers by name, bonkers by nature," Johnny yelled, followed by another spluttering laugh.

They sat silent for a moment, watching the people socialize around them.

"Did you know the man who was murdered? He was from Brooklyn, wasn't he?" Sylvia asked.

"Oh yeah. Terrible shame." Sally shook her head.

"Is it though? Come on, Sal. He was a pain in the ass."

Sally blew out her cheeks and shrugged.

"How do you mean?" Sylvia asked.

"He was Mr Do-It-Right. Complaining about this and that. Writing letters. Making phone calls. If there was one hair out of place, he'd jump up and down... and yet...?"

"What?"

Johnny crooked his head conspiratorially, inviting Sylvia to lean in. She acquiesced and leaned across the table, almost catching the cocktail umbrella in her nostril.

"And yet he let his nephew deal out of his shop."

"Deal? Deal what?"

Johnny held one nostril and sniffed with the other. Sylvia was confused. Did he need a tissue?

"Snow," he whispered.

"Snow?"

Sylvia was even more baffled.

"You know, toot, nose candy?"

"Cocaine!" Sally said, rolling her eyes at Johnny.

"Oh, I see!"

So that's why Giuseppe was arguing with Marco the day before, Sylvia thought.

"Well, that sounds very underhand. I wouldn't have thought Mr Borlotti would have stood for that."

"Yeah, it's surprising what you do for family," Sally said.

"Who knows what will happen to the business now? Marco Borlotti, he's a bad kid, got his scissors in a lotta iffy pies," Johnny commented.

Sylvia screwed her face at the image.

"So, he'll inherit it?"

"That's the rumor."

"How do you know all this?"

"Hey, honey," Johnny reeled back, pushing his shoulders forward and holding his hands out. "You're talking to the best!"

Sally thumped his arm in mock horror and turned to Sylvia, laughing. "No... but he is good."

"What can I say? What can I say? Hey, waiter. Load us up again, kid. That's right, keep 'em coming."

"So, do you think Marco killed him?" Sylvia asked.

"Could have," Johnny said. "But there again, Giuseppe made a habit of collecting secrets. Had his ear to the ground, that one."

"Don't we all? That's why we all report to UGH, right?"

"Yeah, the numbers, what the market wants, but not everyone reports *everything* to UGH."

"Really?"

"We don't report incriminating information about fellow hairdressers."

"Ah," Sylvia leaned in and whispered, "What did he know?"

Johnny put his hand up and shook his head.

"Tenth commandment, no can do."

"Tenth commandment? There are only nine commandments of hairdressers."

"The tenth is unspoken. Never drop a hairdresser in hot water."

"Makes sense, but what if the hairdresser is a murderer?" Sylvia asked.

"Or a murderee," Sally said. "Can't drop him in any more hot water now, Johnny! Come on, what did old Gippy know?"

"OK, you've twisted my arm." Johnny gestured for them to lean in, so their heads almost bumped in the center of the table.

"He found out that a certain hairdresser had more than one wife."

"Polygamy?" said Sally.

"In New York?" Sylvia added.

Then both women, "Who?"

There was a sudden cheer and applause from the Top Knots.

"Look who's here," Johnny said.

The women looked around.

"Everyone's fave judge," Sally squealed, clapping her hands.

Gene Bustle had arrived, and the Top Knots were gathered around him.

"Everyone's favorite?"

"Oh, he's such a sweetie, Sylvia. We all gave him a bad rap at the beginning. I mean, who'd have thought? A gym bunny judge? How could he possibly tell what's a good style from a bad one?"

"Exactly. How can he judge who should win?"

"But it's genius. An outsider brings a fresh view. Did you meet him after the opening night?"

"Oh no. Jet lag got me, coming from Australia, you see."

"Such a cute accent, babe! No, Genie is a doll. Come, I'll introduce you."

"But what about the secret polygamist?"

But Johnny had joined the crowd. The Top Knots, both male and female, shook Gene's hand, or squeezed his titanium muscles. Sally elbowed through the admirers. Up close, his physique was even more impressive than seeing him up on the stage. His skin shone a vibrant shade of orange. It looked as if he had been lacquered from head to toe and smelled like a lightly cooked banana.

"Genie, honey, I want to introduce you to Sylvia Scutlash all the way from Australia. Sylvia, Gene. Gene, Sylvia."

"Hey cutie pie," Gene stooped and kissed her on both cheeks. "Honored to meet a Down Underer. Love that capital city of yours, Sydney, awesome place."

"Oh um, Sydney, well it's…" Sylvia gave up correcting him, making him look dumb in front of his fans probably wasn't a way to win friends.

Just as Sylvia was about to ask Gene how he knew Wiz, someone whipped her away by the elbow.

20

Humphrey bustled Sylvia away from the crowd on the roof terrace. "I've been looking for you everywhere!"

"Hey Humpo! What's up? I was just about to talk to Gene."

"It's Vitale. He's had an accident."

"Oh clippers! Is he OK?" Sylvia asked.

"I don't know. I don't think so. He's hurt his wrist."

"What? No!"

Humphrey marched Sylvia off the rooftop terrace and into the elevator, leaving Gene's many fans to close around him.

"Where are we going?"

"To the gym."

"The gym?"

The Bust-A-Butt gym was full of people dressed in shiny, saccharine-colored leggings, leg-warmers and leotards which threatened to cut the aerobics fanatics in two. As Sylvia and Humphrey approached the bank of running machines, they found Vitale slumped against the side of one, holding his arm and wailing.

"What happened, Monsieur?"

"I came in here to have an exercise."

"You, in a gym?"

"Oui, I got invited…"

"But, you? In a gym? You always say the gym smells like a llama's derrière, and that it makes your mustache flop."

"It was Ramone… again!" Humphrey said.

Vitale tried to move his wrist and cried out in pain.

"One minute you're being detained by the police, the next you're in a gym wailing in agony. Care to fill me in?" she demanded.

"Zay released me. I would never cut wiz the cheap scissors that killed Giuseppe. Pah."

"How do you know they were cheap?"

"They showed me the murder weapon, asked if it belonged to me. Disgusting, this terrible blade, not even silver-plated steel. I retched at zee thought of using them. And covered in blood."

"It was the scissor *quality* you felt sick at? Not the bloodstains?"

Sylvia closed her eyes and shook her head.

"Apparently, everyone confirmed that Vitale only used gold-plated scissors. Made the detective look a bit silly," Humphrey added.

"So, who tampered with your scissors?"

"It was Ramone, I tell you. 'E is determined to get me out of the competition."

"And how come you ended up in the gym?"

"Because that leetle dicksqueak said I was too weak to murder someone, anyway. I tell him I am Mr Muscle and he laughed in my face. He challenged me to a gym workout. I get on zis stupid running machine and it goes faster and faster. And Ramone is laughing and laughing. My legs, they can't keep up and poof! I'm down. Ramone and his gang run away and leave me here."

One of the machines was now cordoned off with tape. Sylvia and Humphrey glanced at each other. A young man stood behind a desk in the corner.

"Excuse me," Sylvia said. "What happened to the machine?"

"It's playing up. Once it hits a certain speed, it won't stop. Sometimes sweat messes with the electrics."

"So, why did you let someone use it?"

"I didn't. I put a sign on it yesterday. Some bozo must have taken it off this morning."

"Hmm, some bozo, indeed," Sylvia huffed. "I'll be talking to Mr Bustle about this."

They lifted the groaning Vitale from the floor, cradling his hand in his arm.

"My wrist! The competition! This is a disaster!" he wailed.

"Lucky you are ambidextrous," Sylvia said.

"And insured!" Humphrey agreed.

Sylvia gently examined Vitale's wrist. He could move his fingers, and through shrieks of pain, bend his wrist. Sylvia judged it to be sprained and bruised, but not broken. Safely back in his room, they knocked him out with a cocktail of champagne and painkillers.

"Help me get Vitale's boots off, would you? We're going to have to look after him, Hump. He's going to be impossible for the rest of the comp."

"I know. At least he hasn't broken it. I don't see how he's going to win it now, though."

Sylvia sadly had to agree. They put a blanket over him. Sylvia's stomach rumbled.

"Dinner?" Humphrey whispered.

"Lead the way, Humph. I could eat a camel!"

They chose one of the dozen restaurants in the hotel and ordered.

"So, how did your date go with Detective Dreamy?"

"It was a police interview. How do you think it went?" she snapped.

Humphrey made a high-pitched ooooh noise. "What's got into

you?"

"Nothing, precisely nothing has got into me, Humphrey."

"And therein lies the problem, sweetie."

"What are you talking about?"

"I'm talking about you and your empty love life."

"It's not empty!"

"Oh come on! When was the last time you...?"

"Humphrey!"

"... had a date?"

"I had a drink with a guy just last week, last month. Oh, I don't know! I don't have time for a man."

"Or are you just terrified?"

"No! Of course not. Just haven't met Mr Right."

"Or are you still holding out for that boy you met in London..." Then he shouted, "TEN YEARS ago?!"

"Who? Sammy? No!" She screwed up her face and shook her head. "No way, uh uh. No. That's history, water under the bridge. Can hardly remember his name..."

"She doth protest too much!" Humphrey said, holding his hand up. "You gotta let that one go, sweetie. He was married to his job, to his boss. And that witch Karla Kreeper was not gonna let him go. Move on."

Sylvia opened and closed her mouth. It was true. She'd never met anyone that excited her as much as Sammy had. She chewed her lip.

"That reminds me. Do you know a hairdresser that has more than one wife?" she said, changing the subject.

"That sounds like the beginning of a bad joke!"

"Apparently, Giuseppe knew someone who was polygamous. Do you think that's why he was murdered?"

"Maybe..."

"It was someone in New York. That narrows it down."

"New York? It could be…"

"Oh, there you are, honey!" A lusty voice interrupted.

Before either of them could say anything else, Clippy had pulled up a chair and sat down. She had regained her upbeat demeanor.

"Hey, dove. How are you feeling?" Sylvia said. "Clippy was a friend of Giuseppe's," she explained to Humphrey.

"Yeah, so sad, awful. I was only talking to him earlier that day. Giving him my spiel on Fritz."

"I thought everyone in America was already using it," Humphrey said.

"Well, he was a slow mover. Needed to take his time." Clippy rolled her eyes.

"I wonder what will happen to his salons now? He didn't have kids, hey?" Sylvia asked.

Clippy shook her head and shrugged.

"Anyway, doll. I just wanted to let you know that I can't get into the storeroom in the salon to give you your first box of product. As soon as the police have finished in there, I'll bring them to your room."

Sylvia blinked at Clippy.

"Your Fritz products! I'm so excited to have you on board! Hope to see you both at the Fritz seminar later! OK, must scoot. Gotta go and talk to Vince Crow."

She waved and set off on her mission.

"She never stops, that woman," Humphrey said. "And what exactly are you 'on board' of?"

"Ah, I may have accidentally agreed to be her sales rep for Australia."

"Accidentally?"

"She sort of railroaded me, took me unawares."

“That's not like you, Sylvia.”

“I know, she's good. She even signed up Jerry.”

“So you're selling Fritz?”

“I believe so. It's actually a good product, Hump. Feel my hair!”

Humphrey combed his fingers through Sylvia's hair. “Looking good, possum, I got to say, it's an improvement.”

Sylvia gave him an 'I told you so' look and picked up her knife and fork.

“No harm in giving it a go.”

Clippy left the restaurant after stopping at some other tables.

Humphrey interrupted her thoughts. “What are you thinking?”

“Something's not adding up. Clippy just said she talked to Giuseppe during the day. But Peggy said she saw her at the salon at 8 o'clock in the evening.”

“Well, look at you, Sylvia Sleutharama! Perhaps you need to go talk to the man himself, eh?”

“Oh shush, Humphrey. It's none of my business. I have my own mission to sort out.”

“Well, that's good because I have a mission, too. I want to tell you about my plan,” Humphrey said.

“You have a plan?”

“I do. I'd bet Madonna's beauty spot that Ramone has the other half of Vitale's scissors.”

“And...”

“We go find them, get the evidence, and leave something in return.”

“I like your thinking, Hump.”

They brainstormed ideas. Humphrey came up with a 'foolproof' plan. Sylvia wasn't so sure, but eventually he wore her down and she agreed to the sting; Operation Scam Ram. Once they had finished, she threw her napkin on the table and pushed back her chair.

"Where are you going?"

"I'm going to find that Gene Bustle of Bust-A-Butt Gyms and complain about his equipment."

"OK. I'll check on Monsieur. Meet me in the rooftop bar later?"

Sylvia agreed and they parted ways.

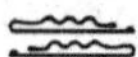

The Top Knots cocktail party on the roof terrace had finished. A few stragglers remained, but most, including Gene, had moved on to eat dinner or enjoy other entertainments. Sylvia looked in the restaurants, the casino and the gym. Ready to give up, she passed the Dynasty Ballroom and saw an A-sign announcing the next event—a seminar by Gene Bustle. She found him limbering up in the Green Room.

"Oh hi, Mr Bustle, can I have a word?"

Gene jumped a little at Sylvia's sudden arrival.

"Hello again. You're the gal from Down Under, right?"

"Yes, Sylvia. I've been meaning to catch you. Have you got a minute?"

"Sure, sure. Call me Gene. We're all friends here. Am I right? I'm preparing for my seminar but..." He looked at his watch, "I've got time for you."

He patted a seat.

"Gotta say I love the smell of the salon. Better than the sweaty old gyms. Am I right?" He laughed a warm chuckle. "Tell me about yourself, Sylvia. What part of Australia are you from?"

"Perth, it's on the west coast."

"Ahhh, the west coast. All the best people come from the west coast. Am I right?"

"I reckon!"

She could see why the guy was so popular.

"Tell me about the kangaroos and alligators you guys have over there."

"Only crocs, no gators and yes, lots of roos. I wanted to ask you about…"

"Crocs, roos?" He widened his eyes. "Never heard of those."

Sylvia laughed. "Crocodiles and kangaroos."

Gene smacked his head and chuckled at himself.

"Of course, I'm a doofus! And spiders, right? Deadly ones?"

"Yeah, but we don't really worry about them too much. So, your gym here in the hotel…"

"You're one tough chick, Sylvia. That's what I love about Australians. They don't let anything scare them."

"Well, our fashion sense is terrifying, but yeah, we're pretty resilient."

Gene slapped his humongous thighs and roared with laughter. He glanced at his watch again and patted her knee.

"It's been a great chat, Sylvia, but I need to prepare for my show. I always pump a few weights before. Sharpens the mind, you know?"

"Of course, Gene. I'm sorry to interrupt. I just wanted to ask you about a piece of equipment in your gym here. It's faulty and frankly, quite dangerous."

"Oh yeah? That's not good. My assistant Wesley manages the day-to-day details of all my gyms. Talk to him."

"OK, will do. Thanks and best of luck!"

"It's all good, honey. Enjoy the seminar! I've got a sweet offer for you beautiful people."

21

Outside the Green Room, guests trickled into the arena taking their seats. Sylvia fished the program out of her bag and dragged her finger down the list, stopping at the current day and time. 'Gene Bustle Presents an Exciting Opportunity'. She figured she may as well stay and listen to what this Gene character had to offer. He was the darling of the hotel right now, and she also found him quite charming. She found a seat and watched the people around her. As usual, Clippy was front and center. She was busy setting up the table and talking to people. Then Jerry approached her, smiling. Her face lit up, and they hugged. Jerry placed a kiss on her cheek. But Wesley, sitting at a table on the far side of the stage, glared at Clippy. He stood up quickly, but MC Brian tapped on his microphone, and the audience hushed. Wesley sat back down and folded his arms. Sylvia hoped Jerry wasn't getting into some love triangle with a man three times his size.

"Good evening, hair specialists and style expressionists! Tonight we have one of our eminent judges talking to you about a fabulous opportunity that'll get your scissors chomping. This man has won five weightlifting titles, runs a successful business, and is a true champion. Let's meet the man himself, Gene Bustle!"

The packed audience cheered enthusiastically as Gene took the stage. He waved them to stop.

"Hairdressers are the nicest people I've ever met!" he said to another raucous round of whooping.

"Thank you, thank you. I really appreciate you coming along tonight to hear my story."

He paused and sat on a stool in the center of the stage.

"I was born in a small town in Alaska. The middle one of five boys. We were broke. My mom was a sick woman. I watched her health go from bad to worse. Every month, a different part of her body failed her. The day my mother died of frostbite, I swore I'd grow up and have enough money to heat the whole town. My father died two years later when I was ten."

The audience was subdued as tears gathered in Gene's eyes. Sylvia wiped a tear away herself.

"My two older brothers went and got jobs. Me and the other two were sent to an orphanage."

Sylvia swallowed a lump in her throat. She knew the suffering of being an abandoned child.

"But I was the lucky one. My youngest brother died of influenza and the other one got caught stealing one too many times and ended up in a kid's detention center. I didn't want to die. I didn't want to lose my freedom, and I didn't want the afflictions of my mom and dad to happen to me."

There was silence.

"So, what did I do, ladies and gentlemen? Do you think I gave up?" Gene held the microphone to the audience.

"NO!" Sylvia yelled out with the rest of them.

"Do you think I cried?"

"NO!"

"Do you think I got sick?

"NO!" they all said.

"Do you think I quit? No, folks, no I did not."

Gene shook his head. He stood and paced across the breadth of the stage.

"No, I did not. You know what I did? I went to the gym!"

The audience was stunned for a moment, but then cheered as it felt the right thing to do.

"The gym saved my life, just like the scissors saved yours, good folks. My mission is for everyone to…" He held up a finger. "Number one: feel good and number two: look good. Bust-A-Butt gyms take care of number one. And you, my friends, take care of number two." He waved the peace sign in the air.

Sylvia's hands were sore from clapping. Gene made a lot of sense. A person couldn't go wrong with a fit, sculpted body and well-coiffed hair.

"I have a dream, ladies and gentlemen. I have a dream!"

Gene moved to the edge of the stage, as close to the audience as possible. He went down on his knees and held the microphone between his hands in a prayer pose. His voice dropped to a low octave.

"We heard the terrible news this morning of our unfortunate colleague. His life bought to a tragic close while he was getting a head massage—God rest his soul. It reminded me that life is but a flick of the hair in the great salon of the universe. You gotta take every opportunity you get in that salon by the short and curlies. You gotta make that opportunity shine like a pelt. And today, I'm presenting you with the shiniest opportunity, the neatest opportunity, the one that's gonna make you feel and look so good, ladies and gents."

He paused, breathing deeply into the microphone. He flung his legs out and round like a break-dancer and sat on the edge of the stage.

"In 1980, I opened my first gym," he continued, leaning in and getting cozy with the audience. "A small fitness studio. I bought second-hand equipment, I borrowed money from dangerous people, I cleaned the gym every day with my own two hands. And eventually, folks, eventually I turned a profit. As I built each muscle in my body, I built each part of my business. I studied at night and coached by day, while running the gym." He paused, stood up. "And now, seven years later, seven years of hard slog later, I own thirty Bust-A-Butt gyms all over America."

Clapping and whooping erupted. He waited for it to die down.

"What has this story got to do with you, I hear you ask? Well, just seven years after opening my first gym, I also opened my first hair salon."

Hair salon? Sylvia, and it appeared the rest of the audience, had no idea that Gene was in the hair business.

"Yes, that's right folks, we're in the same business," said Gene, as if reading their minds.

"You know what I realized?" he continued. "I realized that you people are the smart ones. Yes, you! I'll tell you why. Hair always grows. And hallelujah to that because that means it always needs cutting, and that means money in the bank for you and me. Hair always grows and bodies need to pose. So you see, my dream, our dream, my friends, is to bring the two together—gyms and hair salons. A union of like minds, of good values, of aligned vision. Together, we can help every person become whole, to help them walk in the world..." Gene ran across the stage. "... with a firm stride and head *and hair* held highhhhh!"

Sylvia took an excited breath in. The audience erupted as he held his hands in the air like a true champion. He waited for the furor to die down.

"Bust-A-Cut salon adjoins my flagship gym in the middle of New

York City, right there where the stars shop on Fifth Avenue. And my vision, my good people, is to have a salon in every one of my gyms. From top to toe, from bun to butt, Gene Bustle has you covered!"

The crowd stood on their feet and went crazy.

"Who wants a part of the action?"

Everyone yelled, "We do!"

"Well, I am so honored that you want to partner with me. This is how it works. Bust-A-Cut hair salons are a franchise. You make an investment to buy in, but here's the sweet part: all Bust-A-Cut salons get a 50% discount off hair products. Yes, folks, I'm cutting *your* costs in half." The audience wowed and whooped.

"Now, I know that many of you already own a salon. And I got a creamy deal for you too. Sign up to be a Fritz partner and for every rep you bring in, you get a reward. I'm not gonna bore you with the nitty-gritty details up here today. I'd love you to see my assistant Wesley over there..." He gestured to the table and Wesley lifted his hand.

Sylvia had wondered how Gene had managed to wheedle his way into the hairdressing world and this was how—selling product.

"Wesley will make you an appointment with me or Clippy Feathercombe to go through the details. We can't wait to welcome you to the Fritz family!"

The family? Was Gene part of the Fritz fold?

Gene jogged off stage to a final flurry of applause and an upbeat soundtrack.

"Well, good citizens of the scissors, that concludes our presentation from the esteemed Gene Bustle. Mr Bustle has provided some beverages for you to enjoy while you make your appointments," Brian announced.

A quiet hum of background music came on and the crowd chattered and made their way to the bar set up next to the sign-up table.

Sylvia had already signed Clippy's paperwork. Did that mean she would also get a commission when she signed people up? Now was the time to read through exactly what the Fritz deal meant. On her way out, she bumped into Jerry. He looked like the barber who got the Brylcreem.

"What a woman, hey?" he said, gazing at Clippy.

"She sure is," Sylvia said, glancing at her.

Wesley, sitting next to Clippy, glared back, though Jerry seemed to see nothing else.

"Well, catch ya later, dove," Sylvia said and left.

22

S ylvia rushed to meet Humphrey on the rooftop. She hoped he hadn't been waiting. The bar was quiet while most of the hairdressers were enjoying free drinks after Gene's talk. There was no sign of Humphrey, but she perched at the bar and went to retrieve the paperwork from her bag. There was only one other person sitting at the far end of the bar—Marco. He nodded into a glass of whiskey.

Sylvia ordered a cocktail and found a seat by the pool under a light. She tried to concentrate on the words, but something nagged at her. Gene had said Giuseppe had died while getting a head massage. It was an odd detail. How did he know this? She shook her head, clearing it of the puzzle that was not hers to solve. As she smoothed the page on the table, she was disturbed again by a crash. Marco staggered out of the bar and lurched into a table and chairs. He righted himself but wobbled dangerously close to the edge of the pool.

Sylvia sat up and watched. He swayed and yelled some slurred words and then fell splashing into the water. Without a second thought, Sylvia ran to the edge, flung off her shoes, and jumped in. By the time she swam to him, he was already sinking, as if resigned to his fate. Sylvia cupped his chin and kicked hard to the surface. The two bar staff, alerted by the shouts and splash, were by the edge of the pool and helped drag him out. She hoisted herself out and leaned over him, dripping. She slapped his face, but he wasn't breathing. Sylvia bent down and blew into his liquor-stained lips. She pressed on his chest, counting, and then held his nose and breathed into his mouth again. On the next set of chest presses, Marco coughed and spluttered.

"Are you OK?" she said breathlessly.

Marco retched and spat, but nodded.

"You should have left me," he croaked.

A barman draped a towel around him and Sylvia and told them a first aider was on their way.

"Did you mean to fall in?"

"Yes, no, I don't know. It's all my fault. I deserve to die, not him." Marco wiped snot away from his nose.

"Marco, you didn't kill your uncle, did you?" she asked gently.

Marco's heavy eyes looked at her sharply. "No!" He looked away. "He was right about one thing. I don't have any guts."

"So, why is it your fault?"

"I persuaded him to bring us here. Promised I was up for the competition. But I just needed to find a way to clear my debts. They've got out of hand. Some nasty people have been threatening me."

"Have you told the police?"

Marco shook his head and snorted. "No way! No, or I'll end up lying next to my uncle."

"Well, you nearly did that to yourself, anyway. You should go home and grieve with your family."

Marco coughed and spat out more pool water. "I'm his only family. Everyone else is gone. Part of me is glad he's dead. I was never good enough for him."

"So who did it?"

"I don't know! Someone who wanted something from him?"

"Clippy was with him earlier that night. Did your uncle end up buying the Fritz products?"

"Uh uh, he wasn't interested. My uncle was loyal. He used the same products, did things the same goddamn way forever. No way he was gonna change."

"And how did Clippy take it? She's pretty ambitious."

"She came into the shops all the time. Hassling him, pleading, offering discounts."

"And why didn't he want to give it a go? Couldn't he have used both suppliers?"

"I don't know why. Something in the contract set him off. What's that got to do with anything?"

The bar manager arrived back by the pool with a medic.

"Step aside please, miss. I'll check him over. Now, how are you feeling?"

"He's going to be OK," Sylvia said. She turned to Marco. "Aren't you? You'll inherit those barbershops now. Straighten yourself out. I'm excited to see where you are going to take them. You have vision, Marco. I think you can bring them back into the twentieth century. Jazz them up a bit, you know. Make your mark!"

Marco groaned and gave a deep sigh. "You're off your nut, lady. The sharks are already circling. Bust-A-Butt, Ramone, my debtors. Those salons will be gone as soon as they read the will."

The medic took his pulse, but Marco shook him off. He staggered to his feet and zigzagged out of the bar.

Sylvia was soaked through and shivering. She didn't have the energy to get back to the paperwork. What did it matter, anyway? A lonely old man was dead. Not even a wife to mourn his loss. His only living relative was not really living a life. Everyone seemed to be out for themselves in this world. Sylvia hoped that she wouldn't die without a soul to see her off, but the way things were going, she would be doing just that.

"Another drink, ma'am?" the bartender asked.

"No thanks, dove. Time to call it a night."

Thursday

23

At last, Sylvia's body seemed to get the hang of US time and she slept until dawn. It was already Thursday. Today she would work out UGH's issue. But her first job of the day was to check on Vitale. She would need the utmost of patience to calm him down. Outside his door, she could hear him whining and demanding. She knocked.

"Be there in a tick. His majesty is on the throne!" Humphrey yelled. Sylvia winced and waited. A chambermaid rolled her trolley along the corridor and parked it outside the room opposite Vitale's. She knocked and unlocked and gathered fresh linen in her arms. The lower shelf of the trolley held cleaning materials. There was something familiar about the branding. She lifted a bottle out. It had 'Blitz' emblazoned across the label and then 'Fly through cleaning like a bomb'. At last Humphrey opened the door, rolling his eyes at Sylvia. She put the bottle in her bag.

"How is he?"

Humphrey sighed, closed his eyes and shook his head.

"That bad, huh?"

Vitale sat on his balcony, his bandaged wrist resting on a chair.

"'Orrible," he called out. He stuck his nose in the air and said no more.

Humphrey raised his eyebrows at her.

"Get me out of here! If I hear one more dramatic groan, I'm going to poke myself in the ear with my scissors."

Sylvia patted his arm in sympathy.

"Ready to execute Operation Ramone?" he said.

She nodded. "We'll be back soon, Monsieur. We'll get them to send up some breakfast."

They shut the door on Vitale, grumbling about trying to eat with one hand, and hurried off to Sylvia's room.

Humphrey put his hands on Sylvia's shoulders and appraised her. "Hmmm, what will we dress you in? Let me see what you've got. Get in the shower and I'll pick something sexy out."

Sylvia pulled the hangers out of the wardrobe and dumped them on the bed.

"Oh lord," Humphrey said to the air in front of him. "I'll see what I can do. Chop, chop, in the shower! We need to do hair, makeup..."

Sylvia emerged from the shower to find her clothes ripped and one of her bras draped over his knees.

"What are you doing?" she wailed.

"Updating your look, possum. Now, I've reinforced this brassiere with hair pins. Should give those patties a lift."

Sylvia tightened the towel around her.

"And I've taken your nightie and shredded it to make a skirt. I'm gonna rip..." and he tore the bottom off a t-shirt... "this, tie it in a knot and pull it off the shoulder."

He chucked the ensemble at Sylvia, turned her on her heels, and ushered her back to the bathroom. She came out looking more Madonna than Mother Mary, which pleased Humphrey.

"*Tres jolie*, as our dear friend would say. Now remember, Sylv, we're doing this for him. Let me just... excuse me..."

He looked away but brazenly plunged his hand down Sylvia's top and wedged in a pair of socks under each cup, creating an impressive cleavage.

"Get out!" she yelled, batting him away. She adjusted the padding and straightened herself out.

"Sorry, sweetie, but a man's gotta do... Sit here. Time for hair and makeup."

Within half an hour, Humphrey had dried, crimped, gelled and created a huge back-combed fringe.

"I look like I have a ski jump on my head!"

"Keep still. I need to nail this eyeliner."

He brushed blue eyeshadow below her eyebrows and pink blusher up each side of her face. Finally, a slather of extremely glossy bright red lipstick and he declared her done.

Sylvia didn't recognize the woman she stared at in the mirror and wasn't sure she wanted to. She picked up her glasses.

"No, no. No glasses."

"I can't see a flicking thing without them."

"I reckon Ramone is better as a blur, don't you? You got your story straight?"

"Yes. You know which room he's in?"

"Yes. Ready?"

She took a deep breath. "Ready."

In the foyer, Sylvia approached reception.

"Good morning, ma'am. How can I help you?" a fresh-faced young man asked her.

She thanked the lord for watching hours of American TV and put on her best American accent.

"Hi there, I'm Cynthia Prattle from Airhair Gel International, suppliers to all the best barbers… 'Never a hair dare be in the air with our super strong gel!' I have an appointment with a Mr…" Sylvia grabbed her diary from her bag and opened it. "Ramone Figurelles. Could you let him know I'm here?"

"Just a moment, ma'am. I'll call him for you."

He dialed. After a moment, he spoke to Ramone and then put his hand over the receiver.

"He said he's not expecting you."

"Oh, well, I made the appointment months ago. Tell him I have a very special offer for him," she said, smiling.

"The lady says she has a very special offer for you." A few seconds went by. "He's asking what type of offer?"

"An excellent offer," Sylvia said, raising her eyebrows and sticking her chest out.

The clerk nodded and relayed the message. He listened and then looked at Sylvia.

"Very nice, I'd say five two, curves… yes proportionately well-endowed," he said, looking uncomfortable. Sylvia looked at him thunderously. The clerk replaced the phone.

"Sorry, Miss Prattle, but the good news is he'll be down in ten minutes."

"Perfect. Thank you. I'll sit next to the weeing cherub water feature."

While she waited, Sylvia rummaged in her bag for some chewing gum. She found the bottle of Blitz in her bag and had an idea. She peeled the Blitz label off the bottle and wiped it clean with a tissue. After a few minutes, the elevator doors tinged. She smelled him before she heard him. A tangy aroma of cologne and sweat.

"Hey babe, sorry about the mixup. My secretary didn't tell me about the appointment."

Ramone flicked his mullet behind his shoulders and held out a hand laden with gold rings and chains. Sylvia stood and took his hand. He stared directly at her scaffolded boobs and licked his lips.

"No bother. You're here now. It's so thrilling to meet such a famous celebrity."

Ramone winked at her and basked in the compliment.

"How is the competition going? Third round today—are you feeling confident?"

"Let me give you a tip. I'm gonna win this thing. I'd put some money on it if I were you."

He leaned in close and whispered, "I got a book going. I'm a sure thing." He raised his bushy eyebrows at her.

"Gee, thanks. I'll do that."

Ramone sucked in through his teeth and looked surreptitiously around. "Go see Sandra Tress, she's the girl."

Sylvia nodded. Ramone leaned back in his seat.

"Soooooo, what's this excellent offer you have for me, Cynthia?"

"Well, I represent Airhair Gel International. I have a new product and my boss is a big fan of yours. He wants your face on all the packaging. I mean, who wouldn't? Look at that jawline, the natural sheen on your skin."

"Can't argue with you there, babe. It would sell a million... But I can't."

Sylvia panicked. She needed to give Humphrey enough time to break into Ramone's room and search for the scissor blade.

"Why not? It's a once-in-a-lifetime opportunity."

"You got a strong pair of bazookas to come selling in here."

"What do you mean?"

"This is Clippy's turf, baby. You've heard of Fritz? She's got all the product we need and offering a sweet discount. Besides, most reps wouldn't rock up to her prize-winning cow and steal the cream."

"Stealing? Why? Are you going to be the face of Fritz?"

"When I win this comp, I'll be the face of everything, babe. Fritz, Tatter, billboards, TV. Even Bust-a-Butt gyms. But, hey, that's confidential, babe. Ink's barely dry."

"You're up against a tough competitor, though. How are you so confident you'll win?"

Ramone laughed. "That ain't an option. Besides, there won't be any other product except for Fritz after Clippy is done. Watch out for her, sugar lips. She's got a mean streak."

"Oh, Clippy and I go back years. She wouldn't mind," Sylvia laughed, waving her hands at him.

Ramone nodded, though his expression said otherwise.

"I like a feisty girl. Let's have dinner. Tonight. My room. Maybe just dessert, huh? What do you say?"

His gaze poured down Sylvia's cleavage.

"I... er... am flying back out to LA this afternoon," she said, squirming as far away as she could from his eyeline.

He looked at his oversized gold watch. "I got an hour. What do you say?"

Sylvia recoiled and changed the subject. "Talking about cutthroat, I heard someone was murdered here. Have they arrested anyone yet?"

"Ah yeah, poor old Gippy Bean."

"Gippy Bean?"

"Yeah, that's what his friends called him, Giuseppe Borlotti."

"I've heard of him. The Brooklyn Barber. Why do you think someone killed him?"

"The man was a pain in the ass. Too righteous for his own good."

"How can someone be too righteous?"

"Sometimes ya gotta keep your morals locked up and your mouth shut in this game. Know what I mean?" He tapped his nose. "Now Brooklyn's finest barbershops are all going to that deadbeat loser, Marco. Useless little hair clipping. Gonna be a bidding war for those sweet spots, all for him to pour the proceeds down the plug hole."

"So he won't continue on?"

"Nah, the little punk is clueless. More interested in chicks and cocaine."

"Are you going to put in an offer?"

"Hey babe, give a man some credit! Gip's not even made it to the coffin yet. Day after the funeral, I'm in."

"So we can expect Ramona Foama to expand. Your face on this product would help with that."

"Hey, I got a fine pair of cojones..." He gave his pelvis a couple of flicks. "... and I wanna keep them. Clippy would hang me out to dry by them if I use another product. No can do, sweet cheeks." He looked at his watch again. "I still got time before the comp starts. Wanna check them out?" he said, tilting his head towards his groin. "My cojones?"

"No, no," Sylvia said, standing up. She willed for the appearance of Humphrey, but he was nowhere to be seen.

Ramone sucked through his teeth. His hand shot out, and he pulled her onto his lap. She wriggled to free herself, but his hands clasped her to him.

"Oh!" she called out.

"Heh heh, you like that, hey powder puff?"

Sylvia most certainly did not like it. Nor did she like the searing pain of one of the hairpins in her bra, piercing her skin.

"Let me go!" Sylvia shrieked, the stabbing causing her to speak louder than she meant.

"Chill, baby, chill. Can't blame a man for admiring a hot chick."

"Admiring?" she shouted, trying hard to keep up the American accent and not let her inner Aussie tough chick smack him across the head.

She struggled to free herself from his lap, but Ramone's hairdressing hands kept her pinned down. The elevator dinged, and Sylvia looked over, hoping beyond hope that Humphrey would come out. But it was Danny Good. And with him, his police officers flanked Marco, cuffed and sullen. Sylvia groaned.

"You like that?" Ramone said and squeezed her thigh.

"Get off me!"

Sylvia tried to untangle herself without any more pins sinking into her flesh. Danny, en route to speak to the hotel manager, glanced over at them.

"Oh no," she mumbled.

Danny moved away from the manager and walked toward them, perhaps sensing a damsel in distress.

"Everything OK over there?" Danny called out.

She stopped wriggling and turned her head to face Ramone. She knew she might fool Ramone, who didn't know her from a bottle of shampoo, but she wasn't so sure her disguise would fool the detective. Then, to her horror, Sylvia did the only thing she could think to do. She hid her face by kissing Ramone forcefully on his greasy cheek. After way too long, but enough to be safe, she released the kiss with a sucking noise. With his mind on her lips, his hands lost their grip, and she jumped off his lap.

"Well, thanks for your time, Mr Figurelles. Let me know if you change your mind."

She scanned the foyer. Damn! Danny was still there, but he had his back to her, talking across the desk to the manager. She spun back to the lecherous Ramone, whose hands were already reaching out for her.

"Well, when you don't win, perhaps you'll consider joining us.

Here's a free sample of Airhair for you to try. Enjoy."

She dumped the bottle of labelless Blitz cleaner in his lap and stalked off.

"Hey, babe, where are you going? Hey!" Ramone shouted.

Danny looked around. Sylvia could feel his, Marco and the officer's gaze following her across the foyer. She turned her face awkwardly away from the reception desk, wincing as several hairpins stabbed her in the sides of her boobs. She didn't dare look, but she itched to know why Marco had been arrested for the murder. After fishing him from the pool last night, she knew he wasn't the killer. She felt sorry for him; he was really still a kid and mixed up in all sorts of trouble with no family left to help him.

"Hey!"

Ramone's voice projected across the lobby. She walked faster and turned to look behind her.

"Hey! What's going on?"

Sylvia was relieved to see Ramone had forgotten all about her on seeing Marco in handcuffs.

"Marco, my man, what's happened? There must be some misunderstanding..."

She punched the elevator button repeatedly, still aware of the presence of the men at the reception. The doors opened.

"Thank bloody goodness!"

She was so over the moon to see Humphrey there that she fell into his arms.

"Ugh, what a creep!"

"Who, Detective Good?" Humphrey said, craning his neck around Sylvia to watch the arrest.

"No, Ramone." She shuddered.

Humphrey glimpsed the handcuffed Marco.

"Is that...?"

"Yes, Marco is being hauled away. Please tell me you found the scissors."

"I found the scissors and have the evidence. Mission accomplished, my little possum. When the time's right, we'll let everyone know what a conniving, cheating monster that man is."

He waved the still-damp Polaroid photo in his gloved hand at her. It showed one-half pair of scissors and Vitale's gold ones stashed under Ramone's undies. She went to take it, but he swatted her hand away.

"Fingerprints!"

"Good thinking! You should become an agent like me!"

"If I have to dress up and look like this..." He looked her up and down... "No thanks!"

She punched him in the shoulder. "This is your creation, not mine!"

"Well, let's get rid of Cynthia and resurrect Sylvia. I think I prefer her."

Sylvia winced again and plunged her hand into her cleavage, pulling out a stray pin. "Ouch! If there's anything left of her. "

24

As soon as her bedroom door closed behind them, Sylvia dashed into her bathroom and dismantled Cynthia Prattle. She restored herself to her former glory, putting her hair back in its old-fashioned bob, boobs back in their usual position and unripped clothes back on. She joined Humphrey on the balcony.

"So now we can prove Ramone is definitely cheating. What next? We need to inform the committee."

"No, best not get them involved. Vitale likes to fight his own battles."

"Humphrey, Ramone will get disqualified, and Vitale will win. Simple."

"And Vitale will feel like he hasn't won fair and square against a worthy opponent. It will crush his pride, and he'll feel as humiliated as if he lost to Ramone. No, we keep this in-house."

"And what? Stoop as low as Ramone?"

"Never! We do the impossible."

"Which is?"

"Wait and see, my little possum. I need to talk to the monsieur himself first. Anyway, did you find out anything interesting from Ramone?"

"Apart from being the sleaziest man on the planet, I discovered that Clippy is flooding the market out and will destroy any competition. Even Ramone is terrified of her."

"Sounds like those barbershops were enough motive for murder. Are you going to tell the detective?"

"It looks like they've found the culprit, anyway. Though I believed Marco when he told me he hadn't killed his own flesh and blood. Besides, I can't exactly tell him I was distracting Ramone while you broke into his room, can I?"

"Mmmm, no. Oh well, it wasn't your job to solve the murder."

"No. But I'm not getting any closer to finding out why UGH isn't receiving the data."

"And as far as you know, everyone is still reporting?"

"Yup."

"So, if they are still sending the form back from the *Hair'd Honcho*, where is the information going?"

"That's the question. Where is it going?" Sylvia's eyes lit up. "Hump, you're a genius. I need to check the *Hair'd Honcho*." She drummed her fingers on her lips. "I know! Bonnie will have a copy I can look at."

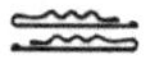

In the week of the Golden Scissors, there was no way the hotel salon could be closed or squeezed into the beauty salon. Salon Sphinx was open again at last. Peggy was back to giving mannies and peddies. The salon buzzed with guests rushing in, asking for towels, spare brushes, clips. Jimmy Baggs and Sorrento Starbright practiced on their models, and a flurry of product was being sold. Bonnie looked strained in the center of the whirlwind. She was on the phone, directing people to chairs and rubbing off the dust the forensics team had left all at the same time.

"You look under the pump, dove. Do you need a hand?"

Bonnie rolled her eyes and nodded desperately. Sylvia pushed her sleeves up, grabbed a towel out of the washing basket, tottering on the edge of the desk and folded it. Bonnie finished the call after scribbling a name in her booking diary and mouthed a thank you at Sylvia who had moved on to gowning a waiting client. Sylvia accepted a box delivered by a bellboy and tidied up a workstation.

"Where do your towels live?" Sylvia asked.

"In the storeroom at the back. Light switch is on the right."

Sylvia carried the tower of clean towels to the storeroom and let herself in. After she stacked the towels on the shelf, she turned and saw a piece of paper crumpled up on the floor. She picked it up and smoothed it out. The heading read 'Agreement'. The Fritz logo, with which everyone was now familiar, was emblazoned on the top of the page. On the back, someone had underlined several points in the body of the text. She looked around the generous storeroom. On the opposite side, the shelving was piled with dozens of boxes of Fritz. A stylist poked their head in the door.

"Chuck me a couple of towels, would you?" they asked.

Sylvia shoved the stray piece of paper into one of the boxes and passed over the towels.

Back in the salon, Bonnie had finally dealt with the stream of requests and was gowning up a client. Sylvia joined her.

"Gee, how can I thank you! You're like my fairy godmother! I didn't catch your name the other night."

"Sylvia, nice to meet you. Fifth rule of UGH; always help a hairdresser in need!"

"Nihil mali capillos!"

"Do hair not harm," said Sylvia, translating the UGH motto. She was pleased Bonnie was a member of the Guild.

"You seemed to know the poor old guy who was murdered? Are you OK?"

"Yeah, Giuseppe's been a regular at the awards for years. He was a stubborn old coot, but we were friends. I can't believe..." Tears sprung from her eyes and the gentleman at the end of her scissors looked nervous.

"Why don't you let me finish up here?"

She guided Bonnie to a chair next to the client and took the scissors. "Sit here and tell me all about it."

Sylvia placed her hands on the man's shoulders. "You just want the mullet tidied up, dove?" The man nodded and relaxed.

"I saw him in here on the first evening," Sylvia prompted Bonnie.

"Yes, he came in for his usual."

"His usual?"

"Yes, a trim. He likes my head massages and we catch up on our year. We always had a cup of coffee before the comps started. I'm from Brooklyn originally, so we had a bit in common."

"Did you work for him?"

"Nah. Giuseppe knew my pa. He used to get his weekly haircut at his place. Gip had inherited the shop from his father, who had won it in a game of cards. From that shop, Giuseppe built a bit of an empire. It's the only thing that survived his old man's gambling habit."

"Was Giuseppe a gambling man?"

"No! Gee, he hated it. Drove him nuts that the Golden Scissors was held in Las Vegas."

"So why did he come?"

"He came for his nephew. I don't know why he bothered. Marco's not interested in being a great hairdresser. The kid's a playboy."

"I just saw him being taken away by the police."

"Really? For the murder? Marco? He wouldn't have the guts or the strength to do that!"

"I don't think so either. Even though he had a motive," Sylvia said.

"A motive?"

"Well, I'm guessing as his only relative, he'll inherit the salons. How many did he own?"

"He's got the three in Brooklyn and the one in Manhattan."

Sylvia whistled. "Manhattan? Fancy!"

"Uh huh. Fifth Avenue. He said that someone wants to buy it but he'll never let it go, though. He promised his father when he died. Told him not to make the same mistakes as him on his deathbed; losing everything to gambling."

"So, if not Marco, then do you have any idea who would kill him?"

"Look, he had strong views, wasn't the most likable of fellas, but why someone would... would do that..."

Bonnie teared up again.

"Did he tell you anything concerning? Like why someone might be after him?"

"We'd just talk shop and about a few old characters that we both knew. I've been here for around fifteen years now, lost touch with Brooklyn. I already told that detective everything I can remember."

"Danny Good?"

"Yeah, that's him. Bit of a spunk!"

"I'll say!" Sylvia blushed.

"Giuseppe was complaining about how all the hairdressing salons look the same in New York, and no one wants to visit the older corner shops. He said how business was down, and he just wasn't interested in new-fangled inventions, products. You know, what all the old folk complain about. 'Things aren't what they used to be'!"

"In my day, we used an open window for a hairdryer!" Sylvia joked.

"When I was a lass, we'd get our hair to shine with spit and boot polish!" Bonnie said in an old voice.

"Back in the day, we'd use a sharp flint to cut hair!"

The women laughed. The man in the chair seemed unable to keep up with tears one minute, cackling the next.

"We shouldn't laugh. Poor Giuseppe. Marco told me he had no other family."

"No. As a young man, he was dedicated to the barbershops. Then he took on his no-good brother's son when he died. Brought Marco up from about the age of twelve. But Giuseppe ended up doing more and more keeping that boy out of trouble. Then, he said the rents were going up on Fifth. Some new landlord squeezing him dry and making demands."

"Poor guy. I hope he's getting some peace with our Lord Almighty."

Bonnie nodded. Sylvia brushed the man's neck and showed him his tidy mullet with the mirror.

"There you go, dove. Enjoy your evening."

The client paid his money and left.

"It's been good to talk, thank you," Bonnie said.

"No worries. By the way, are you still getting the *Hair'd Honcho* from the guild?"

"Yeah, got my copies right here." Bonnie pointed to a pile under the front desk.

"And sending in the report?"

"Sure, I've been a bit late, but yeah, every time."

"Hmm, that's good. Mind if I borrow it?"

"Sure, take it."

"Thanks, dove."

Sylvia went to leave but stopped and turned back to Bonnie.

"Have you read the new magazine that comes with Fritz, *Lighten Up*?"

"Yeah, I really like it."

"Have you got a copy of that I can borrow too?"

Bonnie rifled through a pile of magazines on the reception desk and handed one to Sylvia.

"Thanks so much. I'll give them back to you."

Jimmy Baggs was cleaning up after his practice session, so Sylvia took the chance to talk to him.

"Hi Jimmy! Sylvia Scutlash from Australia." She held out her hand.

Jimmy was dressed in flared red cords and wore a crinkly linen shirt. His long golden hair shimmered over his shoulders.

"Cowabunga, dude!"

"Er, nice to meet you. I read about you in *Hair'd Honcho* last year. Love your style."

"Oh man, you're too kind. It was a sweet piece. Put us on the map in sleepy old Kent!"

Jimmy had taken backcombing to a new level, creating sculpted shapes from clouds of hair.

"I can imagine. You still part of the guild? Still sending in your stats?"

"Fo' sure! I'm a dedicated company man, man!"

"Good to hear. And you haven't heard of anyone forgetting to report, or too busy?"

He shook his head. "No, but it's not a crime not to, hey?"

"No, no. Not a crime. Good luck tomorrow!"

Jimmy raised his fist in solidarity. Sylvia did the same and went back to her room.

25

S ylvia flicked through *Lighten Up*. It was a sleek publication. The images were funky and fashionable. It was colorful and slick with stylized photos of models, news on leading salons, tips and tricks, competitions and even a crossword. She found herself engrossed in an article giving six ways to flick a fringe or bangs as they called them here in America. She tossed it on the bed and took up the *Hair'd Honcho*. It was the first quarter of the 1987 edition, earlier in the year. Everything in it was normal, too normal, boring, in fact. The content felt out of date compared to Lighten Up. Maybe it was because she'd read it before. She turned to the back page of the *Hair'd Honcho* where the HAIRnet form was placed. It had been torn out, which meant Bonnie had sent her data off. Wiz had told her that the data was missing from the last six months, so this should have reached him. Where had it gone? She needed to look at a recent edition with the HAIRnet page intact but didn't want to bother Bonnie again. Sylvia thought about calling home to check her copy, but the time in Perth was around 2 o'clock in the morning. She cursed the time zones.

Sylvia sat at her dressing table and smoothed out the hastily signed paperwork Clippy had given her. The first page laid out the terms. She had agreed to stock Fritz in her salon. It was to be the dominant brand

and she could sell it to her clients. If she broke the contract, she would have to refund the discounted value. Ouch. She could withdraw from the agreement after a trial period of one year. That was a long trial. Sylvia's stomach clenched. What had she done? But then she glanced at her reflection. Her hair looked better than it ever had. If the product was so good, then what was the problem? She turned to the next page. The company had very much entered the spirit of the term 'small print'. The minuscule text was impossible to read. It was time for a helping hand from technology. She folded the paperwork and headed down to the reception to get it photocopied and enlarged.

Sylvia stepped into the elevator and was joined on the floor below by Vince Crow, the only other Australian hairdresser at the Scissors. He was from Melbourne, the funkiest city in Australia, and the only one with any real connection to the fashion world. She had met Vince a few times over the years. He had embraced David Bowie's trans-gender freedom and wore eyeliner, lipstick and nail polish.

"Hi Vince, how's life?"

"Sylv! How ya going, mate?"

"Well done for getting through. Loved your rendition of the mullet."

"Cheers, matey. You not competing?"

"Nah, you know me Vince, prefer to look and learn! Hey, are you still in the guild? Still reading the *Hair'd Honcho*?"

"Yep, though it's getting a bit daggy. You seen the new mag *Lighten Up*? It's got some cool stuff in it. Bit more hip."

"Yeah, I just borrowed a copy from the salon."

"My cousin sent it over from England. Can't wait to get this Fritz stuff in Oz."

"Clippy been hitting you up?"

"Sure has, but I haven't got the time to be selling her gear. You?"

"Yeah, got roped into being the rep! Just going through the paperwork now." She waved it in the air.

"Hah, I'll be in touch with you more often then!"

"You're still reporting to UGH, right?"

"Uh huh, get my assistant to do it every month."

"Good, good. Bad luck for poor Giuseppe, hey."

"Yeah, bad business." He leaned in close and whispered, "There's someone selling alibis if you need one."

"What do you mean?

"You know, can fix you up with a 'date' for the night, retrospectively."

"Really? Who?"

"Oh god, Sylv, do you need one?"

"Well, no I…"

"Hush, hush. Uncle Vince is in the know. Sandra Tress. You need someone to say where you were that night, she'll sort you out. It'll cost ya, but hey better than a shakedown by the Las Vegas Metropolitan PD."

"OK, thanks, Vince. I'm all good," Sylvia said, thinking that a shakedown by one member of the Las Vegas PD might not be so bad.

"No worries, matey. Good to catch up. Be in touch."

He dashed off.

At the reception desk, Sylvia handed over the contract and went and sat in a comfy lounge chair to wait. Sandra Tress, Ramone's model, was not only taking bets on the side but also selling alibis. How dare she redirect the course of justice? Didn't she realize the killer might have bought him or herself a cover? Did Danny know about this?

Sylvia gazed at the baubles with the names of past winners and took stock of what she knew. Number one, for the first time in the history of the Golden Scissors, there was a new judge who was not a member of UGH. Two, a man had been murdered. Three, someone was fixing alibis. Four, Vitale was discovered in a gym. Five, she had a crush on the lushest man in Las Vegas. And six, she had to admit the Fritz shampoo lathered beautifully and smelled gorgeous. None of it made sense, and she was no closer to discovering why UGH was not receiving data from any salons. As far as she could tell, everyone was still sending through their reports. Plus, she had been sending her information through like normal. She sighed. There had to be a valid reason. What was she missing?

The receptionist came over with her photocopies. Sylvia thanked her. Round three was starting any minute. She shoved the magazine and pages back in her bag and headed to the arena.

26

When Sylvia entered the arena, Sandra Tress loitered under the tiered seating, taking bets again.

"Who's the favorite?" Sylvia asked.

"The pilot is getting a lot of love and of course, Ramone. Crassoon's the dog after he got hauled off by the cops."

"But proved innocent," Sylvia said.

"The guy's a walking disaster. Ain't no way he's gonna make it through."

"Is this side-hustle legitimate?"

Sandra chewed her gum and gave Sylvia a withering look.

"We're in Vegas, darling. Try and shut me down and you'll find yourself on your ass in those golden streets."

"Not my business." Sylvia rebuffed the threat. "But I do hear you're in the market for other things?"

"Don't know what you're talking about."

"Oh, I thought you might know of someone who was with me on Tuesday night, before midnight."

"Sold out," she said coldly.

"I thought you were Ramone's model. Shouldn't you be getting ready?"

"I'm always his finals model. Leaves the best till last." Sandra gave her a fake smile.

Sylvia raised her eyes and walked off. So Vince had been right about Sandra Tress selling alibis. But now Danny had interviewed the last suspects and consequently arrested someone; the market was dead.

"Wanna place a bet, then?" Sandra called after her.

Sylvia ignored her and took a seat at the front of the arena. Judging by Vitale's state that morning, she had no idea if he'd be able to compete. She wanted to be on hand if anything else went wrong.

The lights dimmed and she could hear Brian breathing into the microphone. She turned her thoughts to the competition.

"Hairdressers and hair Messers! Welcome to round three, where we're getting to the pointy end of the Golden Scissors. In a few hours, we'll say goodbye to six more talented contenders. Al, tell us about today's heat."

Sylvia wondered where Humphrey was.

"Why thank you, MC Charmly. Charmly by name, charmer by nature." Al gave a flourish to backstage. "Today's round focuses on styling. The contestants are free to create a cut, color, or upstyle to their parting's content. They have two hours to devise a new look. To push their scissors to the edge. To surprise and de-light us with their innovation and flair."

"Let's bring them on folks!" the MC said.

The hairdressers entered the arena to Prince's *U Got the Look*. Ramone ripped his shell suit tracksuit open to his navel and strutted the whole perimeter. The women (and some men) squealed in raptures. Sylvia huffed in repulsion. Gloria Frank came on in goggles and a 1950s-style full pilot outfit. Gonzalo § puffed on a cigarette, then leaned over the barrier and gave it to a swooning fan. Sorrento Starbright had crammed his generous body into a pastel pink suit.

Vince Crow wore a rah-rah skirt, headband and bangles up and down both his arms. Sparkle Jones, Carrie Straw, Billy Torch and Jimmy Baggs all made an entrance, dressed in their best.

Sylvia craned her neck. There was no sign of Vitale. Surely he wouldn't give up? The contestants took their places and looked bewildered as the music played on, waiting for the final competitor. Ramone limbered up, unfazed. Sylvia shuddered at the memory of her contact with him that morning. Along with the other contestants, Ramone arranged his tools and prepared himself. She noticed that his kit was to the left of his model. Then he did his usual and slicked back his hair with his comb—with his left hand.

The crowd burst out in applause as Vitale finally entered, dressed in his black jeans with a silver dinner jacket draped over his shoulders. Sylvia blew out puffed cheeks and then dropped her jaw as he twirled around and whipped his jacket off into the air. Underneath, he had his right hand strapped behind his back in a sling. The spectators gasped and pointed.

"What the clippers is he playing at?"

Humphrey arrived in the seat next to her.

"He's just trumped Ramone, that's what he's playing at!"

Ramone rubbed his upper lip with his fist and scowled. The judges rushed over and spoke to Vitale. After some minutes, they relayed the message to the MC.

"Good people, we have an unprecedented development in the comp. Unprecedented," said Brian, rolling the 'r'. "Vitale Crassoon is so confident in his abilities, he has given himself a handicap by tying his dominant hand behind his back. Our ambidextrous, indefatigable Monsieur Crassoon will attempt to style his model at the very crux of the competition with... one... hand. I repeat, folks, we have a one-handed contestant."

Sylvia put her head in her hands.

"He certainly has a big pair of hairballs, that's for sure," Humphrey said.

"How is he going to pull it off?"

"If anyone can, he can. Let's cross our fingers and combs. Anyway, maybe Ramone will have some struggles too."

"What do you mean?"

"Nothing at all, my possum. I'm just itching to see this round."

Humphrey leaned back in his chair, smiling.

The timer began. Sylvia felt sick with nerves and clutched Humphrey's hand as they watched. Vitale used his fingers, knees, elbow and teeth to juggle the comb and clips, scissors and spray bottle.

"He's struggling," she said.

"Vitale struggles when he's lying on a couch drinking champagne. Life isn't life if he doesn't struggle."

"Yes, but he can't deal with pain."

"I doubt he can even feel his fingertips right now. I don't even want to tell you about the cocktail of painkillers he has taken."

"He's wincing."

"That's just his game face."

The other contestants twirled around their models, piling hair up, pulling it out, coloring and crimping. Humphrey elbowed Sylvia, whose eyes could only be on Vitale.

"What's up with Ramone?"

Ramone's mouth twisted and he seemed to shiver. His body twitched again, and he gave his butt a little shake. He returned to work. But then he gyrated his hips and screwed up his face. His model, whose style looked like she'd swallowed first a hairdryer, then a crimper, frowned as he rubbed himself against the back of her chair. Then he sucked in his mouth like he had bad wind. He wiggled his bottom and jiggled his knees until, finally, he gave in to what was bothering him and stuck his hand down the back of his pants. As he gasped out in relief, the audience gasped in horror. He rubbed and clawed and plucked. The audience laughed in horror and glee. All dignity lost, Ramone attacked the irritation with a hairbrush down the front of his pants. He displayed an expression that is usually kept for the bedroom as he tried to relieve the fire in his groin. Sylvia, Humphrey and the entire room hooted and whooped.

"Was this anything to do with you?" Sylvia asked Humphrey once she controlled her laughter.

Humphrey shrugged. "No!"

"Liar, liar, pants on fire!" They burst out laughing.

"Scratch that! Of course it was me!"

As the itching seemed to calm down, Ramone returned to his model. She jumped up and recoiled from him.

"You're not touching my hair after your hands have been down there!" she squealed, which produced another round of laughter from the spectators.

"OK babe! I'll go wash my hands," he said.

"No way, Mr Figurelles. I ain't having those hands near my head!"

Ramone punched his left hand into his right. He rummaged around in his tool kit and pulled out a can of hair color. Without touching her hair, he sprayed the ends electric blue before dropping some small bows into the radiating hairdo. Every now and then, he gave his bum a shake as another wave of itching threatened.

Unperturbed by the events, Vitale used his entire body to manipulate his model's hair. He held a row of hairpins and a comb in his mouth, had hairspray tucked under his armpit and swung the chair left and right with his knees.

At last, the countdown began.

"Three, two, one! Hairstylists, step away from your models. Go take a well-earned drink while our scrutineers do what they do best."

Vitale sighed. Ramone stalked off after giving Vitale an evil stare. The models were invited up to the stage, and each one was assessed and discussed.

While the judges made their appraisal off stage, Ava Rice swept onto the stage. She wore a gold man's suit with a Liza Minnelli wig and oversized eyelashes. The intro music soared, and in a rich tenor, she sang:

Thank you for comin' here
The chairs are all ready for you
Our games will be starting soon.

These are exciting days
Slowly being whittled away
Just another heat for today
Oh, but we're proud of you, we're so proud of you!
Nothing left to make you feel small
Cos winning is what makes you feel taaaall...
Gold!
Always believe in your goal
You who can finish it all
You're undefeatable
Always believe in
'Cause you're gold!
We're glad you're running this race
Striving to win it with grace
You're undefeatable
Always believe in...

After the hair is done
We hope you find a little more fame
Remember things won't be the same
It is already round three
The best ones will rise to the top
Taking the trophy back to the shop
We believe in you, we believe in you
Nothing will make you feel small
Cos winning is what makes you feel taaaall...
Gold!
Always believe in your goal
You've got the power to know
You're undefeatable
Always believe in, 'cause you're
Gold!

She ended with a bow and gold glitter descended over the stage.

"Ladies and gentlemen, the judges have eliminated the first 5 contestants. We are sorry to say goodbye to Jimmy Baggs, Sparkle Jones, Carrie Straw, Billy Torch and Gonzalo §. Give them a big clap, folks!"

The hairdressers, looking glum, bowed and waved before exiting.

"And two innovators are straight through to the top four. Let's get excited for Gloria Frank and Sorrento Starbright!"

That left the final two places between Vitale, Ramone and Vince. The chatter of the audience grew while the judges deliberated.

"It's not surprising they are in the bottom three," Humphrey said.

"It is surprising they're not out, really," Sylvia replied. "I mean, Vitale was one-handed and Ramone couldn't keep still!" They laughed shortly.

"Vitale's style was good, but it lacked his usual intricacy and detail."

"Ramone's doesn't even look finished!"

"But see Vince's? Absolutely no imagination! No color, nothing new there. It's the innovation round!"

"Glad I'm not a judge. Geez, when will they decide?"

It was another painful twenty minutes before Brian opened the microphone again.

"The judges are ready, folks. Over to you Al."

Al stood on the stage and waited for the chatter to die down.

"Thank you for your patience, one and all. It was a tough one and we've had quite a battle back there." Al glanced at Gene and Emmy.

"Anyway, we have the final two contestants to get through. Please congratulate Ramone Figurelles!"

Ramone jumped up and ran his fingers through his hair. He kissed his medallion and threw his arms in the air.

"Dammit," Sylvia murmured. "Come on, Monsieur!"

"And our last finalist is..."

The crowd took a breath, eyes on Vince and Vitale, quivering on the stage.

"Mr..."

Sylvia gasped.

"Or should I say Monsieur Vitale Crassoon!"

"Mon Dieu!" he cried.

"Thank the Lord!" Sylvia said.

"About bloody time!" Humphrey sighed. "We're gonna need more than a bucket of champagne this time!"

27

Sylvia and Humphrey took Vitale back to his hotel room to dissect the event. Humphrey couldn't keep quiet any longer and admitted to putting itching powder in Ramone's pants.

"You are a genius, mon ami! Zat is the funniest thing! We must go and find him and push zee feather!"

"Yes, let's celebrate!"

"You are both incorrigible! OK, I'll meet you in half an hour. Where?"

"The casino!"

"Humphrey," Sylvia warned. "You promised."

"Just to drink, you silly sausage. Cross my heart!"

"OK, watch him, Monsieur."

Sylvia hurried off. She wanted to visit the gym. Vitale had just got through the round with an injured wrist, but Sylvia still intended to complain about the running machine. The elevator doors slid open, and she locked eyes with Detective Dreamboat. All thoughts dissolved.

"Hey sugar," he drawled.

"Detective! You're still here? I, um, heard Marco had been arrested?"

"Did you? Well, you can't keep things quiet around a bunch of hairdressers, can you?! I *did* arrest him, but for possession and intent to supply, not murder. Another good outcome from the rumor mill!"

"Oh! So we still haven't caught the murderer?"

"We?"

"You, of course, you. How is the investigation going?"

"Slowly. Do you know how many guests and staff there are in this hotel? I'm just heading up to interview the last few."

"Any suspects? Got forensics back?"

Sylvia loved a good Cagney and Lacey and knew the drill.

"Maybe and maybe. You're one curious little lady. Wanna tell me why you're so interested?"

"Just making polite conversation, Detective Good."

She turned her back to him and pressed the 19th floor button. They stood in silence as the elevator went up. She could feel his eyes on her behind.

"Watch any good movies recently?" he asked.

She turned around and nudged him with her elbow. He was smiling.

"Hey, how about dinner?" he asked.

A bolt of electricity went through Sylvia's body.

"OK, but no talk about movies."

"Or murder investigations."

"Deal."

"Meet me at the Eat-All-You-Can-And-More buffet, 7.00 pm."

They arrived at her floor, and she slipped out, turning to smile. She sighed. Her body fizzed. A date, a dinner date! She could hardly wait.

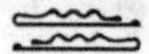

Wesley was in the small office on the phone. Sylvia hovered outside. He had the same build as Gene, flaring from his bottom out to shoulders as wide as a whale. His skin was the same burnished copper tone and looked as oiled as the inside of a sardine can. He wore a neon orange t-shirt with the Bust-A-Butt logo on it. It clashed horribly with his skin tone.

"Yeah, get that delivered to the Brooklyn depot."

He paused as the caller spoke "..."

"Great, thanks. And Gene wants an update on the Glitz labels. The style needs to be the same for all the Hiliterati products."

"..."

"OK, good."

Wesley finished his call and put down the phone. He pulled a sheet of paper from a pile and jotted down some notes. Sylvia tapped on his door.

"Yeah?"

"Hi there. Could I have a word with you about one of your running machines?"

"Er, I'm a bit busy here. What's the problem?"

"My friend, Vitale Crassoon, had a nasty accident yesterday. It could have cost him his place in the competition. You really need to keep your machinery in good working order."

Wesley sighed. "I'm up to my ears in paperwork here, lady. I'll check it out later."

He waved her away. Sylvia balked.

"I don't think you understand how serious this is. Monsieur Crassoon could sue you. This must be a safe place for people to work out."

"Are you threatening me?" He set his pen down with a clunk and glared at her. "I work for a very, very powerful company. You find someone smart enough to come for us, then I wish you luck."

Sylvia put her hands on her hips and glared back at him. "And Monsieur Crassoon is a very, very influential, world-renowned, much-loved hairdresser..."

He picked up his pen, looking her in the eye, and wrote two words on the notepad to the left of him.

"Check machine," he said. "It's on the list. Goodbye."

She scowled at him and left the office, indignation fueling her footsteps. Well, his so-called powerful company wouldn't last long if that was how they dealt with customers and their complaints. She wondered if Gene knew his employee was so rude.

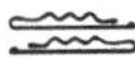

Vitale and Humphrey sat at a table in the bar. Vitale waxed lyrical about his performance and Humphrey looked relieved to see Sylvia. She gestured she would get drinks and turned to the bar. As she turned, she was surprised that Wesley was also at the bar, the orange expanse of t-shirt stretched across his back. How had he managed to get there before her, especially when he said he was so busy? But then the man turned, and she realised it was Gene.

"Hey, Sylvia!"

"Oh, hi Gene." She smiled and shook her head. With all that muscle, bodybuilders looked exactly the same. "I just spoke to your assistant about the faulty running machine."

Gene looked puzzled.

"Vitale, he fell off?"

"Ah yeah, yeah. He made a great comeback!"

"He did, but the point is, your assistant Wesley didn't seem to take it seriously. In fact, he was quite rude!"

Gene closed his eyes and sighed. "He's not a people person like me. That's where we differ. I'll have a word with him. Thanks for bringing it to my attention."

Another voice travelled down the bar. "Hey, toots! What can I get ya?"

It was Johnny Bonkers. Sylvia thanked Gene and joined Johnny.

"Hi, Johnny, thanks, but I'm buying a round for my friends. Have you met Vitale Crassoon?" she asked. "Why don't you and Sally come and join us?"

"Splendido!"

Sylvia returned to the table and gathered extra chairs.

After introductions, Sylvia leaned in. "So, we got interrupted yesterday. You were going to tell me which hairdresser has more than one wife," she said in a low voice.

Humphrey gasped and rubbed his hands together. Johnny lifted his chin and looked them all in the eye.

"You gotta promise me you won't breathe a word to anyone."

They all nodded. "Cross me heart, hope to die, stick a scissor in my eye!" Humphrey sang.

"Bad taste, Hump," Sylvia admonished.

Humphrey shrugged a semi-apology.

"Who?" Sylvia whispered.

"Ramone Figurelles."

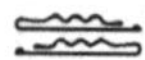

Sylvia went to get ready for her dinner date. Johnny, Sally, Humphrey and Vitale were on a roll. She'd left them as they discussed the list of tricks Ramone had pulled on Vitale. It didn't surprise her that Ramone was a two-timing creep. She couldn't understand why one girl would fall for him, let alone two. She shook her shoulders and turned her thoughts to a man that every woman would adore, buzzing with excitement. Back in her room, she opened her wardrobe. What to wear? Sylvia wanted to look her best for Danny. Her stomach lurched in excitement.

28

S ylvia used all the Fritz products this time. She blow-dried and
styled and combed and sprayed. Her hair had never been so easy
to style. It hung in bouncy waves around her face. She looked at
the label on the bottle of shampoo to see what the magic ingredient
was. But she couldn't read the writing in the steamed-up bathroom
without her glasses.

Danny had suggested the King Midas Eat-All-You-Can-And-More
buffet in the hotel. She arrived there to find him waiting for her at a
table.

"You look stunning," he said as he kissed her on her cheek.

Danny was dressed in his trademark cream linen suit but wore a
fresh pale-yellow t-shirt underneath his jacket. Despite an afternoon
of interviews, he looked and smelled as fresh as a lime spritzer. They
settled themselves at the table and ordered drinks.

"What's the number one thing I should know about Sylvia
Scutlash, Ms?" Danny asked.

"Are you interrogating me, Danny Good, Detective?"

"Maybe. I find it hard to not be on the job."

"Me too. I can tell who a person is just from their hair, you know."

"Oh yeah? Who am I then?"

"A well-conditioned, smooth guy. I reckon you're a perfectionist. Doesn't like loose ends. Makes you good at your job."

"Very astute, Ms Scutlash. You should be in the police force; we could use a keen eye and someone with a feel for people."

"Are you offering me a job?"

The server interrupted and invited them to the buffet. There was a pink fish curled amongst bright green leaves, golden corn chowder, and salads dotted with multi-colored vegetables. Further along; creamy dishes with fish roe, a pig with an apple in its mouth, and sides of beef sliced into fans. To finish; jellies in glasses, layers, slices and rounds of every imaginable food and some unimaginable, all arranged in artistic fashion. At either end of the table, an enormous ice statue of king Midas flanked the feast. Five chefs in tall white hats stood behind the buffet table, looking reluctant to ruin the feast they had so painstakingly prepared.

"Hey there, mate!" It was Jerry. He and Clippy had arrived at the buffet behind them.

"Hi guys! What a spread, hey?" Clippy said.

She had her arm looped through Jerry's. They both glowed. After a few pleasantries, they all headed back to their tables with plates piled high. There was a comfortable silence while they tucked in. Sylvia puffed her cheeks and took a break from the delicious meal.

"So, how long before we're free to leave the hotel?" Sylvia asked.

"Should be done by tomorrow afternoon. I have a handful more people to interview. There can't be that many more left-handed people here."

"Why left-handed?"

"Giuseppe was in the chair furthest to the right against the wall. The scissors were at an angle that could only be dispensed by a left hand."

"Interesting."

Deep in thought, Sylvia glanced over at Clippy and Jerry. They gazed into each other's eyes. Jerry reached for her hand. Clippy gushed more than a faulty faucet. Sylvia would never have put the two together, but then love follows no rules. It has no considerations for continents or convenience. The two mirrored each other, picking up a caviar-stuffed vol-au-vent and feeding it into each other's mouths.

"Ramone!" Sylvia exclaimed. "Have you interviewed him?"

"Who?"

"Ramone Figurelles. I'm sure he's left-handed! And a cheating creep!"

"I can't suspect people on the grounds of being a cheating creep, Sylvia."

"Ah, but he told me he'll put a bid in for the salons as soon as they bury Giuseppe and apparently Giuseppe had some intel on him."

"And what might that be?"

Sylvia leaned in. "He found out that Ramone had two wives."

"Why would a man do that to himself?" Danny said, shaking his head.

Sylvia rolled her eyes. "Some people are just plain greedy. He's got motive, strength and he's left-handed!"

"But he has an alibi."

"Pfft, alibi! Anyone can get an alibi," she murmured.

"What do you mean by that?"

"There was a chick setting people up with false alibis. You didn't know?"

"You're kidding me!" Danny put his head in his hands. "Who? Who is it?"

"Well, you'll never guess who."

"Who?" Danny exclaimed.

"Sandra Tress... who just happens to be Ramone's model."

Danny swore. "Awesome, just awesome. Sorry, Sylv, I have to make a call."

He pushed out his chair and asked the maitre'd if he could use the phone.

Sylvia sighed and took a sip of wine. She watched Jerry and Clippy again. It seemed that now all was not peaceful in paradise. Jerry raked his hand through his hair, his face screwed up. Clippy shook her head. She put her hand on Jerry's, as if asking for forgiveness. Jerry pulled away, his brow furrowed in disbelief. Was Clippy breaking up with him already? Sylvia felt sorry for Jerry. In all the years she had known him, she had never seen him as happy as he was this week. Was love worth it? The pain of unrequited feelings, the compromises, the aggravations?

Danny slid back into his chair.

"Sorry about that. Had to get the wheels in motion to pick up this Sandra Tress. Thanks for the heads up, by the way."

The server came and cleared their table.

"Do you want dessert?" he asked.

"Oh, phoof, no way. I'm as full as a goog!"

Danny gave her a puzzled look. She laughed.

"It's an Aussie way of saying I'm full up!"

"Ah, right!" He chuckled. "OK. Then how do you fancy going back to the hotel nightclub and hitting the dance floor?" He boogied his shoulders.

She smiled and sighed happily. "I would love that!"

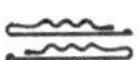

Hairdressers, assistants and hairstyling buffs were packed into the

Nefertiti Nightclub, dancing and drinking. Sylvia loved to boogie, and Danny pulled her to the dance-floor. Colored lights strobed, and the hot, steamy air mingled with spurts of dry ice. Danny had smooth moves. He held her gaze, the corners of his eyes dancing. Sylvia spun and shimmied, feeling free and fabulous. The music faded, and a slowie took its place. He grabbed her two hands and brought their bodies close. Thrills radiated as she placed her hands on his solid shoulders, inhaling his aftershave. She rested her head on his chest. They swayed to Lady in Red. She reveled for a moment in being held—a state she rarely experienced. Her eyelids flickered in the pleasure of it, but she caught sight of two people just beyond the DJ booth, shielded from the dance-floor by a fake palm tree. As the disco lights flashed, she could make out Clippy's fluffy mane and a man with a bulky frame—Gene. Jerry was there too, his hands clenched at his side. Through the strobing lights, Sylvia could see they were arguing. Gene towered over Clippy. She could see his profile; his jaw jutting out, spitting words at her. Jerry put a hand up and pushed it against the mountain of muscle. The big man grabbed Jerry by his shirtfront and shook him. Then Clippy raised her hand and slapped Gene's face.

Sylvia tensed in surprise.

"Hey, sweetcheeks," Danny whispered in her ear.

As the lights flashed on and off the scene, Gene reeled and held his face. He shook his head and leaned towards her threateningly, but Clippy grabbed a full cocktail glass off a high table and threw its contents in his face. She ran into the arms of Jerry. They rushed off, hand in hand. Gene slunk away into the shadows, the great man clearly not wanting to be seen in this humiliating way.

"Sylvia…" Danny breathed and said something in her ear.

She twisted to look further over Danny's shoulder as Gene disappeared out of view. Danny pulled away and put his hands on her arms.

"Sylvia?"

"I'm sorry. What?"

"A little nightcap... in your room?"

"In my room? Oh, uh..."

She looked into his gooey chocolate eyes and her knees wobbled. Oh, the temptation. She could barely believe this was happening. Imagine! The two of them together, in her room, on her bed... in her bed! She'd never quite made it that far with a man—her first marriage being one of convenience. She wouldn't know what to do. But for what? A one-night stand? Her Catholic upbringing pulled at her shirttails; despite the fact she had tried to remove her shirt on many occasions over the years. Danny waited for an answer.

"Come on." He breathed into her ear, running his finger smoothly, suggestively up her arm, her neck and tracing it across her lips. It was electrifying.

"What do you say?" he pleaded, pulling her even closer.

"Danny, I'd love to but..."

Sylvia imagined him in the morning, shirtless and tousled. She put her hand over his and felt the smooth skin along his firm forearm. A movie played out in her mind: She visualized them at his Vegas apartment, which would be cool and open plan, like a studio. He'd have a dog, and they would walk the dog, hiking in the mountains. Then, a child, maybe two or three little girls, and he would solve cases, and she would be at their new house, yes a big house, and she would have coffee with... with? The dream ground to a halt. Who was she kidding? She looked into the melting pot of his eyes, stood on her tiptoes and kissed him squarely on the mouth. The cushion of his lips gave way, and for a delicious moment, they were one. But Sylvia pulled away.

"Not tonight, Detective Good, maybe another time."

He looked at her, more surprised than wounded.

"Ah Sylvia. You're one classy lady."

"Goodnight, Danny."

She pecked him on the cheek and pulled herself outside his magnetic field. There was something going on with Gene, Clippy and Jerry. It didn't make sense. Her scalp tingled. Clippy had persuaded Jerry to join the fold, so why would Gene be angry?

Sylvia headed to the elevator. As she waited, the door of the gents squeaked open and Gene walked out. He gave her a broad smile.

"Nothing like Vegas, hey! You're not at the disco?"

He looked and sounded fresh and chirpy. Sylvia gave him a tight smile and shook her head.

"Well, have a great night!"

Sylvia entered the elevator. The guy was good. He could turn a smile at the drop of a... well, at the drop of a glass of Kahuna Cocktail!

29

Sylvia retired to her hotel room in a daze. She had just turned down the sexiest man in the universe, and seen Clippy slap Gene and run off with Jerry. What was going on between Gene and Clippy? Yesterday morning, he was consoling her at breakfast. Yesterday evening, she was helping him at the seminar. Sylvia was too hyped up to sleep and the thought of turning on the TV now terrified her. Trying to get things straight in her head, she grabbed the hotel writing paper pad and made some notes:

1. Everyone is still reporting to UGH, but UGH is not receiving any information.

2. Reports are therefore being intercepted.

3. The reports are faxed or posted to Wiz's house in Kalbarri.

4. Find out who has access to Wiz's place when he is away.

She sighed and sat on the end of her bed, staring at the orange curtains that were closed against the Las Vegas skyline. She pulled the enlarged contract out of her bag. It now spread over three pages in readable text, but the photocopier had cut off the ends of the sentences.

    1.Pursuant to a binding agreement between the undersigned party and Hil
signee has been granted a license to market and distribute Fritz products.

2. The signee shall consent to being inducted as a member of HUH and disen
professional groups and organizations within the industry.

3.The signee shall undertake to provide HUH with regular updates & detail
concerning all commercial activities related to the business.

4.In the event that the signee entertains the idea of divesting their bus
they shall be duty-bound to formally notify HUH of such intention and abid
a stipulated period of three months,during which HUH reserves the right to
an offer to acquire the signee's assets and other interests.

Now, therefore, it is hereby agreed between the parties hereto as follows:
The undersigned party shall, act in accordance with the aforemention
& conditions, & any violation thereof shall be deemed to be a material bre
agreement.

Report all data to HUH? What is HUH and who is Hil...? She shuffled through the papers to find the original contract to read the end of the sentence, but it wasn't with the photocopied sheets. The receptionist must have forgotten to give it to her. Sylvia swore.

If she understood any of the convoluted language, by signing this, she had agreed to leave UGH and report to this HUH. Her stomach turned. She couldn't believe she had signed the papers without even seeing what she had got herself into. Damn Humphrey and his gambling habit! She wondered if Clippy caught everyone unawares with her busy talk and powers of persuasion. Only a person with supercharged eyesight and an ability to translate legalese would be able to read and understand these terms. She knew that very few hairdressers who signed up would read all the small-print. They wouldn't even realize they had agreed to send their data to them. But Fritz had yet to hit Aussie shores. So if they had defected to HUH, that still didn't account for the missing Australian data. And finally, what did an 'offer to acquire the signee's assets and other interests' mean?

Sylvia recalled the paperwork she found in the storeroom at

Bonnie's salon. Could that have been Giuseppe's? Was he also questioning the small print? Perhaps that's why he refused to sign up, thus enraging Clippy. Bonnie had said he was a stickler. She wished she had kept the page she found in the salon to see if Giuseppe had the same concerns as her. Was it enough to get him murdered? Did Clippy murder Giuseppe? The thoughts made Sylvia's scalp itch and her mouth go dry. Peggy had said Clippy was in the salon with Giuseppe that evening. But that was earlier, and Giuseppe's time of death was around eleven o'clock.

Sylvia needed to find out who was behind this HUH. Who was Clippy ultimately answering to? She noted the time. It was ten o'clock, which meant it was 1.00 pm in Perth. She picked up the phone and asked for an outside line and dialed. The landlord of the Sip & Snip that fronted Wiz's house, Gary, kept an eye on it for him when he was away.

Gary answered.

"Hi Gaz. It's Sylvia. How you going?... Yeah, sounds like you're busy in there... Lunch time rush? Blimey, I've just had my dinner!... I'll be quick. I'm just wondering if anyone has been into Wiz's place while he's been away... They haven't? Are you sure?... Oh, what sort of security has he put in place?... CCTV? What's that?... So he can watch his own house on the telly?... Extraordinary! Trust Wiz to have the latest gadgets! Thanks for your time, Gaz. Yes, I'll be up for a visit soon."

She placed the receiver back down and looked at the ceiling.

"So where the devil is the information going then?" she said to the room.

Sylvia opened the copy of *Hair'd Honcho* Bonnie had given her and dragged her finger down the inside of the front page until she found the address and fax number; PO Box 60, Main St, Kalbarri. Something wasn't right with that. She knew that Wiz received the data directly. She needed to talk to Jez and dialed out again.

"Hey, dove!"

"Sylvia! How's Vegas?" Jez shrieked.

"Flashy, fun and, well, fatal. Listen, Jez, can you do me a favor? Go into the storeroom and find an old copy of the *Hair'd Honcho*. Find the one from a year ago."

"Hang on."

Sylvia could hear the TV in the background, the trickle of a running tap and the crackle of cicadas. In that instant, she missed the Wavy Lady and Hardup and Jez, and even the old ladies she cut and colored every week. She heard the thump of magazines being tossed to the floor in the back of her salon.

"OK, I'm back, love."

"Flick to the front page where the address is and tell me what it says."

"60 Main St, Kalbarri. Fax number 09 258741."

Sylvia reread the details back to Jez to confirm.

"It definitely does not say PO Box 60?"

"No, just 60 Main St."

"Well, I'll be blown over! Jez, can you get all the copies and tell me when the address changes from 60 Main St to PO box 60 Main St?"

Sylvia basked in the familiar sound of the salon—the gentle hum of the drier, the squeak of the cupboard door. Jez came back on the line.

"It changed six months ago, Sylvia. What's going on?"

"I'm not sure yet. Thanks so much, dove. I'll be back in a few days. Love to all!"

Sylvia said goodbye and hung up the phone, gazing at the magazine in her lap. The address in the latest copy was: PO Box 60, Main St, Kalbarri, fax number 02 258741. Someone had subtly changed the address and fax number before the magazine went to print. Which meant that someone had either deep pockets, influence, or both.

She leafed through her address book and dialed a new number—the Kalbarri post office. These calls were going to cost her a fortune. She'd have to bill Wiz.

"Hi, Ron. It's Sylvia from the Wavy Lady... Good thanks. How's Mary's perm holding up in the heat?... Yes, I know it's a shocker! Look Ron, Wiz is having a spot of bother with his post. I don't suppose you can tell me who PO Box 60 belongs to? Someone told me they'd sent a letter there by accident. I know you're not meant to divulge the names but... Yes, I'd come up to Kalbarri myself to sort it out, but I'm in Las Vegas and Wiz is off somewhere... Yes, I know, it's very snazzy here!... It's just the letter is quite important, and I need to get it to him."

Sylvia was running out of the appetite for deceit, but she didn't know how else to persuade Ron, the Post Office manager, for the info. He came back on the line.

"So you're saying that any post that comes into that box gets immediately redirected? To America? Can you give me that address in America, Ron?" Sylvia winced in hope.

"OK, yes, I've got that." She jotted the address down. "Higher Union of Hairdressers, New York, you say? Fifth Avenue. That's a long way from Hardup. Thanks so much, Ron. I'll have to chase up this Higher Union of Hairdressers and try to get the letter back. What a mix-up. I don't know what the world is coming to. Send Mary my love. Next time I'm in Kalbarri, I'll give her a free cut and color. Bye. Bye. Bye, Ron."

"Who are you?" Sylvia said to herself.

There were still a lot of unanswered questions, but she had made progress. With the satisfaction one gets from unraveling a large knot of wool, Sylvia fell into a deep sleep.

FRIDAY

30

The restaurant was quiet the next morning. She suspected most guests were ordering a breakfast of anti-acids and orange juice in their rooms after the drinking and partying the night before. Sylvia sipped her coffee and curled a finger around her soft, pliable locks. Her thoughts flitted from the delicious kiss with Danny to her mission and back to Danny again. They were from such different worlds, yet they seemed to fit together. He laughed at her jokes. She loved his dedication to creating a safe city. And then there was that firm body, those lips. She sighed, wishing she had accepted his offer for a nightcap in her room... but then, no, she was on a case and couldn't afford any more distractions. She needed to find out who was behind HUH. Who was creaming off the years of hard work Wiz had put into UGH by illegally changing the address in the *Hair'd Honcho* so that all reporting was made to them instead? Where could she source that kind of information? Then a memory of the previous night intruded; his fingers trailing up her arm, the imprint of his warm hand at her waist. His penetrating desire. She bit her lip. No, no, no. She needed to go to a library and find a directory. Who would have access to information about organizations like HUH? The police? She sighed. All thoughts seemed to lead to Danny Good. Yes, Danny could help.

Perhaps they could help each other out again. It seemed that he was getting nowhere with the murder investigation and she had already proved to be of some assistance, professionally speaking, of course.

"Dime for your thoughts?" Danny slid into the chair opposite her.

"Wow, g'day, detective. You're at work early this morning."

"I couldn't sleep, had too much to think about." He smiled at Sylvia, who blushed and raised her shoulders coyly.

"Yeah, this murder case has me stumped," he said, rubbing a hand over his smooth, square jaw.

Sylvia's shoulders dropped.

"I know how you feel. You know..." she glanced at him, "maybe I can help you. Two heads and all that."

He leaned back in his chair and tilted his head at her.

"OK, you *did* help me last night." He pinged back to the table and took a moment. "I can't find a motive for this murder. Giuseppe was well-respected. He didn't live a very exciting life."

"Giuseppe's barbershops in New York are a goldmine. Apparently, a lot of people want to get their mitts on them. Like I said, Ramone. Did you interview Sandra?"

"In the process. She's giving us the names of every last person who bought an alibi from her. But it hasn't got us any closer; just revealed a few people spending time with people they shouldn't have been." He bunny-eared 'spending time'.

"And what about Ramone?"

"Er, he had a grand total of five females confirming he was firmly ensconced in his bed that night."

"Ugh!" Sylvia screwed her face up.

"By the way, we're taking a look at the polygamy rumor."

"That's good. Hey... What if he hired someone?"

"What do you mean?"

Sylvia leaned across the table and whispered. "You know, an assassin."

"I think you've been watching too much TV." He smiled and winked.

Sylvia felt the blood rise to her cheeks; the one side indignation, the other embarrassment. She crossed her arms.

"Fine, work it out for yourself. I'm just trying to help!"

"You're right. No, you're right, Sylvia. I mean, they left no fingerprints. Could be a pro job. I'll get the boys to run some checks, see if there is any M.O."

"Good idea," Sylvia smiled. "So, if Ramone turns out to be a cheating creep and not the murderer, who else could it be? Even though Marco denied topping his uncle, he had plenty of motive and no way of proving his alibi with the drug dealers. He could have done it in a drug-crazed fury."

"Except we have an undercover man on the inside. He was with Marco on the night of the murder. That's how we got him on drug possession."

"Wow. OK. Not Marco, didn't think so. So, who are your prime suspects?"

"I'm not meant to divulge this, Sylvia. I don't know how you've managed to get this much out of me!"

"Hairdressers are trained to extract information."

Danny laughed as if she was joking. Sylvia raised her eyebrows and tilted her head. She went through her own list of suspects in her mind.

"Does Clippy Feathercombe have an alibi?"

"Yes. Why?"

"Maybe she wasn't the murderer, but I can't help but think Clippy had something to do with it. She was the last to see him alive, even though the time of death was around eleven."

Danny rubbed his hand over his top lip. "Go on."

"Well, she was desperate to get Fritz in his salon for some reason, or at least her boss was hell-bent on him stocking it. He told her to do what it takes to get the deal."

"Who's her boss?"

"The man of the moment; Gene Bustle."

"Maybe with Giuseppe out of the way, she could convince Marco, though that seems somewhat extreme. She had keys to the salon, and she followed Giuseppe after his fight with Marco at the karaoke bar."

"They had a fight?"

"It was pretty nasty. There was no love lost there." Sylvia shook her head. "Even though he'd turned Clippy down countless times, she told me she was giving him a demo. Peggy saw them in there."

Danny's thoughts swirled in his eyes.

"Interesting, but I have several people confirming she was in the casino, too."

"I wonder if she's left-handed."

Danny took out his notebook. "I'll check, but I don't think she has the strength."

"You're right. What about Gene Bustle? He and Clippy had a big row last night."

"An argument isn't proof of anything."

Sylvia thought for a moment. She remembered the conversation she overheard next to the milk fountain.

"It didn't mean anything to me at the time, but on Tuesday, I heard Wesley saying that Giuseppe rented one of his shops from Gene. The same building as his flagship store on Fifth Avenue."

Sylvia paused. Her eyes searched the air in front of her, recalling the words.

"And?"

"And that Mr Borlotti could get in a coffin if he didn't cooperate. Gene was very keen to get his business. Said he'd fire Clippy if she didn't find a way. Perhaps Clippy and Gene worked together?"

Danny thought about it.

"That would explain how he knew Giuseppe got a head massage from his murderer," she added.

"What are you talking about?"

"Giuseppe's hair was damp and tousled when he was killed. Gene mentioned in his seminar that he died whilst getting a head massage. If he wasn't the murderer, how would he know this?"

"Huh," Danny grunted. "But he's a businessman, not a thug. Plus, his alibi is watertight. I've got every guest in the hotel telling me how he entertained them in the casino that night."

"I wonder where the other half of the scissors are? Have you looked for them? Only someone prepared with a small screwdriver or strong enough to pull them apart would be able to separate those scissors. The other half were not on the scene, were they?"

"Huh. Good point. I've overlooked that there must be another half." He swore under his breath and squeezed his dimpled chin. "We need a search warrant to find them, but I don't have the manpower to search every nook and cranny in the hotel."

Sylvia sipped her coffee. Danny smoothed his hair behind his ears.

"Thanks," Danny said, touching her hand. "This has been a great help." He paused and looked into her eyes. "Sylvia?"

"Yes?"

"Can I take you out again?"

She wobbled her head from side to side. Did she really want to fall for this guy? Out here so far from home? She looked into his eager eyes, those lashes. He trusted her, he listened to her. She felt special in his company. She tipped her chin and took in his gorgeousness.

"How about I show you a bit of Vegas?" he said.

How could she resist a bit of sightseeing with a handsome man?

"You could ride shotgun, and I'll take you to some of my favorite spots?" he urged.

Sylvia's shoulders lifted again. "I'd love to, as long as I'm back in time for round four this afternoon."

"Great! I'll meet you in the foyer in an hour."

Danny took her hand and kissed it. "Until then."

He strode smoothly between the tables and out the door as Sylvia watched his tight, linen-clad bum.

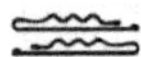

As the detective left, Humphrey came in.

"Hump, where have you been?"

"Never mind. I have intel."

Humphrey shot a look around them and leaned in close.

"Earlier, I overheard Danny and one of his officers talking."

"What did they say?"

"The full forensic report has come back, and Giuseppe was drugged before he was murdered."

"Drugged? He didn't mention that."

"Who?"

"Never mind. That would explain why there was no sign of a struggle."

"It was a hallucinogen. And the pen Danny found had Giuseppe's fingerprints on it."

"Do you think he was in there doing the crossword?"

Humphrey shook his head.

"Me neither," Sylvia agreed.

"But why would someone drug him?"

"Maybe there were two people involved. The washer and the killer could have been working together. Clippy got him to the salon. She could have drugged him and let someone else make the fatal blow."

"But then, why didn't she just poison him?"

Sylvia shook her head. "Giuseppe wasn't very popular, and he owned all those barbershops. Maybe they were trying to scare him."

"Or bribe him," Humphrey suggested.

"He was an old man—don't think he would have put up much of a fight."

Humphrey glanced at his watch.

"Flick-a-doodle, is that the time? I need to get back to Vitale. He's in the bath. Gotta make sure that nobody puts him off his game today. See you in the arena."

Humphrey gave Sylvia a quick kiss on the cheek and dashed off.

Sylvia chewed pensively on a slice of toast. Fifth Avenue had come up three times now. Both Giuseppe and Gene had their businesses there. And the post for UGH was being redirected there. Was it a coincidence? There was one piece of evidence that might help. The papers she found in the salon storeroom. Perhaps they would uncover a motive or even have fingerprints. She wondered if Giuseppe had had the same reservations as her. Could that be why he was murdered? She shivered. Maybe Clippy was guilty of more than being an aggressive salesperson. She needed to get that paperwork, and if her suspicions proved correct, she needed to warn Jerry.

31

Sylvia decided to get ready for her lunch date first and then call on Bonnie. She grabbed a small clutch and emptied out her big handbag, tossing the *Hair'd Honcho* and *Lighten Up* magazines on her bed. Then her fingers landed on the label from the bottle of Blitz cleaner she'd given Ramone. She smiled, wondering if he had tried using it yet. The label was curling at the edges, and she smoothed it out absentmindedly. The Blitz font was a similar style to Fritz and, she remembered now, the Mitz nail varnish. She inspected the label which had the name 'Hiliterati' on the top. She fetched a bottle of Fritz product from the bathroom and scrutinized the label. Sure enough, Hiliterati manufactured the shampoo too. She was sure Wesley had mentioned that name, along with the fact he worked for a powerful company. This brand seemed to have its fingers in a lot of hair. Sylvia's scalp tingled, and that was never a good sign.

She leafed through Lighten Up, passing over the pages she had read the day before. She stopped at a headline that said:

Higher Union of Hairdressers Highlights

There it was again. A union for hairdressers, and this time being featured in the magazine. She read on.

> The hairdressing industry worldwide is delighted to announce the formation of this new association; The Higher Union of Hairdressers (HUH).

Of course! HUH was the acronym for the union. She berated herself for not making the connection. It went on:

> This fantastic new association goes above and beyond to serve all workers in the follicular industry. HUH affords many benefits to its members. These include the protection of employees' rights. It lobbies for better renumeration in an industry that is notoriously poorly paid. HUH advocates for hairdressers and provides information and advice. Membership with HUH also offers a wealth of bonuses, like discounts and competitions. One

such competition which
has got salon owners very
excited is the chance to win
a year of free advertising or
a salon makeover.

Membership requires that
salons send their statistics
to compile all the latest
industry trends. Find the
form at the back of the
magazine.

Sylvia flicked to the back page. The form was almost identical to the one UGH published in the *Hair'd Honcho*. She opened her copy to compare the two. The address and fax number of both were: PO Box 60, Main St, Kalbarri, 02 258741. Her blood ran cold. Whoever was behind this operation was the one diverting data away from UGH.

She searched for the enlarged contract on her desk. The cut-off word 'Hil' must be Hiliterati. Hiliterati, HUH, the magazine and even their product seemed to trump anything UGH offered. Sylvia retrieved her notes from earlier. She added:

1. Hiliterati makes a range of products, including Fritz, Mitz, Blitz, Glitz.

2. The sales rep contract was with Hiliterati and they seemed to be affiliated with an association called HUH.

3. The small print on Clippy's paperwork required all reps to

be members of HUH only, therefore pushing out UGH.

4. HUH's address was in Kalbarri and being redirected to New York.

5. Gene is selling Fritz in his franchises. Is Gene employed by Hiliterati?

6. Wiz brought Gene in as the new judge, so who is Gene to Wiz?

Sylvia checked the time. She could make it to Salon Sphinx before lunch and see if the discarded paperwork was still in the storeroom.

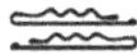

The salon was as busy as it ever was. Vince Crow was showing impressed stylists how to create the perfect shag. Bonnie was on the phone and Sylvia mouthed she wanted to get some Fritz from the storeroom. Bonnie nodded.

Sylvia made her way to the storeroom at the back of the salon and opened the door. To her horror, the room contained a tight pair of buttocks, jiggling in front of her. Fritz product was dashed off the shelf to the floor. Sylvia's jaw dropped as Clippy squealed at the interruption, and Jerry released her ankles to the floor.

"Oh my lord!" Sylvia stammered.

She slammed the door closed and put her back against it. Whatever had been troubling the lovebirds last night was clearly resolved now. The door pushed against her back and she released Clippy and Jerry as they straightened their clothes.

"Clippy was just showing me some of her product," Jerry rasped.

"I bet she was," Sylvia said.

They looked sheepishly at each other, their mouths holding in smiles. They slunk off and Sylvia giggled with stunned eyes. She wasn't sure if she wanted to go into the storeroom again, but she took a breath and opened the door wide. She grabbed a pair of plastic gloves used for applying hair dye and put them on.

There were fewer boxes on the shelves now, but she had shoved the paperwork underneath the bottom of the pile. Clippy and Jerry's 'product display' had dislodged the boxes, leaving a corner of a page sticking out. She extracted it, grabbed a can of hairspray, and made her escape.

Bonnie was at her desk as the two lovers dashed out of the salon. She screamed and dropped the phone.

"I know," Sylvia said. "Get a room!"

Bonnie stared out of her salon like she'd seen a ghost.

"Bonnie, dove, are you OK?"

"Yes, no. I mean yes, but..."

"What's wrong?"

"That was Detective Good. He thought Giuseppe's will might shed some light on who would want him dead."

"I told him his barbershops were valuable."

Sylvia felt a little smug that she had helped him pursue an avenue.

"He left them to me." Bonnie hiccuped and burst into tears. "And now they'll think I killed him." She slid to the floor and sobbed. "I had no clue! He never told me, and now they'll say I did it."

Sylvia sat beside her on the floor. "No one will believe for a moment that you had anything to do with Giuseppe's death. They'll just ask you some questions. This is great news."

Bonnie let out a flurry of tears and laughter, followed by more tears. Sylvia put her arm around her.

"Excuse me." A voice chirped over the counter. "I have an appointment."

Bonnie blew on a tissue, wiped her eyes and straightened herself out. "Of course, ma'am," Bonnie got back on her feet. "Take a seat. I'll be right there."

32

Sylvia checked her appearance one last time in the mirrored elevator wall. She had dressed in Capri pants and a neon pink t-shirt. After reapplying a slather of cerise lipstick, she ran her fingers through her glossy hair and deemed herself good to go. She fizzed with excitement. The smell and atmosphere of foreign lands brought her alive. When she visited a new country, everything always seemed brighter, bigger and better than sleepy old Hardup, a small suburb in the most remote city in the world.

Las Vegas did not disappoint. They pulled onto the main boulevard, 'the Strip', in Danny's police car. Her head swiveled from side to side, taking in the flashing lights, huge hotels, fancy restaurants. Elvis lookalikes jostled for space with cowboys. She felt like she was in a movie set. Danny pointed out various landmarks, giving her a potted history of the city.

"So who are you investigating today, detective inspector?"

"You."

"Me?"

Sylvia blinked. Was she a suspect?

"Yes, I've lured you away to give you a thorough interrogation."

She looked at him in alarm, but his eyes crinkled in humor.

"Ha ha. Very funny."

She relaxed and gazed out at the kaleidoscope whizzing by.

"I saw Bonnie earlier. She told me about the inheritance. She's in shock, had no idea she had inherited the salons."

"Anyone can bring on tears and act innocent."

"That's nuts! Bonnie is not the culprit."

"Find me the evidence, Sylvia, and I'll believe you."

Her thoughts whirled. She had to prove Bonnie was innocent, and the only way of doing that was by finding the real murderer.

"How's Marco holding up?" she asked.

"He's got the shakes and cries a lot."

"Poor kid."

Danny cocked his eyebrows at her. "You make your choices."

"Sometimes we don't get a good range of choices."

"And sometimes smart people make the most of what they got." He looked at her pointedly.

"True," she conceded. She was a case in point.

They sat in silence again.

"Do you think Giuseppe had a choice in his demise?"

"I don't draw conclusions until I have the evidence in front of me."

"Well, let's pick up where we left off earlier. What if I told you I might have some evidence? Would I get anything in return?" Sylvia played her card.

Danny looked at her in surprise, and to her annoyance, mild disappointment.

"Yes, you would. An arrest for withholding evidence and bribing a police officer."

"Do you do everything by the book?"

"I didn't get to being a detective by making up my own rules. Spill it, what have you got? It could be important."

They pulled up outside the police station. She said nothing.

"Come on, you either go in a free woman or in handcuffs. That enough choice for you?"

This time, he wasn't joking. Sylvia was beginning to think he was no fun at all.

"Jiminy clippers! Anyone would think you don't have any leads."

Danny stiffened at her cheekiness and looked at her with raised eyes.

"OK, OK. Keep your hair on." She pulled Giuseppe's paperwork out of her cavernous handbag. "I found this in the storeroom at Bonnie's. It was on the floor."

Danny put a glove on and took it, glancing over the page.

"What is it?"

"It's one of Clippy's contracts. She gave one to me as well, and when I read the small print, I realized there are some pretty shady moves going down. Someone, and I'm assuming it was Giuseppe, underlined the same clauses that concerned me. Apparently, he was refusing to sign."

"Apparently? Why do you think that?"

"I overheard some of their conversation when I was in the salon the day before the murder. Plus, Bonnie told me he was an old stick-in-the-mud."

"Doesn't sound like a motive for murder."

"I know, but Gene was hellbent on getting Giuseppe's business. He told Clippy he'd fire her if she didn't get the contract signed. Something is telling me it's a link."

"OK, I'll send it to forensics." He was silent for a moment. "And what might you want in return for this so-called evidence?"

Sylvia smiled. He wasn't so bad after all.

"I need to find out who owns a company called Hiliterati."

"And why do you need to know this?"

"I have my own investigation going on, as it happens."

"For the murder?"

"No, silly!"

"Hmm. Mysterious, but I guess I can find that out for you. As long as this has no bearing on my investigation."

"Of course not!"

Danny escorted Sylvia into the police station. He got her a coffee from the vending machine and invited her to wait. Another police station experience to chalk up. There was the usual march of felons, petty thieves and prostitutes. After fifteen minutes, just as her coffee was cool enough to drink, Danny reappeared.

"I made a call to the Securities and Exchange Commission. Get this Sylvia, Hiliterati is owned by Gene Bustle. And not only that. Hiliterati also make Glitz cosmetics, Critz pet shampoos and Splitz dance & leisure wear. Flitz airline is about to open up. Then there is a gross-sounding Gritz food and a record label called Hitz."

"Gene Bustle? I should have known. Bloody hell! He's trying to take control of every commodity on the market. Ramone told me Clippy wanted Fritz to be the only hair product range. What if Gene Bustle is not only after monopolizing the hair industry but all the other industries, too? All along he's acting so dumb and sweet, and in reality he's a greed-crazed megalomaniac."

Danny nodded. "Thing is, it's all legal and above board."

"But not necessarily ethical."

Danny shrugged his shoulders. "Not my jurisdiction, I'm afraid."

"Look, I better get back to the hotel. The next round kicks off in half an hour."

"I'll drop you. Still got a couple of people I need to talk to."

Back in the hotel lobby, Sylvia turned to the DI.

"Thanks, Danny. I really appreciate your help. It was a lovely drive.

You live in a great place."

"Always my pleasure to spend time with a beautiful woman. Perhaps I could round it off by showing you Vegas by night? It's a whole other experience. Dinner tomorrow?"

Sylvia's heart soared. She tried to temper the huge smile breaking onto her face. "I'd love to!"

33

The arena was more packed than ever with hairdressers, stylists, barbers and models as the competition progressed.

A drumbeat burst from the speakers. **Dum**... dum dum **dum**, dum dum duuuuuum. **Dum**... dum dum **dum**, dum dum duuuuuum.

Ava Rice burst onto the stage. She wore patent white platformed wrestler's boots to her knees, tiny shorts and glittery top. A white silk cape, edged in gold brocade, flowed out behind her. She had a headset microphone attached because she wore boxing gloves, and she pumped them with the next round of **DUM**... DUM DUM **DUM**, DUM DUM DUUUUUM. She came to the front of the stage and sang...

Gowning up, back in the seat,
Trained so hard, made advances.
Went the distance, now I stand on my feet,
Just a stylist and a will to survive

Do the cut, give the dryer a blast
Another head, another story
Keep on going, move those scissors so fast

Wash, color, cut, comb, primp and blow-dry

Ava flicked her wrists, and the gloves flew off to reveal a comb in one hand and a pair of scissors in the other. The crowd went wild.

It's in the eye of the styler
It's the thrill of the cut
Rising up to the challenge of our rival
And the last happy client
Who sits his butt in the seat
Puts their hope, faith and trust... in the eye of the styler!

She strutted the breadth of the stage, flashing her gargantuan eyelashes to the audience, while the music pumped.

Hand to head, his life is complete
Psyching up, drinking coffee
The smell of shampoo and hairspray so sweet
To win this comp is his way to survive

It's the eye of the styler
It's the thrill of the cut
Rising up to the challenge of our rival
And the last person standing
Is the cream, the elite
The Golden Scissors is in... the eye of the Styler!

DUM... DUM DUM **DUM**, DUM DUM DUM, DUM DUM DUUUUUM
The eye of the Styler

Ava collapsed into a dramatic crouch, head down, scissors and comb held aloft. The crowd clapped and whistled, but Sylvia was distracted. She had to tell Humphrey about the unsettling discovery that Gene Bustle was muscling his way into her industry, along with many others. Ava broke into another number and Sylvia made her way to the Green Room.

The room was abuzz. The contestants limbered up in their unique ways with their supporters helping out. Ramone was shirtless and punching the air in front of him like a prizefighter. Gloria stared into the burning end of her cigarette, and Sorrento ran worry beads through his fingers and seemed to be praying. But Vitale was not there.

"Jiminy Clippers!" Sylvia mumbled. "Where is Monsieur?" she asked the model waiting nearby. The girl shrugged.

"Have you seen Vitale?" she asked Sorrento and a few others. Someone said he hadn't shown up yet.

Ava had maybe one more song after this before the round started. Sylvia ran to the elevators and struck the call button over and over. She arrived at Vitale's floor and rushed to his room.

"Monsieur! Are you in there?" she yelled as she pummeled on the door.

"Zank see Gods of Hair! Help me, Sylvia!" Vitale's voice was muffled.

"Open the door!"

"I cannot! I'm stuck in zee bathroom. Zee stupid door won't open!"

"The competition is about to start! Where's Humphrey?"

"There will be no Humphrey when I get my fingers on him!"

Sylvia looked frantically up and down the corridor but there was no one in sight.

"Hang on, Monsieur!"

She rifled around in the bottom of her bag and pulled out two bobby pins. With nimble fingers, she fashioned the pins into right angles and twisted off the ends. Then she gently inserted the pin into the keyhole and gave it a wiggle, flicked it up and across. The door opened.

"I'm in!"

"Get me out of here!" Vitale wailed from the bathroom.

Sylvia tried the door, but it didn't open.

"Is it locked?"

"Non. I never lock."

She banged her shoulder on it and rattled the handle. "Then why won't it open? It's like it's stuck fast."

At these words, she saw a rock-solid drip of glue oozing from the doorjamb.

"Oh no. Someone has super-glued the door shut."

"*Merde, merde, merde*! Get me out, Sylvia!"

The semi-final of the Golden Scissors was starting in a matter of minutes. There was no time to call for help. Vitale was freaking out. He yelled and banged on the door.

"Calm down. I've got this," Sylvia said through the door.

Once again, she delved into her bag of tricks and pulled out the nail varnish remover Peggy had given her. She squirted it around the door frame.

"Monsieur! Squirt your toothpaste around the edges of the door. It'll help dissolve the glue!"

"*Oui, oui*! But hurry, Sylvia!"

"Did you hear anyone come into your room?"

"Non, I fell asleep in zee bath."

"Asleep? How can you fall asleep at a time like this?"

"My wrist is so sore. I took some painkillers and poof! I was out."

Sylvia shook her head. She got the nail file out of the kit and began sawing the gap between the door and the frame. The glue was loosening now.

"Where is Humphrey?" they both said together.

"Ah! I can see the file poking through," Vitale cried.

"Stand back! I'll try opening it."

Sylvia heaved her shoulder on the door. She went flying into the bathroom and into the arms of a naked Vitale.

"Jiminy Clippers! Get dressed!"

He kissed her on both cheeks, and she tried not to look at his bare bottom as he turned to his wardrobe.

They rushed to the arena and got to the Green Room just as the ecstatic applause wore off and Ava was leaving the stage. Ramone gave Vitale and Sylvia a scowl as they arrived as he punched the air to hype himself up. Brian's voice boomed out.

"Hair Stylers and Scissor Smilers, let's welcome your judges to the stage... Al Fa'Rou, Emmy-Lou Bangs and Geeeeeeene Bustle!"

The judges ran on. Al resplendent in a mustard yellow boxer's get-up. Emmy-Lou in red, and Gene looking very comfortable in blue silk shorts and a matching singlet that was no competition for his pectorals and biceps. They all wore boxing gloves and did a choreographed fight, ending in them all being winners as they held their joined hands in the air.

Sylvia took a seat and scanned the auditorium for Humphrey. Jerry and Clippy were in the front row, snuggled together and talking animatedly. Bonnie was there too, sitting with Peggy. The two looked to be back on good terms.

"And now for our fabulous, fingers-on-fire finalists..."

The contestants entered the arena one by one to the quieter backtrack of the 'Eye of the Styler'.

"Mr Ramone Figurelles!"

Ramone came on, still shirtless. His chest was slick with oil. A thick patch of black hair cushioned a medallion.

Gloria Frank and Sorrento Starbright arrived to applause and cheers.

"And Monsieur Vitale Crassoon!"

In comparison, Sylvia had never seen Vitale look so diminutive. His heeled boots, designer jeans and black T-shirt only accentuated his small wiry body. She took a deep breath and blew it out of her lips loudly. Four live models sat in chairs, gowned with damp hair. Lights flashed and dry ice rose from two jets.

"Al Fa'Rou, tell us about today's round," Brian asked.

"There are no limits to what you can do with a head of hair. When you polish the crowning glory of a human being to a shining jewel, when you treat your canvas as the most precious thing, when you make your riches by tending each filament with awe, you are at the top of your game. We urge our semi-finalists to allow their creativity to flow like a golden river to produce a hairstyle that says, 'All that Glitters'."

Vitale had thought long and hard about which cut and color to do and had discussed it in much detail with Sylvia and Humphrey. Should he play to his strength with a classic or show his innovation as Humphrey urged him to? Should he push his scissors to breaking point and attempt a 'Louis 18th Mohican'?

"Our models are lined up, caped up and ready to go. Two of these talented top knots will be leaving the competition today. Emmy is heading down into the arena to have a chat with our contestants."

Emmy-Lou appeared on the floor with a microphone and approached the first finalist.

"Howdy, Ms Frank, can I call you Gloria?"

The Amazonian Gloria cranked her model's chair up until it almost swayed. She pulled a pair of thick goggles down over her face.

"This is why they call you 'the Pilot', Gloria. Can you tell us why you wear the goggles?"

"I don't vish to get any fluids in my eyes."

"Fluids?"

"In my line of verk, I get back splatter. It is not nice."

"In your hairdressing line of work?"

"No, in my assassin line of work," she said with deadpan seriousness.

The audience and Emmy laughed. "You guys and your hair salon humor!"

She moved on.

"Mr Starbright! Do you moonlight as anything else? You certainly have the name for it!"

Sorrento was a gargantuan man, but not in the same way as Gene. Loose folds of chin wobbled as he talked. As usual, he wore a suit, though his jacket looked more like a tent. His dainty hands held his scissors aloft, and it was a wonder they reached his model over the barrel of his body. He glanced at Emmy-Lou over the top of his round glasses and shook his head.

"I am a purist, Ms Bangs. I deal with hair and only hair. It is my one love."

"Ah, a romantic! My favorite kind of hairdresser."

She moved on to Ramone.

"Our reigning champion, Mr Figurelles. How ya feeling today?"

"On top of the world, cutie. Wanna be my date for the award ceremony? Have this winner take you out for dinner?"

"Wayell, if confidence ain't your middle name, I don't know what is!"

She bumped Ramone with her hips and moved on.

"And last but never least, the eminent Monsieur Vitale Crassoon! I heard the queen is offering you a knighthood. Is this true?"

"Peut etre oui, peut etre non. Zees rumors!"

"You'll always be my knight in shinin' armor!"

While Emmy Lou was doing her rounds, Sylvia assessed Gene. Had he infiltrated the music industry awards with Hitz? Had he attended aviation conferences, spruiking Flitz? Was he hitting up Jane Fonda with his Splitz leotards? How much power did he and his business have? And how would she find out? He was the owner of a powerful company which was sticking its fingers in a whole heap of industries. If he knew about the valuable data all the hairdressers sent to UGH, then would he somehow try to redirect it to his business? She needed to get some more information on him.

But first she had to find Humphrey. There was nothing on earth that would stop him from being here to protect Vitale and cheer him on. Something was up.

34

Though Sylvia was loath to leave Vitale in case of any more foul play, the round was going smoothly. She slipped out of the arena and crossed her fingers that Ramone had learned his lesson.

There was only one place Humphrey would be—the Tutankhasino. Sylvia fast-walked through the slot machines and pushed the doors into the casino proper. As usual, it was busy. She scanned the room. The roulette was quiet apart from the rattle of the dreaded ball, heralding ruin. Humphrey wasn't playing craps or blackjack. She ran around the many tables, but Humphrey was not there. She couldn't think of anywhere else he would be. His loyalty to Vitale surely trumped anything else? Maybe he was sick. She asked the concierge if anyone was in the sick bay. No. She went up to the roof bar, the restaurants, the shops, but she couldn't see him. Bonnie hadn't seen him. Time was running out. She needed to get back to check on Vitale. She tried Humphrey's room in vain. Perhaps he had gone to the washroom. She doubled back to the casino, and the scene was much the same. As one of the bronze-chested security guards opened a concealed door and entered, she heard people arguing. She rushed over and put her ear to the door.

"My dear fellow, I refuse to leave. I have paid for my room and I assure you, I'll pay this little debt. Just give me one more round."

"Rules are rules, sir. You have extended your casino marker and now you're causing a scene. It's time to leave."

Sylvia pushed the Head of Horus on the panel and the hidden door swung open. The room was like the inside of a pyramid with fake ancient Egyptian chalices, gold jewelry and statues. The card table was a glass-topped sarcophagus with a wrapped mummy inside. The Casino Manager, security guard and another man all turned to look. Humphrey raised his chin to the pointed ceiling and slumped his shoulders. "Sylvia! What are you doing here?"

"What am I...? Humphrey, A: you promised me you had stopped gambling and B: Vitale is cutting for his place in the bloody final... ALONE!"

Humphrey sighed and ran his fingers through his hair. "I can explain..."

"No, I don't want to hear it." Sylvia turned to the manager. "What does he owe?"

The manager nodded to his assistant, who wrote a figure on a notepad, whipped it off and handed it to Sylvia. She looked at it and her eyes popped out of her head.

"Flicking hell! A little debt! How could you let this happen? You and you!" She pointed to all the men in the room as her voice got louder. "This is a lifetime's savings. Humphrey, what have you done?"

"I'm sorry!" Humphrey stammered. "They say I have to leave."

"You can't leave now. He can't leave!" Sylvia turned to the manager.

"Rules are rules, ma'am."

She took in a deep breath and put her palms together in front of her lips. "What can I do?"

"You can pay the debt."

Humphrey stuttered, "No, no, no..."

Sylvia thought for a moment. She didn't have time to babysit Vitale for the rest of the competition. Not only was she on the edge of discovering who was sabotaging UGH, but she was also falling for an amazing man who seemed to like her back!

"If I vouch for him, will you let him stay?"

"What will you vouch? As you can see, this is a considerable sum."

"Yes, a considerable sum *you* lent him. I'm sure this so-called free loan is now accruing a nice sum of interest?"

The manager shrugged. "I don't make the rules. I just keep 'em. Now what will you vouch for Mr Lebonne?"

"My salon. I will hand you the deeds until Mr Lebonne has squared up his debt."

"There is no way I'll let you do this, Sylv. You can't risk your livelihood for me. I'm not worth it. Just forget it. I'll work it out. I'm going."

"Not so fast, matey," Sylvia said in her most commanding voice and grabbed his arm.

"You don't get to run away from your friends, your debts or your responsibilities. It's not an option. I know you'll pay the debt."

"You still trust me? This stupid idiot who breaks promises, who has no self-control?"

"Yes. I do. Go and check on Vitale and I'll do what has to be done here."

The Casino Manager nodded, and Humphrey escaped out of the tomb.

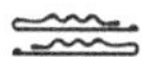

After Sylvia had signed her life away, she needed a moment to sift through her feelings of anger, fear and disappointment. She went to

her room and flopped on her bed. She was sick of people trampling on each other to get on the highest pile. Whether it was money, fame, business or winning, it brought the worst out in people. This casino would not get away with it—preying on vulnerable punters—she'd make sure of that. There was a murderer in their midst, and no one would sabotage her precious United Guild, either. Wiz, Al, Emmy and she had all worked too hard. She sat up and pulled her sweater over her head and pulled a new disguise out of her wardrobe.

Back down at the front desk, dressed in a white blouse and black skirt, she ordered a sandwich and a banana smoothie with an umbrella to be sent to Mr Gene Bustle's room. At the room service kitchen, she hid behind a pair of curtains, waiting for the tray to leave the kitchen.

After a few minutes, the tray emerged, and the waiter entered the service lift. She followed. The elevator went up and up and up to the uppermost floor. The waiter turned left and stopped at a door. Sylvia hovered just out of sight. She grabbed a duster from the housekeeper's trolley. The waiter knocked. There was no reply. He knocked again. Then he called "Room service" and left the tray outside the door. Sylvia dusted a painting as he returned to the elevator. She hurried to the door and extracted a hairpin from her hair. With a little wriggle and a deft flick of the wrist, the door clicked open.

Gene's room was one of the much-lauded luxury penthouse suites. Sylvia entered a grand sitting room with floor-to-ceiling windows along the entire wall. In a corner, a bar stocked an array of colorful bottles of liquor. Another shelf was stacked with protein powders called Builditz. There was a vast desk upon which sat Gene's beloved mobile phone, plugged into an enormous charger. An untidy pile of computer printouts took up a large part of the desk. In the center of the room, there was a bank of modular sofas, one of which had a pillow and a sheet strewn across it. Sylvia stood still and listened, ensuring there was nobody else in the suite. She crept to the bedroom and inched open the door. There were crumpled sheets scattered across the bed, but it was otherwise empty. Lastly, she checked the bathroom. It was spacious and sumptuous, complete with a spa bath. A range of Fritz lined the vanity, along with creams of teeth-whitener, tanning cream and baby oil. She used a flannel to pick up the tanning cream and sniffed it. It was familiar; the smell she had detected at the murder scene.

Back in the sitting room, Sylvia peered at the computer printouts. They were huge, perforated pages studded with holes at the edges and filled with rows of figures. She pushed her glasses up as if that would make them somehow work better, and tried to decipher the data. It was all gobbledygook figures until she recognized a name. The Fluffy Coif was a salon in London. She looked for the next break in numbers. Jim's Trims was another salon. If this wasn't HAIRnet data, she'd be knocked over by a hair tie. She lifted the top of the concertinaed sheets, but the next sheet slid off the table. The pieces fell, one after the other, like a slinky.

"Flicking hell!" she muttered.

She gathered the sheets in her arms and arranged them back on the desk. In doing so, a familiar name caught her eye. On an A4 sheet of paper, the contract named Emmy-Lou Bangs and the Tongs as the signee, and as she read further, she understood they had been signed by Hitz record label. So Emmy-Lou had succumbed to Gene's charisma too. Sylvia shook her head in dismay.

Next, she snooped around the bedroom. She found a stack of Gene's publicity photos, a pair of woman's panties, dumbbells and a wardrobe full of gigantic shirts, shorts and workout clothes. One last look around the sitting room and she had done her sweep. Tap-tappity-tap.

"Housekeeping!" a woman's voice called out from the corridor. Sylvia gasped. The keys rattled in the lock. Sylvia ripped off her shirt and skirt and jumped onto the sofa. She pulled the sheet over her. She would pretend to be a floozy of Gene's if discovered. If not, she'd hightail it once the maid went to clean the bathroom. The girl pulled her cleaning trolley through and closed the door behind her. Sylvia held her breath and clutched the edge of the sofa. She could smell the tanning lotion on the sheet and tried not to retch. Her fingers landed on something cold and sharp in the gap down the back of the sofa. The maid headed into the bedroom and Sylvia emerged from the sheet. She pressed back the sofa cushion, revealing half a pair of scissors wedged down the back of the couch. Her blood ran cold, her hand flew to her mouth. With the edge of the sheet, she prised the scissor blade from its hiding place. They could be from any pair of scissors, but in all her time in the salon, she rarely saw a lonely blade. She turned it to inspect the blade. The screw was missing, and they were slightly bent from being wrenched apart. The tap in the ensuite turned on, then the bathroom door clicked shut. If these weren't the other half of the murder weapon, her name wasn't Sylvia. Evidence, hard, cold evidence. But how could she explain it to Danny? He would be furious if he found out she had broken in. She could hear the rustle of the room-maid's hosiery coming towards the door. She wedged the scissors back, threw on her clothes and tip-toed out of Gene's suite.

Dressed now in her normal clothes, Sylvia arrived next to Humphrey back in the arena. The contestants were concentrating on their styles, which all looked impressive.

"Where have you been? Is everything OK? Look, I'm so sorry, I promise I'll..." Humphrey gushed.

"Never mind that now. It's Gene! He's behind everything!"

"Behind what?"

She told an impressed Humphrey of her sleuthing.

"If this is true, you need to find Danny," he said.

"I can't tell Danny what I found without him arresting me for breaking and entering."

"He wouldn't!"

"Wanna bet?" Sylvia raised her eyebrows. "And besides, the evidence would be inadmissible."

"Maybe you can persuade him to get a search warrant?"

"But everyone adores Gene. No one would believe me, and Danny would need to know why."

"So you need to find more evidence," Humphrey said.

"But what? How?"

They both fell silent.

"I know it's him. I just need to prove it," she surmised.

MC Brian interrupted their conversation by breathing into the mic.

"OK Chair Twirlers and Hair Curlers, we're approaching the final minutes of the round. Judges, take us through today's styles."

One by one, the judges visited each contestant.

Ramone's red-headed model resembled a cockatoo on heat. He had shaved the sides of the model's head, cut a short fringe and smoothed the sides out with a small flick. An explosion of hair arose from the top of her head in an arch, like a bird's crest cascading over her face. He had studded diamond-like jewels throughout, which caught the lights of the arena.

Sorrento went for an extreme Farrah flick. Billowing wings of platinum hair exploded from his model's head.

Gloria had created a sculpted reverse mullet. Her model's black hair was short and spiky at the back and a long straight fringe covered one eye. She had scattered diamante jewels throughout, reflecting at least some light in the darkness.

Vitale had swept his model's blond hair back at the sides and back-combed the top into a towering bouffant. He finished with a long, crimped fish-tail plait at the back. It looked like a mixture of a French 18th-century courtesan and 1980s rock chick. He burnished the curls with a metallic spray and swept her face with gold dust.

Brian got the audience to count down, and the round ended with a spray of sparklers.

"The judges have a tough job here today. This may take some time. So let me welcome to the stage for your enter-excite-ment our very own Ava Riiiiiiiiiiiice!"

Ava Rice burst on stage and sang a rousing rendition of Madonna's 'Material Girl'.

At last, Al took the loudspeaker. "It gives me the greatest of glee to announce the 1987 Gold Scissor Award's finalists... Mr Ramone Figurelles and Monsieur Vitale Crassoooooon!"

Sylvia and Humphrey hugged each other and jumped up and down, and for a moment, they both forgot their troubles.

Saturday

35

S ylvia had fallen asleep, twisted and uncomfortable. They had celebrated too hard at the Pyramid rooftop bar. The telephone sounded like it was keening. She looked at the time on the digital alarm clock built into her bedside table. 4.12 am. She coaxed the feeling to come back into her arm, and once she had convinced it to pick up the insistent telephone, she croaked, "Hello?"

"It's me, Humphrey. Jerry's dead!"

"What?"

"Someone just found him in the washroom at the casino."

"No! No! Are you sure? Oh, Humphrey... was he murdered?"

"They're blocking it off now, but someone said there was a lot of blood. So, yeah, killed in cold blood."

"This is just terrible. Horrible!" Sylvia put her hand over her mouth. "What did he do to deserve that? Is Danny there?"

"Yes, just got here."

"I'm coming down now."

"Oh, now you're coming... to see Danny boy?" He said in a sing-song voice.

"For Jerry. He was a friend, Hump. I've known him for years!"

"OK, OK. Sorry, Sylv. See you down here."

By the time Sylvia had dressed and made her way to the scene, the police had cordoned the area off and Danny was inside. A policeman guarded the door. Clippy was in floods of tears. Sylvia waved at Humphrey, but instead of joining him, she ducked under the police tape. A rusty rivulet of blood had congealed on the tiles. Sylvia shuddered. A man was taking photos, the flash escaping under the cubicle door of which Danny was now backing out.

"Jesus, Sylvia. How did you get in here?"

"Who's done this?" She said, tears springing. "He was a good guy. Never hurt a flea. I can't believe it." She sniffed two short snorts. She sensed the now familiar aroma, a sweet, slightly rotten smell.

"How did he die?"

"Come on, this is no place for a lady." He tried to usher her back out the door.

"No, Danny. I want to see him. He's my friend."

"All the more reason…"

But she pushed past him and stepped in front of the cubicle. The forensic photographer's camera flashed at the slumped body of Jerry, his pants around his ankles. Dried blood stained his shirt and arms. The flashes seared the image on her eyeballs. Someone had stabbed a half pair of scissors into the left side of his neck.

"Someone killed him on the dunny?"

"The what?"

"The toilet. Someone killed him while he was taking a…?"

"That's right," Danny interrupted.

"From the same pair of scissors that killed Giuseppe?" Sylvia asked, a shiver of dread going through her.

"It's looking like it."

"Are you sure? The same murderer? A serial killer?" she squeaked. She clutched her hands to her face.

"OK, settle down. We'll have to wait for forensics to…"

"Oh no, oh heavens, it, it…" Sylvia sobbed.

"Calm down. I'm not making any assumptions. You're in shock."

"You don't understand. I… I…"

"I'll find out who did this. Trust me. I know he was a friend. I'm really sorry, Sylvia."

"He… I… I should have…"

Hot tears burst down her cheeks and her stomach clenched. Danny wrapped his arms around her, and she sobbed into the soft linen of his shoulder.

"Sylvia, come on, come with me. You're not allowed in here. It's the men's and a crime scene."

They left the crime scene to the forensic crew. Humphrey, who was hovering outside, passed her a hanky. She hiccuped and composed herself.

"Any reason why someone would want him dead?" Danny asked.

"No," she said, wiping her eyes. "He was just a sales rep for Latherlongs. A good guy. Everyone liked him." She broke into sobs again. "What if I had… If only I'd…"

"OK, breathe. It's OK," Danny soothed. "What's Latherlongs?"

"It's… it's the brand of product most of us use in Oz." She sniffed and took in a deep breath. "He'd travel around the country with their new products."

"Well, he rubbed someone the wrong way here."

One of Danny's men interrupted. "The forensic team seems to think the victim died of razor blade cuts. The scissors were stuck in afterwards."

"Razor blade? OK. Get me the forensic report on the scissors asap. We need to work out if this is the same guy, or not connected."

"Yes sir," the man affirmed.

"And check any records of hotel guests for incarceration," Danny added. "Razor kills are the work of past felons in my experience. Might give us a lead."

"A razor?" Sylvia echoed. "It was a razor blade?"

"Looks like it," Danny responded.

A small rivulet of relief flowed through Sylvia.

"Poor Jerry," she sobbed, wiping her tears away with Humphrey's proffered hanky. "Do you think they'll cancel the competition?"

"I doubt it. It's so close to the end now and the only time the Scissors had to stop was when everyone got food poisoning."

Humphrey put his arm round her, but all Sylvia could think about was the touch of the scissor blade hidden in Gene's sofa. She couldn't tell Danny she broke into his room. He would be furious. If only she had taken the scissors, then maybe poor Jerry would be alive now.

"I can't believe Jerry's dead. He's just hit it off with Clippy, too."

They glanced at Clippy, who was as white as an over-bleached blond and shaking, her cheeks wet with tears.

Another policeman called out to Danny.

"I've got to go. See you later, yeah?" Danny left Sylvia with a tender touch on the elbow and moved towards Clippy, who was now being comforted by Wesley.

"I know Gene did it," Sylvia said forcefully. "If that son of a gun is left-handed, then it's one more piece of proof."

36

Sylvia pulled herself together and scoured the hotel. The desire for retribution, for justice, coursed through her heart. The dining room was subdued. Not many people here knew Jerry, but another murder in the hotel was not good news. She searched the casino, which was practically a ghost town. The arena was busy being set up for the finals, but no judges were there. She was exhausted yet restless, angry and terribly, terribly sad. She couldn't believe how Jerry had been caught up in all this. If Gene was the murderer, why would he do such a thing? And if not, were there two killers on the loose? Her scalp told her it was Gene. He seemed to be involved at every turn. She stood outside his room, but all was quiet. At last, she found him in the gym. He was grunting as he lifted weights, Wesley spotting for him.

"More!" Gene ordered.

Wesley put another weight on the end. Gene strained, but managed to lift it.

"Again!"

Wesley shook his head, but Gene insisted. "I said one more. I can do it!"

Gene's muscles bulged out of his neck with effort, but he lifted the bar briefly before it crashed to the floor. As he recovered from the lift,

Sylvia made herself visible.

"Hi Gene, impressive weight you're lifting."

"Well, thank you. The only way is up. Am I right?"

She wanted to scream at him. She controlled her voice with a forced lightness. "Could I ask you a favor?"

"Sure!" He grabbed the towel Wesley held for him and sat on the bench. He gulped down water, his skin shining with perspiration. Sylvia caught a whiff of that smell again; now she knew. It was the scent of fake tan and sweat, the same smell she had detected at both Jerry and Giuseppe's murder scene.

"I... er... would love your autograph."

"Sure thing! Hey Wesley, grab me a photo for Sylvia here."

Wesley went to the office.

"Have you heard there's been another murder? Jerry Latherlongs, brutally stabbed. I'm terrified," she said.

"Yeah, shocking, shocking," Gene replied.

She watched him closely. A face twitch, a shifty look away, a change of subject? Nothing. This guy was good.

"Who would do such a thing?" she probed.

"Beats me! Maybe this Jerry was a bad guy."

"Oh no, he wasn't. He was a friend of mine." Sylvia's eyes sprang with hot with tears. "Did you know him?"

Gene shook his head.

"Well, I did. He was funny and helpful and friendly and now he's dead. And you, *you*..." She wanted to punch him, to beat him for killing an innocent man, her friend. She curled up her fists, but Wesley came back with a photo.

"Here boss. You got to get ready for the comp, so make it quick."

"OK, bro. Calm down. Can't you see the lady's upset? Her friend is the dead guy."

Sylvia let out a sob. Wesley shrugged and tossed over a still of Gene in a tiny pair of shorts, posing to show every last muscle in his body. Sylvia regained her composure. Gene grabbed the pen Wesley held. Sylvia took a little in-breath as he signed with his left hand in the corner of the photo: 'Dear Sylvia, the only way is up! Gene Bustle X'.

Sylvia took the photo and held it up. "The person who killed these men will be caught. I'll make sure of it."

She looked them both in the eye and hurried away from the gym. She had to find Danny. He had to re-interview Gene. If Giuseppe was indeed preventing Clippy from flooding the market with Fritz, then finishing him off would be a quick fix. And if by befriending Clippy, Jerry and his products were a threat to Fritz, then there was a motive. Gene had even suggested Jerry was a bad man. She wondered if Clippy knew Gene was a murderer. Was she in on the crimes, too? Perhaps Clippy had confided in Jerry. They had got very close over the course of the week.

The elevator arrived at the foyer. She asked the concierge if he'd seen Detective Good. He hadn't. She wanted to find Humphrey, but she knew he would be guarding Vitale as he was about to head into the final round. She wouldn't interfere with that delicate predicament.

37

Sylvia felt sick. Her head spun with grief, lack of sleep and over-thinking. She made her way to the arena and spotted Humphrey. He waved her over.

"How did it go?" he asked.

"I nearly punched the creep, ugh. But he is left-handed."

"Not firm evidence, but enough to get the detective to look at him again?"

"I don't know. It's worth a try. At least we can keep an eye on him while he's judging."

"He's so high profile, I don't know how he manages to squeeze in murder."

"Two murders! And not only murder, he's a thief."

"Gee, possum, you've really got it in for him."

Sylvia scowled at Humphrey. "He _is_ guilty of murder. I just want justice! Why don't you believe me?"

"Goooood afternoon, Highlighters and Lowlighters!" Brian purred. "Well, it's been one heck of a week, but today we have our final contestants in the hair-raising competition for the incredible, dazzling Golden Scissors! Are you ready?"

The audience cheered. Once they had calmed down, a gentle

drumbeat emanated from the sound system.

"But before we begin, put your clippers together for Emmy-Lou and the Toning Tongs singing Kool and the Gang's 'Victory'…"

Everyone except Sylvia and Humphrey leaped to their feet and danced. Al and Gene joined the band, Gene dancing awkwardly out of time to the beat and Al writhing his way exotically around Emmy-Lou. The band brought the song to a close, and the judges remained on stage, bowing and breathless before running off. The lights dimmed. Everyone went quiet. The tension in the arena felt like it was high on hairspray. Light beams strobed down and bounced around the stage. Piped music built to a thunderous classical crescendo. The judges returned; Emmy-Lou in a floor-length swathe of black starched silk with sharp razors of fabric shooting out from her shoulders. Al was also dressed in a full-length gown in black and white African print. Gene's orange skin and pumped body were barely contained in a dinner suit and a huge pair of silver sneakers, and on his head, he wore a gold crown.

"Who does he think he is?" Sylvia couldn't believe it. "King Bustle?"

But before Humphrey could reply, MC Brian came back on.

"Ladies and gentlemen, here we are at the grand final of the 1987 Golden Scissors. We have two extraordinary competitors this afternoon. Winner of the last two years, reigning champion Ramone Figurelles…"

Ramone's fans woohooed and whistled as he strutted into the arena like a cougar about to finish off his prey.

"And the world-famous stylist to the stars, the one and only venerable Vitale Crassoooooon!"

A huge roar rose from the auditorium as Vitale jogged on. He put his hands in the air and spun on his heels as he greeted his fans.

"These two amazing hairdressers have wowed us with their expertise, thrilled us with their technique. And on this auspicious day, we will witness their own unique innovation!"

The models came on stage dressed in black t-shirts, leggings and white stilettos. Vitale and Ramone took them by their hands and led them to the salon chairs. Sylvia was pleased to see that Sandra had not made it to the floor. She had hoped Danny would tie her up long enough to miss this.

"Al, tell us about tonight's theme."

"Thank you, Brian. We have seen hundreds of talented stylists here this week. And all of them, bar these two champions, have fallen by the wayside. We see before us the two greatest hairdressers in the world." Al took the microphone off the stand and stalked across the stage. "A hairdresser is not merely one who arranges the follicles of humans, who teases tresses or tames tufts, no. A hairstylist is an artist! He is a creator, a communicator, a pioneer. He pushes boundaries, he communes with God, with spirit, to innovate and articulate the language of hair. Today's theme tests our finalists to produce something that has never been seen, that has never even been imagined! Today's theme, ladies and gents, is 'Out of this World'. The winning style will be featured on the front of *Lighten Up* magazine. We are sublimely excited to watch the wonder of these gentlemen this afternoon. Take it away, Brian."

"Hang on a minute!" Sylvia hissed to Humphrey, doing a double-take. "The winner always appears on the front of the *Hair'd Honcho*. Since when did *Lighten Up* get the rights?"

"Fritz has sponsored the event. Guess that's the payoff," Humphrey said.

"I still don't understand. Why didn't Wiz sponsor it like usual?"

"Maybe he's broke?"

"Maybe. Still, it looks like this Hiliterati crowd is pushing UGH out."

Sylvia chewed her bottom lip. Nobody seemed to care about the guild anymore. It seemed as if it was becoming invisible, outshone by a dazzling new jewel—Hiliterati and the Higher Union of Hairdressers.

"Let me hear you, scissor-breakers and comb-shakers! All together now... ten, nine, eight..." MC Brian counted down, helped by the spectators. The final began.

Ramone rolled his shoulders and cricked his neck. Before seeing his model to her seat, he grabbed her with one hand around her waist, tossed her back and kissed her full on the mouth. Wolf whistles erupted from the crowd. Vitale stared at Ramone, shaking his head. He took his model gently by the hand, gave it a quick kiss, and twirled her to her seat. Vitale opened his tool kit. Sylvia knew he had checked and double-checked and kept it under lock and key. He pulled out his special scissors and comb, holding them ready.

"Three, two, one... scissors away!"

The audience cheered and the two finalists set to work. The hairdressers concentrated on their models while the judges paraded, and MC Brian kept time. They reached the halfway mark. As Vitale applied the third color to his model's hair, the girl's head wobbled. Vitale held her head and adjusted the angle, but the minute he took his hands off, her head dropped forward and she slumped in the chair. Vitale stepped back. His model was a rag doll. He ran to the front of the chair. The spectators were on their feet.

"What in the name of finger rolls is going on?" Sylvia said.

"There seems to be something wrong with Monsieur Crassoon's model," Brian announced. "The girl appears to have fainted. Can the medics please attend the stage?"

"Oh no! No, no, no, Sylv. Ramone has got to the model! That

flicking ducktail. I've been glued to Vitale for the last twenty-four hours, and so he's only gone and sabotaged the bloody model. I'm going to kill him!"

Humphrey started towards the arena.

"Wait, Hump. Calm down!"

"Calm down? Calm down, Sylvia? What's V going to work on? He can't lose now, after everything."

Humphrey looked like he was about to burst into tears. Sylvia looked around her, huffing. "I don't know. There's got to be something we can do. Is there a spare model?"

"No, he never has one."

"Why doesn't he have a backup model?"

"You know him and his superstitions."

"What?"

"He says he's asking for trouble if he has a second model because he can never decide which one to use."

On the stage, Al flicked his fingers across his neck to signal the timer to be stopped.

"Mr Figurelles, please step away from your model. We have stopped the clock. We have a medical emergency."

Ramone threw his arms in the air and chucked his hairbrush onto the counter, uttering a volley of swear words.

Sylvia clutched her fingers in her hair.

"How could Vitale get through without a model? After all we've done to get him this far."

Vitale gesticulated towards Ramone and shook his head.

"He's going to be disqualified."

"No, no. Wait... I've got it. I'll do it."

"Do what?"

"Be his model."

Humphrey gasped.

"Are you sure? You never let anyone near your hair."

"Last time I sat in a hairdresser's chair, they shaved my head. I have trust issues!"

"That was ten years ago. You've never had a trim?"

"No, I do it myself."

"Figures," Humphrey said, raising his eyes at her hair.

She slapped him on the arm. "Come on, I'd better get down there."

Humphrey gave her a quick hug and grabbed Sylvia by the hand. They raced down to the arena.

Sylvia jogged to Vitale whilst two hotel staff carried the model's slumped body out. Vitale paced up and down, swearing in French.

"Monsieur. Let me sit for you. I'll replace your model."

"Ma cherie! Are you sure?"

She nodded. Vitale eyed her hair for a moment. Giving a brief shrug of acceptance, he took her face in his hands and kissed her with a sucking noise on each cheek.

"Sylvia, you are an angel!" He helped her into the chair. "Judges! I 'av a new model. Please let us continue."

The judges inspected Sylvia. They made sure her hair was not prepared in any way and gave her a gown. They left Vitale with a look that said, 'good luck with that!'.

Vitale stood behind Sylvia and touched her hair. He lifted a few strands, then swept it to one side, then the other. He stepped back, his mind working. Sylvia chewed the bottom side of her lip. Her cheeks colored, hating her hair that behaved like an unruly child in front of all to see. Vitale took a few more moments of consideration, then dived in. He segmented it, then sprayed it three different colors, then clipped and back-combed. He pinned on extensions and put them in curlers. Facing her, he gathered her hair in his hands and teased and tousled, lacquered and added more streaks of color. As she watched herself transform, she zoned out. Her thoughts kept returning to Jerry, lifeless and bleeding in the cubicle. And Giuseppe, cold and stiff in the chair. Who would do such a thing? Tears flowed down her cheeks.

"*Ma cherie*, I have to do your makeup now and zees tears will not help." Vitale stared into her eyes.

She nodded, and he handed her a tissue, then tenderly took to her face with a brush. Her skin turned pearlescent with powder, and he applied rainbow eyeshadow and huge false eyelashes.

Ramone concentrated hard on his model, seemingly unaffected by Vitale's mishap. He had colored his model's hair a burnished silver. He tightly wound her hair into a thick ring, pulling down a veil of strands over her face and all around.

"Five minutes to go, folks. Make your final adjustments."

Ramone crimped the wisps of hair he'd pulled out, and Sylvia couldn't help but let out a snort. The resulting hairstyle looked as if the model's head was a UFO, a wacky flying saucer. The model did not look happy, and Sylvia could only imagine the number of bobby pins holding it all together. Meanwhile, she could barely recognize herself. In the mirror, a magical, mystical beauty reflected back at her. Above her hairline, Vitale had sculpted a silver unicorn horn. The rest of her hair extensions shimmered and flowed like a rainbow mane around her shoulders.

As the final few minutes ticked on the clock, the contestants had laser-sharp focus. They spun the poor models around this way and that. Their arms in a whirlwind of activity as hairspray was pumped and product was rubbed. They teased, tousled, twisted and manipulated every last hair into the exact place.

"Thirty seconds to go!" Brian called out. "Let's count them down, ladies and gents, twenty, nineteen, eighteen... Three, two, one, and time's up!"

Fireworks exploded from the four corners of the arena, throwing sparks into the air. The crowd cheered and broke into applause. More pyrotechnics sprayed out around the room, lighting up the whole arena.

The crowd went crazy as the hairdressers led their models to the stage for judging. But one corner of the audience seemed to be shrieking rather than cheering. A few heads turned towards them. They screamed in alarm. A swathe of spectators moved like a Mexican Wave and fled along the seating. A flicker of flame rose from the seats closest to the arena. Soon the whole audience caught on in alarm, and a mass of bodies pushed to the exit. Smoke billowed from the chairs and the fire alarms erupted into action.

Brian's panicked voice yelled through the speakers, "There's a fire! A fire! Everyone RUN..." There followed a magnified bang of the dropped microphone. Chaos ensued as people rushed to escape. The two competitors and models on the stage were slow to catch on. A spluttering noise issued from the ceiling. All four looked up and a shower of water met their upturned faces.

38

"*N on, non, NON!*" Vitale squealed and flicked the bottom of the gown over Sylvia's head. Vitale pushed and bumped Sylvia to the exit. Bodies pressed around her, yelling and wailing. Sylvia and Vitale were caught in the crush. She couldn't see a thing as Vitale herded her to safety. At last, she felt the warm air of Vegas catch her legs and the siren's racket faded.

"Can you take this off now, Monsieur?" she begged.

Sylvia lifted the gown so she could see what was happening. Everyone had been evacuated outside the front of the hotel to the blaring of fire trucks. The guests clumped around the fountain that cascaded impressively into a gold-lined pool. The fire brigade rushed in, dragging a huge hose with them. A harassed-looking hotel manager came out to the top of the grand steps that led to the hotel foyer. He spoke to the crowd through a megaphone.

"Thank you for your hasty evacuation. Please report to the hotel staff so we may account for everyone. As soon as the building is safe, you'll be able to get back to your..."

Emmy, Al and Gene arrived on the steps. Emmy-Lou grabbed the megaphone off the surprised hotel manager.

"Hey folks! Folks!"

Everyone hushed and looked at her.

"Thanking y'all for your cooperation. It's terrible timing, but the show must go on!"

Everyone whooped. The hotel manager scowled. He went to take the megaphone, but Emmy-Lou would not let go. "What do you think you're doing, lady?" the manager blustered, wide-eyed. "There's a fire in the hotel."

"And there's the Golden Scissors Awards to judge, mister," Emmy-Lou jabbed the megaphone into his chest. She put it to her mouth. "As I was sayin', we're still obliged to pass judgment on our two finalists today. So, could I ask you to come up on the stage, um, steps?"

She motioned for the two soggy finalists to join her with their models.

"Come on up here, you champions. Now, first, I want to apologize to you for being so rudely interrupted."

The poor hairdressers looked shell-shocked, but they nodded in assent.

"So let's take a look at your hairdos. Please talk us through your style today."

The bedraggled models stood before the judges and the crowd of hair experts.

Ramone had not been as quick thinking as Vitale, and his style had not fared well. The roll of hair had sagged down over his model's eyes and the crimped fringe stuck to her face. Her make-up ran in coppery drips down her face. The spectators clapped politely, a few die-hard fans whistled.

Vitale unveiled Sylvia's do. Though her unicorn was at a slightly less jaunty angle, the style was still intact, a sculpture exploding with color. It wasn't half bad for a rush job, and the people cheered and clapped.

The judges found a place to convene. Sylvia wished she could hear the conversation but she couldn't break away from Vitale and Ramone. She caught Humphrey's attention and flicked her eyes to the judges. Humphrey frowned. She huffed and snaked her hand up to her earlobe, pretending to scratch it. Humphrey twigged and wove his way through the crowd, arriving behind the judges.

Gene seemed to be doing all the talking. Emmy-Lou and Al looked uncomfortable. Sylvia tried to lip-read, but it was not something UGH taught in the training of agents. She made a mental note to have Wiz include it. The judges had reached their decision and the three split apart. Emmy-Lou took up the megaphone. "Ladies, gents, firstly I want to thank you for your patience. We have been informed that the fire is out, and no one has been injured."

Everyone applauded.

"Now, the news you have all been waiting for… and I'd like to invite our guest judge to announce this year's winner. Please put your hands together for Gene Bustle." She was more subdued than her usual enthusiasm.

As Gene joined Emmy-Lou, his odious assistant Wesley stood to the side, his tree-trunk arms crossed. Sylvia was anxious enough about the competition without having to listen to Gene. Humphrey pushed his way around to where she stood, a serious expression on his face. Sylvia moved towards Humphrey.

"Sylvia!" Vitale cried as she left his side. She waved a hand at Vitale and leaned in to hear what Humphrey had to report.

"You were right, possum," he said. "Gene told Emmy-Lou that he was rethinking her record contract."

"You're kidding? And Al…"

"Al? Even Al has an Achilles heel. It seems Gene had promised him lifetime first-class travel on his new airline."

"Wow!" she said.

"Sylvia, *venez ici*. Come here!" Vitale hissed.

Sylvia stood to attention next to Vitale. He clutched her hand, silent prayers moving his mustache.

"It is my honor," Gene said with his hand pressed to his heart, "to announce the judges' unanimous choice…"

Everyone held their breath…

"Mr Ramone Figurelles!"

Vitale slumped beside Sylvia in a half-faint. Sylvia caught him. The audience clapped, though many looked somewhat astounded.

Sylvia's jaw dropped. "What? No, no no!"

Ramone leaped up and air-punched his fists. He strutted the edge of the steps. Gene took Ramone's hand and held it in the air.

"No, no way. This isn't happening," Sylvia yelled. "Can't anyone see what a dingo's breakfast his style is?"

She snatched the megaphone from Gene's unsuspecting hand and took a deep breath. She could feel the unicorn horn quivering over her, and it seemed to give her a boost of power.

"I object!" she yelled.

Everyone was making too much noise. She stuck her fingers in her mouth and whistled into the megaphone. The crowd winced and shushed as they turned to the stage. "He's a cheat," she said, pointing at Ramone.

The crowd erupted in surprise and shock before quieting again.

"This man," Sylvia said, gesturing toward Ramone, "is a cheat."

"Sylvia!" Al interrupted.

"No, let me speak," Sylvia held her hand up to Al. The frenzied look in her eye was as dangerous as a real unicorn. "Monsieur Crassoon has been beset with challenges this year. At every turn, he has endured pain and discomfort, yet he has pushed through. But these incidents were not mere circumstance."

The crowd murmured. She went on. "Ramone purposely set traps to put him off his game."

Sylvia could sense Ramone shifting nervously.

"Vitale's biggest rival knew he was no match for our maestro. First, he tricked him into drinking a burning cocktail. In round one, he squirted chili hairspray at him. Before round two, he had hot coffee poured in his lap and tampered with his tools. Then he lured him onto a faulty running machine where he badly strained his wrist, and finally today, he drugged his model."

Al rushed to Sylvia and took the megaphone from her hands.

"What is this?" Al said.

"This is crazy, Sylvia. Stop now!" Emmy-Lou added.

"This woman is deranged!" Gene said.

"I'm not. You can hear me out or I can mention some other arrangements that you have made with Gene."

"You don't know what you're talking about," Gene growled.

"Sylvia, we know you want Vitale to win, but..." said Al before Sylvia cut him off.

"But you really want to travel first class, hey Al? And you, Emmy-Lou, a lucrative deal for your band? Do you want me to let the audience know that even the judges cheated for their own gain?"

The judges were silent. Sylvia grabbed the megaphone back and faced the audience. "Ramone Figurelles has been sabotaging Vitale for the entire competition."

Uproar ensued. Ramone threw his hands in the air in disbelief.

"Do you really agree that this..." she pointed to Ramone's model. One side of her spaceship unraveled over her mascara-smudged face. "Over this?" She twirled her hand around her horn.

The audience yelled out a few boos and nos.

"This is bull," Ramone said, tossing his chin in the air. "These judges have watched my skill and found me the winner. Somebody call security."

Wes barged onto the steps and grabbed Sylvia's elbow.

"Get off me!"

She tried to pull her elbow out of his grip but failed. He dug his fingers in.

Humphrey leaped onto the steps in glee. "We have evidence," he yelled and held up the Polaroid he took in Ramone's room. The judges pulled his hand down to look at the half of Vitale's gold-plated scissors in Ramone's suitcase.

"Let her go, Wesley," Al said, inspecting the photo.

Sylvia and Wesley glared at each other murderously.

"I also asked the breakfast waiter and the barman. They both admitted to receiving a very good 'tip' for serving a hot cocktail and pouring coffee over the monsieur," he added.

"And he has been taking illegal bets on the side," Sylvia said. "While his partner-in-crime, Sandra Tress, perverted the course of justice by selling false alibis."

"These accusations are outrageous!" Gene exploded. "Ramone has won fair and square. What sort of show are you running here?" he said to Al and Emmy-Lou.

But they were no longer running the show. The hairdressers took justice into their own hands. Ramone fled from the steps, but they caught him and flung him onto their outstretched arms. They crowd-surfed him all the way to the fountain, stripped him of his clothes and dumped him between the ears of the jackal Anubis statue. The hotel guests booed and splashed water at him. Vitale and Sylvia laughed at the spectacle. The judges gathered and made a show of inspecting the photo with Humphrey. Al took the megaphone and regained the audience's attention.

"It seems there has indeed been foul play here. We are stripping Ramone of his title and declare Monsieur Vitale Crassoon the winner of the 1987 Golden Scissors!"

Once again, the feral crowd went wild. Some jeered at Ramone, who was still wedged between the ears of the god of embalming and the dead.

"My dear friends. I zank you from zee tips of my mustache!" Vitale cried out.

"Congratulations, my friend!" Humphrey shook his hand.

"Yes, well done, Monsieur. Your hairstyle is amazing!" Sylvia said, smoothing her hands over her head.

"Thank you, Sylvia! Once again, you saved my sausage."

"I think you mean bacon? But you're welcome."

"Let's go celebrate, oui?"

"I'll meet you guys in the bar. I just have to collect something," Humphrey said.

Once the furor had died down, the competitors were allowed access to the Green Room to collect their tools from the abandoned arena. The water had soaked the floor and the acrid smell of burnt fabrics and plastic filled the air. The award ceremony the next day would have to be held somewhere else.

39

As the adrenalin dispersed in Sylvia's body, she remembered her friend Jerry. His body cold and stiff, lying in the morgue awaiting a long and lonely trip back to Australia to be buried by his family. She needed to unwind before her date with Danny, as well as try to numb her lingering sorrow for Jerry. Vitale insisted on celebrating with the finest champagne. Humphrey had joined them in the bar with a flush on his face and a smile never far from his lips. He kissed Vitale on his cheeks, ending in a big one on his lips. They sat on the bar terrace sipping bubbles while Sylvia's silver unicorn horn glinted in the setting sun. They retold the story of Ramone's humiliation every which way. Sylvia drained the last drop of champagne.

"OK, I'm off to find Danny. I need to let him know I can't go out with him tonight," she said as the night lights took over the city. "I'm too sad about Jerry. It feels wrong to enjoy myself."

Humphrey and Vitale's words jumbled together. "Nah uh, no way, you must go on zis date!"

"I can't, guys. I'll stay with you, drown my sorrows in Champagne."

"Now look here, possum. That guy is a catch. You like him, right?"

"Yes, of course. He's amazing."

"And he likes you?"

"I think so. He keeps asking me out on dates."

"Would your friend Jerry want you to give up a golden opportunity wiz zis beau?" Vitale added.

Sylvia shook her head.

"Right. Off you go. Put your glad rags on and get out of here. Have fun, possum!"

She knew better than to argue with the two of them, and she left to get ready.

Sylvia didn't have the heart or energy to deconstruct Vitale's masterpiece. She wiggled out of her shirt and put on a lilac jumpsuit, and touched up Vitale's makeup. Danny was waiting for her in the foyer. He whistled.

"You look... magical!"

Sylvia smiled as he took her hand. Guests stared and gave a round of applause as the winning hairstyle paraded through. When the last guest had taken a photo and even a few autographs, Danny said, "You hungry?"

"I'm starving. I couldn't eat breakfast or lunch after what happened this morning. It's been a long day."

He stopped and took Sylvia's hands in his. "Are you OK? I know Jerry was a friend."

"I will be. Forgive me if I burst into tears." She gave a weak smile, and he kissed her gently above each eye.

Sylvia melted. Humphrey and Vitale were right; spending time with Danny would be the best remedy for grief.

"Come on. I'll take you to my favorite place. It's halfway down the strip. Fancy a walk?"

Sylvia agreed and they set off. The town at night was even more dazzling than by day, alive with flickering lights of every color. Signs for casinos, cabarets and diners reflected across her face, matching her rainbow extensions. Large cars cruised along the street. A hundred billboards jostled for airtime, clamoring emporiums, coffee shops, souvenirs. Towering hotels bedazzled her with their architecture, size and names—Moondust, Caribbana, Napoleon's Palace. The moon was full, and she could make out the Red Rock Canyon, creating a dramatic backdrop for the town.

"It's like a wonderland!" she said, snuggling up to Danny's arm.

The smell of fried food and car exhaust fought with his aftershave and the dry desert dust that coated the street. Danny breathed in. "Can't beat Vegas. It's on the up, this place. We've chased the mafia out of town and soon it will be all above board and safe."

"Still murderers around, though," she said sadly.

Danny stopped and faced her. He took her hand and squeezed it.

"I'm so sorry this happened."

Sylvia's lips wobbled. Danny pulled her into a hug, and she surrendered into his chest, her lacquered unicorn horn almost taking his eye out.

"Don't worry, I have a list of suspects, and my money is on one in particular."

She pulled away and looked at him.

"You do? Who?"

"Well, you were right to consider looking at an assassin."

Sylvia looked surprised. "I was?"

"It was something Gloria Frank said yesterday. I've done some digging. Interesting background. Anyway, I have surveillance on her."

"Gloria?"

Something didn't gel. The woman was scary for sure and dark as the devil's plughole, maybe even a murderess, but when Sylvia thought about the crime scene, something didn't fit.

"Wait a minute... it wasn't a hairdresser who did it!"

"Say what?"

She knew from the tips to the tops of her follicles it was Gene. She just needed proof.

"If the person who washed his hair is the killer, they weren't a hairdresser."

"Honey, my impression of you is plummeting. What are you talking about?"

Sylvia balked at his condescension. "Anyone." She emphasized the word again. "*Anyone* could see that the person who tied the gown was not a hairdresser."

"Huh?"

"There are many ways to securely attach a gown—velcro, a popper, a button, or a tie. Bonnie's gowns are the old-fashioned wrap-around. The ties are knotted at the back, not at the front like it was on Giuseppe. No client wants tickly hairs or drips of water down their neck. The person who loosely knotted that gown was not a hairdresser. Especially not someone as precise as Gloria Frank."

Danny pondered this new evidence.

"Not only that," she continued, "the third law of UGH is 'never leave a client unfinished'."

"What law?"

"A hairdresser never leaves a client without finishing the job."

"I'd say someone finished the job good and proper."

"You're right, but I'll bet my best pair of scissors it wasn't a hairdresser."

Danny nodded. Sylvia could see his brain computing.

"Interesting observation. Of course, we can't prove the hairwasher and the killer are the same person, but maybe I should hire you as a consultant on the case."

Sylvia couldn't tell if he was joking or not. She didn't think he knew either.

They had stopped outside a building. Red lights framed the door in the shape of lobster claws.

"This is the restaurant."

A person dressed as a lobster welcomed them. "Welcome to the Lobster Mobster! Love your hairdo. Wanna swap?" The lobster said, motioning to his massive antennae that dangled off his lobster headpiece. Sylvia shook her head. The lobster shrugged and led them towards a table. The interior was bright pink-red, and the waitresses wore skimpy lobster dresses. A whole wall of fish tanks contained live crustaceans slowly waving their claws as if crying for help. Sylvia's stomach went queasy. They got shown to a table, and the server covered their laps with napkins. Danny reeled off an order without even looking at the menu.

"Is this your first time in America?"

"No, I've been a couple of times. Never to Las Vegas though."

"I've never been out of Las Vegas."

Sylvia gulped. "Never?"

Danny shook his head.

"Do you want to?"

"Nah, all the excitement I need is here."

"It _is_ a thrilling place, but how about experiencing something new? Somewhere different, just for a holiday."

"I can sit down and watch the TV and see everything I would want to. Besides, I have too much to do here. I got to clean this city up, so it's safe for lovely ladies like you."

They smiled, though Sylvia suspected for different reasons. All she had ever wanted was to travel the world. Though she couldn't imagine ever leaving Perth for good, she still wanted to explore other places. A huge platter of lobster arrived. Danny rubbed his hands together and tucked his napkin firmly under his chin.

"Dive in." He gestured to the pile of food.

Sylvia looked at her dinner like it was a puzzle to be solved. She hovered her hand over the plate but detoured to her glass of wine. Danny's eyes sparkled. Sylvia reached for the safety of a wedge of lemon and squeezed it. A spray of lemon juice shot into Danny's eye.

"Ow!" He blinked and winked and scrubbed his napkin over his face.

"Oh, I'm so sorry. I... uh... I've never had lobster before."

Danny laughed, though one eye was squinted.

"Here, I'll show you."

Danny snapped open a claw and pulled out a delicate pink strand of meat. He fed it into Sylvia's mouth.

It really didn't taste of much. "Mmmmm," she lied.

Danny took a mouthful and rolled his eyes in delight. Sylvia picked up a piece and turned it over in her fingers. Greasy juice dribbled on to her hands. She tried to crack it in half, but the whole thing flew out of her hands and across the table. It hurtled past Danny's left ear and landed on the tray of a server as she carried an ice bucket of champagne and six glasses. The thud of the flying lobster on her tray upset her balance and the whole lot went crashing onto the floor.

Sylvia put her hands to her mouth. Danny, having ducked and then watched it fly through the air, burst out laughing. He threw some bills on the table, took Sylvia's hand, and pulled her out of the restaurant. They stood on the sidewalk, which glowed with flashing lights, and laughed.

"Anywhere sell burgers around here?" Sylvia asked once they had caught their breath.

Danny's eyes creased at the edges, and his bright white teeth beamed at her.

"Sure. This way."

<h1 style="text-align:center">40</h1>

Fifteen minutes later, Sylvia and Danny sat on high plastic chairs in a fast-food joint called Burger Burper. The burger was the tastiest Sylvia had ever eaten and neither spoke as they worked their way through them. As promised, they both let out a belch after the last bite.

"You know, the reason I came here was for an investigation of my own?"

"You mentioned it earlier. I thought you were joking."

"No jokes."

"Don't tell me you're a private detective masquerading as a hairdresser to uncover a massive fraud in the hairdressing world."

"As it happens, I am a hairdresser. I do undertake some sleuthing here and there, and there is something dodgy happening in the hairdressing world."

Danny looked amused. "Go on."

"It seems that someone is diverting all the data from UGH."

"What's UGH?"

"The United Guild of Hairdressers. It's our main industry association. It usually sponsors the Golden Scissors. I have a suspicion that the new hair products that Clippy Feathercombe is selling have something to do with it."

"You think Clippy is involved?"

"Possibly an accessory, or at least is close to the murderer."

"Why do you think that?"

"She works for Gene Bustle. I think that maybe, um, Gene could be the one. We know he owns Hiliterati. I need to find out who HUH is, the entity that is trying to call the shots in this contract."

"HUH?"

"The Higher Union of Hairdressers."

"Huh," he grunted. "You want me to do some more digging." It was a statement more than a question.

"I'll do some for you if you do some for me," Sylvia said sweetly.

"Are you saying you don't think I can do my job?"

"Well, I have been useful. You would never have known that a hairdresser didn't fix Giuseppe's gown. And I found some evidence."

"True, it has given us a motive. Though the fingerprints only put Miss Feathercombe in the frame. But I can't just use our system to do favors for a beautiful woman, you know."

"You wouldn't say no to a unicorn, would you? A unicorn doesn't ask a favor from you every day."

"OK, OK, you make a good..." Danny looked at Sylvia's hair, "...point!"

Sylvia groaned. "Don't give up your day job, detective."

"So, what do I get in return?" he asked.

"I hope you're not suggesting..."

"No, I wasn't, only intel... though if you have other ideas?"

Oh, she did, but she wasn't going to admit that. This was her chance to uncover Gene, but what could she tell him? Not that she had broken into his room. And not that she had smelt the same strange aroma on him and at the crime scenes. He would think she was crazy.

But she was leaving in just one day and needed to solve this mystery soon.

Danny scrunched up his napkin and brushed his hands together. He stood up and slurped the last of his soda.

"Come on!" Danny cocked his head. "Let's go and do your digging." She gave him a gooey smile of thanks.

At the police station, Danny said, "You can sit here and wait for me. I'll be back soon."

Once again, she found herself in the stark waiting room. The police station was chaotic. Cops dashed in and out. Drunken gamblers hollered and sirens wailed as the cars skidded off. Danny's colleagues bustled about. As promised, it wasn't long before Danny reappeared.

"Well?" she said, jumping up. "Did you find anything?"

"The Higher Union of Hairdressers is actually an incorporated club, not strictly a union."

"A club?"

"Yeah, looks like it's protecting the rights of hairdressers, organizing events, lobbying for better pay."

"So, by signing this, I automatically join the club and agree to abiding by these rules?"

"That's right."

"And if I break the rules or cancel my membership, they can legally claim back my discounts with interest and have a right to take my assets?"

"Yep, at a very high interest rate, if you were dumb enough to sign it. You would be legally bound to their terms. Smells like a scam to me."

Sylvia swallowed and dropped her head. "Flicking hell," she mumbled.

"Oh Sylvia, you didn't sign it, did you?"

She looked at Danny, not wanting to tell him the truth.

"OK, not good. Well, just don't buy any product. There must be a way out of it. A cooling-off period?"

"I'll work it out. Thanks for checking."

"Do you want the very bad news?"

"Go on," she sighed.

"Gene Bustle is also on the board of the Higher Union of Hairdressers."

"Oh no. Is he the CEO?"

"No, some guy with a weird name, Wizard Blowave, holds that position. Got to be a joke, right?"

The blood drained from Sylvia's face.

41

"**A**re you alright, Sylvia?"

"Wizard Blowave?"

"Yeah, that's the name. Do you know him?"

"He's the head of UGH! My boss, a friend, too."

"Why the white face?"

"I... I'm shocked that Wiz is on the board of an organization which is in competition to his own. I don't understand."

"But not the end of the world."

"No." She paused. "Can I run a theory past you?"

"Sure."

"Gene has set up multiple businesses, perhaps all with some sort of pyramid scheme attached. He has one aim; market domination and he doesn't care who he takes down. Clippy told Gene she had the key to the salon. He knew she was seeing Giuseppe to demonstrate Fritz and try to make the sale. Then Clippy must have gone back and told him she had failed despite using a drug to help him sign the papers."

"Wait a minute. How do _you_ know he was drugged?"

"Um, I overheard something... Anyway, the only thing between Gene and his total domination of the market was Giuseppe. He buttered up Marco, assuming he would be the inheritor so the barbershops would be open for Gene to either buy or at least stock Fritz, Blitz and Mitz."

"He's a businessman, not a murderer. And why would he go for Jerry?"

"Who knows? Maybe Jerry found out about it. He and Clippy have been pretty close. She could have told him. Plus, only a left-handed person with a great deal of strength could stab the scissors in at that angle. I asked him to sign his autograph, and he is left-handed."

"I don't know, Sylvia. This is one wild theory. Besides, he has a watertight alibi. Plenty of people were with him in the casino. He bought the drinks all night!"

"Is that what Sandra Tress said?"

"No, it's what half the hotel said."

"Well, I know he wasn't there all night. My friend and very helpful night porter, Brad... remember him? He met Gene in the elevator at about 11.30, after he fixed my TV. He has Gene's autograph to prove it."

"OK, let's go and talk to him. I hope you know what you're doing here, Sylvia."

"I do. My scalpy sense is never wrong!"

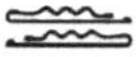

Back at the Pharaoh's Palace hotel, Sylvia found Brad at the concierge desk and convinced him to give her his coveted autograph.

"Promise you'll give it back!" Brad pleaded.

"You might not want it after this," Sylvia replied enigmatically.

The casino was as busy as ever. Celebrations were in full swing, and the guests were making the most of their penultimate night in Vegas. Danny and Sylvia wove their way through the tables. A large group of guests crowded around one, including Vitale, being celebrated and congratulated. Humphrey spied Sylvia.

"Hey possum, how was your date? Your face is telling me it didn't go well!"

"The date was fine. I'll talk to you later."

She hurried to Danny. He nodded at some of the guests, who parted as he went into the group to find Gene.

"Sorry to interrupt your fun, people, but I need to have a word with Mr Bustle."

Gene was mid-throw of dice. Wesley shouldered his way to stand between them. Gene turned his face and smiled at the detective.

"Sure, sure. Stand down, Wes. Always happy to help the police force. What can I do for you, Danny?"

Wesley looked grim as Danny led Gene to a spot away from the crowd.

"Some evidence has come to light that you didn't spend the entire evening in the casino, as per your declaration."

"I don't know where you've got that from. Apart from some breaks to the little boy's room, I was here all night with my new friends." He waved his hand to the group, who had gone very quiet, straining to hear.

"I see. Then can you explain why one of the night porters told several of his colleagues about meeting his hero in the elevator?"

Sylvia held the docket up in the air. Danny gave Sylvia a withering look. The eavesdroppers gasped.

"And not only that, but this man was given the opportunity by the great Wizard Blowave to judge the Golden Scissors when all along he has been undermining him, and all of you, by diverting all salon data to his organization, HUH!" Sylvia declared.

The crowd took a unified in-breath.

"Sylvia, please!" Danny hissed. "This is a murder investigation which I am in charge of!"

Gene turned to Sylvia. "Well, you got it all worked out, haven't you, dear? I _was_ in the elevator with the bellboy, you're right. I was coming back from my room after taking a phone call. My cell phone needed charging, so I took the call in my suite."

"Can you prove this?" Sylvia asked.

"Sylvia!" Danny yelled.

Sylvia tried to look sorry.

"You can check the phone records with my provider or ask the person I was talking to," Gene answered calmly. "And who were you talking to?" Danny managed to get the question in.

"Am I under arrest? 'Cos if not, I don't have to answer your questions."

"No sir, we just need to double-check your alibi."

"Your evasiveness suggests you weren't talking to anyone or even in your room." Sylvia couldn't help herself.

"OK, back off Sylvia. Let me ask the questions." Danny held his hand in front of her.

Gene's orange-hued skin turned puce. He stepped closer to her, and she could smell the now familiar aroma. She knew she had him.

Gene smiled. His ultra-white teeth glinted. "I was talking to... Wizard Blowave himself."

Sylvia's head spun. She shook it in denial and to clear the stars that appeared in her vision.

"You're lying. There's no way you can get hold of him."

Gene laughed through his nose. "I don't know what I've done to upset you, lady." He shook his head at her and appealed to the crowd, who now looked at Sylvia with ill-disguised hostility.

Humphrey stepped in. "Please forgive her, Mr Bustle. She's very upset about Jerry's death. Grief looks for blame." He hissed at Sylvia to zip it.

"Quite alright, my friend. There is a perfectly good explanation and I'm so sorry for not recalling this on the night. Too many Crazy Kahunas! Mr Blowave is only in range at certain times and when he is, it's usually in the early hours. We have a mutual business interest and I've been keeping him up to date with the competition. Call the phone company. The records will show exactly where I was at the time of that man's death."

Sylvia's neck flushed hot, followed by her cheeks. "I don't believe you. I could smell you in the salon, and in the washroom where poor Jerry was butchered." Sylvia flew at Gene, her punches ricocheting off his solid pecs. Wes rushed in and held her wrists. Humphrey and Danny hauled her back.

"And he has bribed the judges. He's a cheat and a murderer!" she screamed.

"Unless you have a shred of proof of this ridiculous accusation, get her out of my way."

"He's lying. The other half of the murder scissors were in his room," she blurted out.

Everyone stared at her. "I expect," she whispered.

Danny's delicious lips went so thin she almost didn't recognize him.

"Thank you for your time, Mr Bustle. I will take a look at those phone records, but until then, apologies for this. Please..." Danny motioned for Gene to get back to the blackjack table.

Humphrey took Sylvia firmly by the elbow and led her away. "What are you playing at?" he growled.

"I know it's him."

"Gene is not a murderer, Sylvia."

"It has to be him. It all fits—his strength, he's left-handed, he has motive, that funky, lingering smell. He's trying to take over the world. And he's the one who's diverting all the data from UGH right under Wiz's nose, while buttering him up. He's got you all fooled."

"It's been a long week. All the hairspray has addled your thinking," Humphrey said.

"My thinking is fine, thank you very much," Sylvia huffed and shook her elbow free of Humphrey's grip. "I'm going to bed. And I will prove he did it." She stabbed the air with her finger and glared at Danny, who looked as far from amused as a turkey before Thanksgiving.

Humphrey was right about one thing. It had been a long week, and she was tired and sad, but she knew in her scalp Gene was up to no good. Even if he hadn't murdered Giuseppe and Jerry, he was moving in on the hairdressing industry. She just wondered how she could prove he had arranged the change of address in the *Hair'd Honcho*.

That night, Sylvia lay awake in her stuffy hotel room. All she could think about was how and why Wiz was heading an association that was in direct competition with his own. And if he knew the existence of HUH, did he not know that the data was going there? Just as she had thought she had solved one mystery, a deeper layer waited. There was no sense to any of it. She closed her eyes, but the riddle rattled around her mind. Her body twisted with it until she was entangled in the sheets.

SUNDAY

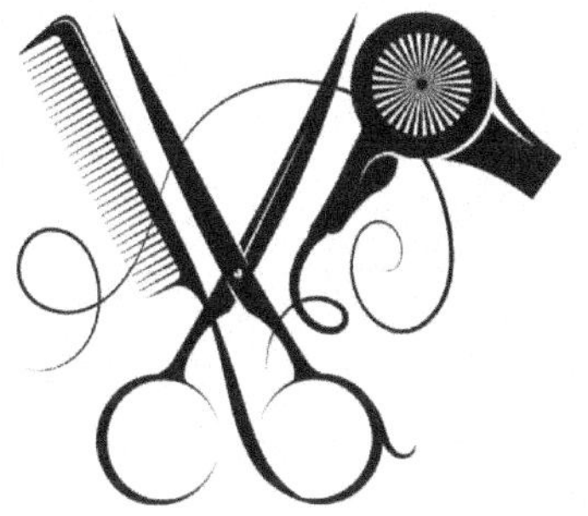

42

S ylvia awoke to a tapping noise. It was her final full day and night in Las Vegas and as her mind came into focus, she remembered with horror the terrible fool she had made of herself the night before. The hotel guests had shaken their heads at her outburst—no, attack—on Gene. And Danny, he couldn't even look at her. Even Humphrey had been incredulous. She groaned and turned over in bed to pull the sheets over her head and wished she could die. But she noticed a square of paper had been pushed under her door. She got out of bed and retrieved the note. On the hotel paper, she read:

'Meet me in the Dynasty Ballroom MC booth at 8.00 am. I know who the murderer is. Danny X.'

Sylvia's heart jumped. He wanted to see her and signed off with a kiss. He must have had a breakthrough in the night. It was 7.40 am. She washed her face, dressed and squirted her hair with Fritz hairspray. A coat of lippy, and that would have to do.

As she stepped out of the elevator on the second floor, a voice called to her.

"Hey Sylvia." Clippy had spotted her. "I need to talk to you."

"Hi Clippy. Look, I don't have time right now."

"It's about Jerry."

"I know, dove. I know you two were... I'm devastated too, but I can't talk now."

All Sylvia wanted was Danny's forgiveness, his approval, his arms, his lips.

"It's important..."

"I'll find you later, promise. I have to meet Danny in the Dynasty Ballroom right now."

Sylvia dashed off to the arena. The ballroom was still cordoned off after the fire. She gave a quick glance over her shoulder and ducked under the barrier tape, pushing the door into the room. It banged behind her. She winced at the acrid smoky stench. The carpet was squishy, and black soot marked the corner where the fire had broken out. The place was a mess, with overturned chairs and eerily quiet. She walked up the steps to the side of the stage and pushed her way through the heavy curtain. It was dark and damp. She took the staircase up to the MC and lighting booth. There was a shuffling noise in the booth.

"Danny?"

No response. She knocked on the door. It opened, but instead of a handsome face, a rough hand grabbed her elbow and pulled her in.

"Danny?"

"You got my little note, huh?"

"Wesley! what are you doing up here?"

"I'm putting a stop to you and your big mouth."

The room was small, and the sickly, sweet aroma hit her again. She swallowed. "What do you mean? Where's Danny?"

As she said the words, she knew Danny had never sent her a message. It was a trap. She turned around, but Wesley reached across and slammed the door onto the enclosed space.

"You shouldn't go around accusing people of murder. Especially if it's my brother."

"Your brother?" A wave of understanding washed through Sylvia. "Your brother. Of course, you're Gene's younger brother—the one who had been in jail..."

"And I'm not going back. I knew you'd worked it out when you got the photo off Gene."

"Worked it out?"

"That little mule Giuseppe didn't play nice with my Clippy."

Then Sylvia did work it out. Wesley had killed Giuseppe, not Gene. And it hadn't been Gene that Clippy argued with at the disco that night. It was Wesley. She kicked herself for not picking up the family resemblance.

"I don't know what you're talking about!" She played dumb.

"He wouldn't sign the paperwork and buy her shampoo and stuff. What's wrong with the guy, eh? He's a barber—didn't the man need shampoo?" Wesley whined.

"But he didn't have to buy Fritz. There are hundreds of other products he could use."

"Oh yeah? You too? You gonna squash her dreams as well? If Gene fires Clippy, she'll leave. She's my princess, and she gets what she wants. And I'll get her."

"You killed Giuseppe. For Clippy."

"She's a cut above. I'm not having anyone upsetting her."

"And Jerry?"

"That creep was pushing himself on her, hanging off her ponytail."

Sylvia swallowed. "You killed Jerry because he was in love with Clippy?"

"And she fell for his charms. We had a thing, Clippy and I. She was *my* girl. I had that scissor blade left over. Waste not want not. But it was useless as a knife, dunno how anyone cut hair with it. Had to finish the job off with my first choice."

He kicked his foot up on the wall and pulled a razor blade from his boot. Sylvia backed away from him, her heart pounding, but he stepped across the small room and grabbed a fistful of her hair.

"Ow!" she yelled. "Let me go!"

He shoved her against the control panel. Sylvia's fingers landed on the console.

"Got to tie up this one loose end."

He yanked her head back and Sylvia squealed. She frantically pressed her fingers on the buttons of the soundboard.

"You won't get away with three murders," she croaked.

"Won't I? Everyone thinks it was Marco who popped his uncle off."

"Marco?"

"Yeah, to get the salons that the old boy left him. And now he will take the fall and sell the salons to Gene."

"It was you who set up the deal with Marco and the Las Vegas drug ring on the night of Giuseppe's death?" Sylvia's mind ran over the events of the week.

"Yeah, I got brains too. Not just Gene that can do the thinking."

"I saw you disappear with him from the casino. If Marco provided his alibi with drug dealers, they would have killed him. But there was an undercover cop there. The police know Marco is innocent."

"Shut up! Think you're a right little Columbo, don't you?"

He pulled her head further back. She could feel her follicles popping.

"You won't get away with this," she gurgled, head bent backwards.

"Watch me."

Sylvia lashed out with a fist, but his abs were as solid as a washbasin. She kicked out and caught his shin. In a deft move, he released her hair and pinned her arms behind her back.

"Who you gonna pin Jerry's death on? Marco was in jail, an alibi as tight as a hairdresser's plug hole."

"You, the jealous lover."

"Me and Jerry?" Sylvia tried to twist out of his grip. "Help!"

"Yeah, two little Aussie lovers. Your nutty behavior yesterday proved that in front of all the casino. Now you're gonna pop yourself off too."

"With a razor blade?"

"Nah, with Blitz cleaner." He dropped the razor and grabbed an open bottle from off the floor. "Now drink this!"

"You're crazy!"

He sloshed some of the cleaner out of the bottle. She closed her mouth, but Wesley grabbed her by the chin and squeezed her jaw open.

"Drink!"

He brought the bottle to her mouth. The antiseptic citrus tang grabbed her nose, and she pulled away. Wesley clamped her throat so tightly that she couldn't imagine swallowing anything.

"I can't. You're choking me!"

Wesley released his grip slightly. She took the opportunity and swung the bottle up, sloshing it in his face. He groaned. His hands flew to his eyes.

"You..." He swore at her.

Sylvia pushed his bulky body away, but the booth was small. He grabbed at her torso blindly. She slipped in the puddle of cleaner on the floor, and her jaw smashed against the console.

"Help!" she yelled. "Help me!"

"Ain't nobody here to save you. They're all getting ready in the King Tut function room." He plucked her from the floor with one hand as if she was a dummy made from plastic. Sylvia pounded her fists against his solid body. He crashed her down on the console, the buttons grinding into her back.

"Now drink this!"

He swooped up the bottle.

"Help!" Sylvia screamed again.

The door crashed open. Danny, Humphrey and Clippy crowded in the narrow staircase. Sylvia couldn't see who pounced on Wesley but she suspected it was Danny. She felt herself being lifted out of the room, her face ringing in pain.

"Sylvia, possum. Are you OK?" Humphrey had got her into a chair backstage.

"He's the murderer, he tried to kill me," she sobbed, holding onto her jaw.

"It's OK. Danny's arresting him. Clippy followed you in here. She knew Danny wasn't in there, because she'd just left him in the incident room. Then she heard your voices over the loudspeaker and alerted us. Well done, Sylvia!"

"He's Gene's brother! Where is he? That man is behind all this, I swear!"

"That's what I was trying to tell you," Clippy squealed. "Wesley told me what he'd done on Thursday night, declaring his love for me. I was so scared, I told Jerry. Then Wesley found out we'd gone to dinner, and he went crazy. He threatened to kill Jerry at the disco."

"Why didn't you go to the police?" Humphrey asked.

"I couldn't. Wesley was on my tail constantly. Jerry and I tricked him when we saw you in the All-You-Can-Eat."

"But you were the last one to see Giuseppe. Did you slip him the drugs?" Sylvia asked.

"Yes, Gene and Wes told me he would be more suggestible if I gave him a sedative. But he fell asleep when I was giving him a head massage.

He wouldn't wake up, so I left him there."

"Did you lock the door after you?"

"No, I left it open for Giuseppe when he woke up."

"Wes must have waited until you were back in the casino and then gone to the salon," Sylvia said. "And when he was sleeping on the sofa in Gene's suite, that's where he hid the other half of the scissors."

"You see? Everything comes out in the wash," Humphrey said. "Now let's get you checked out."

"I think I want to go home," Sylvia said through a veil of tears. "Give me snakes and spiders and boring old ladies who want a wash and blow dry any day."

Humphrey shushed her.

"It's the award ceremony this afternoon. We can't miss it. Vitale would never forgive us. We have to go, then first thing on Monday morning it's back home to sleepy old Hardup for you."

43

The hotel medic checked Sylvia over. Nothing broken, but she was sore with bruised ribs and jaw, but Humphrey and Vitale fussed over her like she was a princess about to get married. She struggled to get into her awards ceremony gown—a black satin dress with pearl detail, a large lace bow and train at the back. She winced as Humphrey zipped her up over sore ribs. Humphrey wore a black dinner suit and Vitale a golden one. She whistled in approval when they came to collect her from her room.

"I just spoke to Detective Good. Wesley will be locked away for a long time."

"What about Gene?"

"Apparently, he knew nothing about it. He's furious with Wesley and disowning him."

"I still don't believe him, Hump. There's something not right. I mean, he'd rather throw his brother out with the hair clippings than lose his empire."

Following the destruction of the arena, the final event was now to be held in the King Tut function room. Sylvia had never seen such sumptuous grandeur. Gold swathes of cloth hung from the high ceiling, the massive pair of golden scissors dangling in the center.

There were dozens of round tables laid with damask tablecloths to the floor, and the chairs were dressed in gold covers. Huge yellow and white flower decorations filled each table with gold sprayed leaves. The guests poured through the wide doors in their finery and fluffery. A waiter held a tray of towering champagne flutes as they walked in. A live quartet played 'Golden Years' by David Bowie. They found their table, which was right at the front. The lights dimmed, and the chatter died down. Ava Rice stepped onto the stage. She wore a long silver-sequined dress and a blond wig that cascaded over her shoulders. She looked demurely at the ground to one side.

"I don't wanna talk
Of all the styles we've been through
Though good memories,
Now it's hair-story."

She looked endearingly at the audience.

"I've done all my cuts
And that's what you've done too
I think I've done okay,
There's no more hair to spray."

Then she belted out to the crowds' rapture.

"The winner takes it all
The loser feeling small
Hairdresser victory
That's all I want for me!

Not fooled by your charms
Even though I loved your hair
I figured I had a chance
You led me on a dance
You tested all my wit
Thinking you had got me there
You thought I was a fool
But I was just too cool

The judges make their call
They think they've seen it all
But this hairdresser here"

Ava swept her arm to Vitale. "He hears the audience cheer!"
The audience did cheer, and Ava invited them all to sing along.

"The winner takes it all (takes it all)
The loser feeling small (feeling small)
But never feel the shame (don't feel shame)
We're all winners in this game (winning at this game!)

So let me take your hand
As comrades in this race
Let's all own the victory
As a community
Somewhere deep inside
You take your fall with grace
But what can I say?
The victor takes the day

Ava gestured towards the guests…"Let me hear you!"

The judges make their call (make their call)
They think they've seen it all (seen it all)
Spectators of the show (of the show)"

The music continued as everyone clapped, and Ava spoke over the instrumental. "Good people, Hair Shavers and Dream Saviours. Let's welcome our winner to the stage. The indestructible, the indomitable, the incredible victor of the Golden Scissors 1987… Monsieur Vitale Crassoooooon!"

Vitale rose to go on stage, accepting back slaps and kisses from his table. He bowed in his golden suit and held his hands up to the adoring crowd. The judges, emerging from the wings, clapped towards the beaming Frenchman. Al took the microphone.

"Well, Monsieur Crassoon, it has been a momentous competition. You have battled through many mishaps, but still produced outstanding, innovative results. We are thrilled to present you with the Golden Scissors of 1987!"

Vitale stood in anticipation, his mustache quivering. Nothing happened, and the audience was tired of clapping. Al looked stage-left for the trophy to be wheeled out.

"The trophy please, Emmy-Lou!" he called out.

The music stopped and a percussionist from the quartet made a drum roll. There was an awkward moment: Vitale standing expectantly, Al staring into the wings, the audience miraculously silent. The drum roll drumming. Emmy-Lou ran on stage empty-handed, a look of horror on her face.

"It's gone!" she squealed. "The trophy, it's not there!"

The drum roll finished in one final thump.

A wave of murmurs went through the diners. There was a beat of silence, then a blast of trumpets. A spray of sparklers rushed across the front of the stage, followed by a flurry of confetti. A clanking noise came from the top rear of the auditorium. The audience and those on the stage raised their heads to the ceiling. A wiry man wearing a white studded leather jacket and matching pants shot down a rope. He held the Golden Scissors in his arms, and as he flew onto the stage, everyone gasped.

"Wiz?" Sylvia and Humphrey said in unison.

The spectators were on their feet, and as they each realized who had arrived, they clapped and cheered. The judges grinned, and Vitale's mustache quivered up at the ends as his trophy careered towards him.

Wiz landed on the stage to tumultuous applause. He unclipped himself from the rope and took the microphone from Al, who hugged him. He handed the trophy to Emmy-Lou, who kissed him. Sylvia's sore jaw hung open. Where on earth had he come from?

Wiz smoothed back his mass of white hair, which was tied back in a plait. Then, removing a small hairdryer from inside his jacket, he blasted it in the air three times and yelled out, "Surprise!"

The room erupted again. Sylvia and Humphrey looked at each other in amazement. Wiz hooted a laugh of glee and gestured for quiet.

"I've been keeping up to date with the competition and, my dear friends, I'm so sorry I could not come earlier. However, I'm delighted to get here just in time to present this fellow here with the Golden Scissors award. Congratulations, Vitale. Well done!"

Emmy-Lou handed him the Golden Scissors, and he hoisted the award at Vitale. With a huge grin, Vitale gave a small bow and held the trophy aloft. All the hairdressers stood up, celebrating Wiz's appearance as much as Vitale's victory. Wiz and Vitale shook hands and then hugged. Al did the same, and Emmy-Lou kissed him on both cheeks, one, twice, three times. At the side of the stage, Gene appeared.

"What's he doing here?" Sylvia hissed.

Sylvia watched Gene's face. Though he had a fixed smile, there was a look of fear in his eyes. Before Gene could get near them, Ava Rice burst back onto the stage. Everyone else exited as the spotlight fixed on her and she belted out another number.

Sylvia jumped up and ran backstage. Already, a knot of eager people surrounded Wiz; everyone clamoring to talk to him. She elbowed her way through.

"Wiz, where have you been?" Sylvia asked. He looked as lean as ever and well-toned. She swore he looked younger every time she saw him.

Wiz hugged her. "And hello to you too, Sylvia. I've been on my own mission, my dear. Now tell me. Do you have news?"

"Yes, I do…" For the first time all week, Sylvia's shoulders released. Just as she was about to explain, the hulking back of Gene cut in front of her.

"Wiz! Welcome, welcome. You should, er… could have warned… let me know you were coming."

"Gene, my good fellow. I do love a surprise, don't you?"

Sylvia pushed around Gene's bulk. "Well, that's good, as I have made some surprising discoveries. Can I talk to you in private?"

"Give the man a break," Gene interrupted. "Come, come—let's find you a room."

"No, no, Wiz, please…" she implored.

"To be frank, Wiz buddy, this lady has been throwing around some wild accusations."

"Your brother murdered two people and then tried to kill me with your cleaning product."

"You provoked him."

"I did not. I thought you were the murderer," she yelled.

"You see? Wildly ridiculous," he said to Wiz. "As I said to the police, I am deeply regretful that you went through that and for the loss of those fine men," Gene said with a look of concern etched on his face. "I no longer recognize him as my brother."

Wiz looked concerned. "Good heavens! Are you OK, my dear?"

Sylvia wasn't OK. It hurt to breathe and talk, but at least she wasn't dead. She nodded.

On the stage, Ava Rice's song came to a close. A hotel manager hurried to the group. "Lunch is about to be served. Could everyone make their way to their tables, please?"

"Let us speak after our meal. I've had a terribly long journey and I'm ravenous!" Wiz said.

Gene's dazzling smile was back. He put his arm behind Wiz's shoulder and steered him away.

44

S ylvia arrived back at her table. She scowled as she lowered herself into her chair.

"Did you talk to him?" Humphrey asked.

"I tried, but Gene has commandeered him."

The waiting staff served soup, then plates of delicious food, but Sylvia found it hard to eat, and not only because of her bruised jaw and trouble with breathing. Gene sat next to Wiz on the neighboring table, telling jokes, working the table, his white teeth flashing. He slapped Wiz on the back and they all laughed. Clippy was the only one not joining in. She said something to the guests, and the conversation subdued. The other diners looked down, no longer laughing. Sylvia wished she could hear what they were saying. The quartet played a heartfelt version of 'I've had the Time of my Life', drowning out any chance of eavesdropping. As the desserts were served, people swapped tables and mingled. Sylvia couldn't contain herself any longer. She had to tell Wiz that Gene was the snake. As soon as Gene was busy with a group of squealing apprentices, Sylvia took her chance and pulled up a chair next to Wiz.

"Ah! Sylvia, my dear. I'm so glad you're here. I've been hearing about the terrible events of this week. Poor Giuseppe. I knew him well many years ago, but we had lost touch. And our own Jerry. So shocking, so shocking." Wiz shook his head.

"I know. That's what I wanted to talk to you about. It's…"

Still shaking his head, he interrupted. "My dear, would you take the stage and give a tribute to our dear departed friends?"

"Me? On stage?"

"Why yes. You always say the right words."

"Wiz, I think that's your forte. As head of UGH…"

She trailed off, wondering if she should mention his role with HUH.

"I fear I'll shed a tear if I try, but it feels fitting that we honor them before we all part our ways."

"Um…"

Wiz's pale blue eyes searched her face.

"OK," she swallowed.

Wiz took her hand and led her onto the stage. He signaled for the quartet to stop and tapped the microphone. "My dear friends," he said. "I hear there have been some terrible crimes committed here this week. I understand the murderer has been caught and detained. So, I have asked my good friend Sylvia to speak about Giuseppe and Jerry. Please give her your attention."

Sylvia cleared her throat and gazed upon the sea of faces that were untidily arranged around the room.

"Uh, hello."

Gene watched, tight-jawed. Humphrey leaned back in his chair grinning. Vitale looked like an expectant puppy. She cleared her throat.

"When I arrived at the Pharaoh's Palace hotel earlier this week, I saw a bunch of happy people. A crowd excited to put their scissor skills against each other in good spirit and honor. But when the hair was parted, and the skin was scratched, I saw a deep, dark emptiness."

Everyone went quiet.

"This emptiness is a cavern of wanting, of desire that cries to be filled. We have lost two loved associates this week. For what purpose?"

She paused. Not a breath could be heard.

"I'll tell you. For the urge to fill that space. For greed. And while the murderer has been caught, we should look into our own inner being to see if greed is digging a hole there.

"You might say Wesley Bustle murdered for love. No, he murdered because he couldn't get what he wanted. He took the lives of our friends because he was greedy for the love of a woman."

Sylvia glanced at Clippy, who had tears pouring down her cheeks.

"You might say Ramone cheated for glory. No, he cheated because he was greedy for fame and fortune, for the Golden Scissors."

A few boos spread through the room.

"You might say the gamblers who walk these casino floors risk their money for fun."

She looked at Humphrey.

"No, they are greedy for the thrill of winning."

She paused.

"We all harbor an emptiness, a yearning. There is no sin in that. What we must not do is throw our fellow humans under the limo to fulfill that desire. Because it is the people in our lives that bring meaning to the money, the fame, and the glory. It is by sharing with the good people in our world that they breathe life into the love we seek.

"The Golden Scissors is a symbol of success, but it is all of you who are the real prize. It is the ability to share in the winning that has the greatest value. A value that has been hugely lessened by the loss of Giuseppe and Jerry."

For once, the crowd responded quietly with raised glasses. Wiz, still standing beside her, clapped. "Beautifully put, my dear, thank you!"

This was her chance. Gene was watching from his table at the foot of the stage. Sylvia clicked the button to off on the microphone. The diners went back to their chatter and clinking of glasses.

"It's Gene, you know, behind the missing data," Sylvia said to Wiz.

"Gene? What are you saying, my dear?"

For some reason, there was a sudden lull in the noise of the room. Gene raised himself up. She glanced in his direction and saw him coming.

"Gene is infiltrating the hairdressing industry. He owns Hiliterati and the Higher Union of Hairdressers."

"Yes, I know. I'm on the board."

Al, Emmy-Lou and Gene approached the stage.

"I don't understand, Wiz. You've worked so hard for so many years to build it up. How can you be on a board that's cheating UGH, that's pushing out the Hair'd Honcho?"

There was movement in the wings as the judges approached via the stage steps. But Gene simply leaped onto the stage with his powerful thighs.

"Pushing out?" Wiz echoed.

"It's Gene who's stealing our data. He's the reason UGH is no longer receiving anything, and nobody even knows it's happening..."

Gene had yanked the cord of the microphone and it went crashing to the ground with an almighty 'bonk'. It was then Sylvia realized the mic was still on and the entire room had heard the conversation. There was a clamoring and confusion. A few shouted out, "What's going on?" "Stealing?"

Wiz furrowed his eyebrows, a calculation flickering across his face. He turned to Gene, who stood before him. Gene opened his hands wide and pulled his chin back.

"Wiz, this girl has been pestering me all week. I don't know why she has taken such a dislike to me, but this is all nonsense!"

"I saw the printouts on his desk."

"You saw them on my desk? How did you get into my room? How dare you! I'm calling hotel security!"

"That's nothing compared to what you're attempting!" She turned to Wiz. "He's tricking us all to sign up to selling his product or franchising his salons."

"Tricking? My business is all above board and legal."

"It's a scam. The small print is too small to read and in such obscure language, nobody knows what they're getting into!"

By now, the hairdressers had flocked to the edge of the stage.

"Tricking us?"

"Yes, Giuseppe, being the stickler he was, had actually read the small print. That's why he wouldn't agree to sell Fritz."

"It's up to everyone to read the terms. I have done nothing wrong here," Gene huffed.

"Maybe it could be argued that you have done nothing illegal, but it is unethical," Sylvia retorted. "Why are you involved with him, Wiz?"

"How could I have been so blind?" Wiz muttered.

"Hey buddy, we used each other. Am I right? We had a mutual need. I needed a product. You needed funding."

Sylvia cringed at Gene calling Wiz 'buddy'. No one had ever shown him that much disrespect.

"Yes, you did need my product." Wiz nodded.

"What product?" Sylvia asked.

"Fritz. I've been working on the formula for many years, but I needed an investor."

"Fritz is your invention?"

"Of course, my dear. Have you tried it?"

"Yes. It's amazing! That's why everybody is so keen to stock it and sell it."

"I've used Australian flora. There are so many qualities to tea tree, eucalyptus and myrtle."

"That's it. Eucalyptus... I couldn't pinpoint the scent."

Wiz beamed. "Thank you, so kind! Now, how to get out of this sticky mess? I never intended the business model to be a pyramid scheme."

Gene squared his enormous bulk to Wiz, towering over him. "Look buddy, you agreed to be on the committee of HUH in return for me manufacturing Fritz. You been getting all the minutes. You agreed to the change of reporting address. Business is business, am I right?"

"I did not receive the minutes, and I did not agree to the change of address," Wiz said slowly.

"Well, a no-show automatically goes to my vote; says so in the constitution." Gene dazzled the stage with his teeth.

Wiz's slight frame seemed to double in size. He took a breath in.

"Fritz will no longer be sold by Hiliterati."

Gene laughed. "I'm afraid you awarded me the license to sell it."

"And I am afraid I have the patent to do with it as I wish."

Gene's face fell. "The patent?"

"Yes, I took the precaution of registering my invention with the patents office."

"But you sold the formula to me!"

"Just the license which I am revoking."

Gene's fists closed, opened and closed again. The smile was replaced by a sneer. "Wes..." he remembered his assistant was no longer there. He spun on his sneakers and stalked off the stage.

"I shall be advising my friends in the aviation, music and beauty industries to look over their contracts too..." Wiz called after him.

The hairdressers booed Gene as he pushed through the room. He glared at them and slammed through the doors at the end of the gilded function suite.

45

The dining room cheered. The waiters weaved through with bottles of Beaujolais Nouveau and Champagne. Ava Rice sung more songs. Brandy and liqueurs accompanied coffee. Despite a long week, the hairdressers partied like it was 1999, and Emmy-Lou and the Toning Tongs finished with Prince's iconic song. Wiz jumped up on stage with them, playing the air guitar. Sylvia, awash with relief, knocked back every glass of whatever was offered. The pain in her jaw and ribs magically subsided, and she danced with Humphrey. He hung his tongue out.

"I need water. Come to the bar with me," he said.

"Hey, you've been like a Cheshire cat with a comb-over since yesterday. What's going on?" Sylvia said in the relative quiet of the bar.

Humphrey grinned and swayed his arms above his head, wiggling his hips. He clapped his hands and punched the air.

"Oh yeah, baby! Remember that bet I placed with Sandra?"

"Yeah, even though you promised me not to."

"Well, thanks to our detective work and uncovering that cheating pig, I won. A lot. She had stacked the odds against Vitale, and so, voila! You can tear up that guarantee you gave the casino. It's all paid up."

Sylvia's jaw dropped, which hurt. Instead, she held her hand up and they high-fived, interlacing fingers and he did a little dance. The murderer had been caught, the mystery solved, Humphrey had won the money he'd gambled back from his bet on Ramone, and she was in love. As she swayed to the music, she admitted to herself that Danny had not only saved her life but also captured her heart and the criminal.

They went back to the party and danced on the tables. As she closed her eyes, threw her arms in the air and ugly sang to Fleetwood Mac's 'Big Love', she heard her name. She looked down from the table to see Danny's eyes crinkling at her.

"Danny. My hero," she squealed and leaped into his arms.

He caught her and swung her around.

"Dance with me," she yelled over the music.

Emmy-Lou and her band brought the last song to a close. They bowed to uproar. The curtains dropped.

"Let's partay," Sylvia shrieked.

The hairdressers stumbled, danced and twirled out of the ballroom, unwilling to call it a night. Some dispersed to the casino, others to the disco.

"Let me show you the nightlife of Vegas," Danny suggested to Sylvia, Humphrey and Vitale.

They all roared a yes in unison.

The Strip was alive. Neon lights flashed through Sylvia's blurred eyes. Stretch limos cruised with bass pumping from inside. Tourists jostled the sidewalks. South American beats wafted out of doors. Disco ball lights flickered from clubs. The greasy smell of burgers mingled with exhaust fumes and cigarette smoke. Danny led them inside the Shark Club, the bouncer letting them through the queue like royalty. The music belted out and a mass of sweaty bodies grooved on the dance-floor. High-heeled women danced on podiums, multicolored lights strobed, and the clientèle were dressed in silver leotards, and teeny shorts with leg-warmers. Sylvia and Humphrey squealed and disco-ed their way behind Danny to the bar. He ordered shots which the barman lined up, and with a one, two, three, they downed the liquor. The party joined the writhing bodies, whooping and looping on the dance floor.

A few hours later, they stumbled out onto the street. Humphrey and Vitale held each other up. Sylvia twirled and swirled to the beat that still coursed through her veins, along with several more shots of tequila.

"Let's go dance some more," she slurred. "It's too early for bed." Though she had no idea of the time.

Danny caught her in his arms and kissed her. She melted into his solid chest and would have indeed slumped to the ground without his strong embrace. Humphrey and Vitale wobbled on and off the sidewalk, singing. A car sped by, sounding its horn.

Danny's eyes sparkled, and he laughed.

"Sylvia, I've never met a girl like you."

"Me neither," she said and giggled. "I mean, a boy, no..." she dropped her chin and tried to look serious... "a man like you."

She ran her fingers up his muscular arms and took his face in her hands. They kissed until air forced its way between them and into their lungs.

"Marry me," Danny murmured into her neck.

Sylvia pulled away. "What?"

He looked at her, his usually piercing gaze now goofy and soft. He dropped to one knee and took her hands.

"Will you marry me, Ms Sylvia Scutlash?"

"Marry you?" she giggled. "Marry you? Yes! Yes, I will, Detective Danny Good."

He jumped up and cheered, catching her in his arms and spinning them around. Their lips hungry for each other, they embraced. Then Sylvia unattached and yelled, "Hump, Monsieur! I'm getting married!"

Her friends paused their precarious jaywalking and ran back. "She's getting married? Sylvia's getting married!"

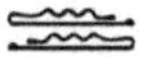

And so it was that Sylvia Scutlash woke up the next morning, draped across Danny Good. Every part of her body ached. Her head, her lips, her jaw, her ribs, between her legs and her feet. She opened and closed her crusty eyes and peeled her tongue off the roof of her mouth. She rubbed her hand over her face and caught sight of a ring on her finger. Slowly, in shock, she turned her head to the man sleeping next to her. Fleeting memories flashed through her mind. She gawked at the ring. She rolled over to gaze upon his face. So handsome, so perfect. So married?

"Danny, Danny." She clutched the sheet to her and wiggled his shoulder. "Wake up!"

He yawned and saw Sylvia. A huge smile spread across his face. "Good morning, Mrs Good." He pulled her towards him.

After she pulled away from his delicious lips, she said, "So, it's true? We got married?"

Danny laughed. "You don't remember?"

"Yes, yes, I do... And that's exactly what you said last night."

"But we hardly know each other."

"Oh but we do," he said, stroking his fingers up her arm. She shivered.

"Wait until Jez hears about this." She sat bolt upright. "Jiminy

Clippers! Jez—it's her wedding next weekend. The hen night is in three days. I'm her bridesmaid and best girl."

She looked at the clock. "Oh flicking hell, it's already eleven! My flight leaves in four hours. I have to pack."

"Mrs Good," Danny drawled in a voice so delicious a thrill shot through her. He grabbed her and drew her in, breathing in her hair, which probably did not smell so good after the previous night.

"It's our honeymoon," he whispered. "Stay."

She melted into his arms for a moment, then pulled away.

"I have to go."

She jumped up, swaying with the pain that fought for supremacy in every part of her body.

"I've got to get back to Australia. Jez is getting married and I need to be at the salon..."

The words tumbled out of her mouth. Reality hit. Danny raked his hands through his hair. Sylvia threw her clothes into her suitcase, washed her face and tried to keep her stomach from escaping through her mouth. They agreed she would go home and see Jez married. Danny would organise their honeymoon as soon as he could get away from work, and Jez was back from her honeymoon.

"Come on, let's have some breakfast," he said. "You need to go home on a full stomach."

Sylvia burst into tears.

"Hey, come here." Danny gently drew her back under the sheets and kissed away her tears.

"It's been a long time since someone cared about me having a full stomach, or holding me, or, or even looking out for me..."

She sobbed for a moment before passion overcame them.

MONDAY

46

S howered, packed and satiated, they left the room. Danny had placed the plastic wedding wreath from the Nile Aisle chapel back on her head. In the restaurant, they filled their plates from the breakfast buffet. Sylvia was both starving and unable to eat a thing. She looked at her husband.

"I have to say goodbye to Bonnie."

"I'll wait for you in the foyer." Danny took her hand and kissed her palm, holding onto it until she finally pulled away. She bit back tears, missing him already.

Salon Sphinx was a hive of activity as usual, but this time the guest hairdressers were packing away and the staff tidying up.

"Hey Bonnie, I've come to say goodbye," Sylvia said.

"Oh honey, it's been a pleasure meeting you. How are you feeling?"

"Still sore." Sylvia tentatively wiggled her jaw that sported a gray bruise. "How long are you staying here before you head to New York?"

"A few more weeks before I hand over to the new manager. By the time I'm settled back in New York, the probate will be sorted, and I can get into the Brooklyn shops."

"It's so exciting. I'm really happy for you. Will you look after Marco when he gets out?"

"Yes, we all need second chances, don't we?"

"That's my life motto, dove!"

Sylvia hugged Bonnie and promised to visit her one day. She headed to the rooftop bar to take in one last look over Las Vegas. The city was fresh and sparkling in the new day as the sun rose, coloring the backdrop of hills a soft red. She and Danny had yet to make plans for their life but she couldn't wait to be back here again soon.

"Vegas puts on a show no matter what time of the day."

Sylvia turned to see Al.

"It sure does," she said.

They stood side by side in awkward silence. Sylvia wanted to broach Al's indiscretion.

"You said that bribery never happened in the Golden Scissors."

"I also said all that's gold does not glitter. I don't always heed my own wisdom. Such is my weakness."

"I don't blame you, Al. Gene had everyone eating out of his hand. We all have our Achilles' heel."

Al turned and looked at her.

"I should have listened to you. You are a marvel, sister."

Sylvia smiled.

"So, what will happen to Gene?"

"The FBI has taken him in. He'll be tied up with them for a good few weeks. Hopefully, he'll have screwed up and broken the law somewhere, but he can afford a decent lawyer."

Sylvia humphed. "But once the newspapers get hold of the story, no one will touch him with a long-handled hairbrush."

"I hope so. I will do what I can."

He took her hand and turned her finger so the ring glinted in the light.

"I see congratulations are in order?"

Sylvia smiled. "An unexpected outcome..." she bit her lip.

"It'll work out one way or another. Love knows no distance."

"Talking of distance; did Wiz stick around?"

"He had to leave, but he asked me to give you this. Said he'd be in touch."

She took the manila envelope Al held out.

"What is it?"

Al tilted his head to one side and shrugged his shoulders.

"I think my next mission will be to find out exactly what Wizard Blowave has been doing to put UGH in such danger. He really needs someone to manage it if he's going away all the time."

Al nodded. "Well, until next time, my silvery sister."

Al kissed her hand and left her with one last glance over the city.

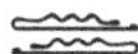

The foyer of the Pharaoh's Palace whirled and swirled with bodies, streaks of neon and the perfumed aroma of hair product. The hanging golden scissors were being lowered to make way for a giant pair of stilettos, which depicted the upcoming fashion show. Sylvia took a breath in and smiled. She found Sol's bauble. He would be pleased that Ramone hadn't taken his title. Sol deserved to keep it. She winked at the glass ball.

"Hey doll. All packed and ready to go?" Clippy had emerged from the elevator and joined her.

Sylvia nodded. Clippy gushed on. "I cannot wait to come over to Australia. A whole new world."

"You're going to love it, dove. And all the salons are going to love Ultra Gold Hair."

"Wiz is a good boss, isn't he?"

Sylvia wasn't sure if she was asking a question or making a statement. She felt sorry for Clippy, who had poured her heart and soul into Fritz, only to find the company was a scam. Still, once the rebrand had happened, she would be able to regain the trust of the salon owners.

"He is, dove. He really is, just a little tricky to pin down sometimes."

"I'll manage," she said brightly. "I'm good at pinning." And Sylvia knew she would.

Danny arrived and encircled her waist, snuggling his face into her neck. She squealed and spun around. She rested there a moment, breathing in the smell of his clean shirt, feeling the seam of his linen lapel on her cheek, the relief, the joy of being held by a strong man.

The elevator dinged again, and Humphrey struggled out with his suitcases.

"Get a room, you two!" he joked. "V is coming down to say goodbye."

"So he's staying on to style for next week's fashion show?" Sylvia said.

"He is, and to bask in the glory of winning. He has three interviews this afternoon with Tittle Tattle, Dish and Blather."

On cue, Vitale arrived and swaggered towards them, receiving congratulations along the way.

"Sylvia, ma cherie. I want to zank you. I couldn't 'av managed without you and Humphrey."

"Always at your service, Monsieur."

Vitale's face froze. The elevator had opened, and Ramone and his one remaining supporter, Sandra Tress, stepped out. Vitale turned to face him. Ramone stopped in his tracks. The lobby fell silent.

Vitale cocked his head a fraction in greeting and expectation. Ramone narrowed his eyes. Vitale glared at him. Ramone tipped his head to one side, his eyes scanning the room. Vitale raised his eyebrows. Humphrey and Sylvia, flanking Vitale, crossed their arms. Vitale's mustache tilted as he nibbled on his bottom lip. Ramone's nostrils flared. Sandra Tress chewed gum noisily. Ramone took a step closer. Vitale put his hands on his hip, his heeled boot tapping. Ramone's stiffness left his body. Relenting, he marched forward and held his hand out.

"Well done. You beat the greatest. See you next time." Ramone ground the words out.

Vitale returned the handshake, his lips fighting a smile that shook his mustache. Ramone released Vitale's hand, and the hubbub of the lobby returned. Ramone and Sandra turned to leave.

"I guess that's the closest you'll get to an apology," Humphrey said, shaking his head.

But Danny said, "Before you go, Mr Figurelles." The lobby quietened again.

Ramone turned back and saw Danny retrieving a pair of handcuffs from his pocket. "Your under…"

Ramone shoved Sandra out of the way and bolted for the exit. Not missing a beat, Danny grabbed the wreath from Sylvia's head and threw it at the polygamist, catching him behind the knees. Two of Danny's officers closed in and hauled Ramone to his feet. "Book him. I'll meet you at the station soon."

Sylvia hugged her man. She had never felt so happy.

"Well guys, it's time to say goodbye," Sylvia said to Humphrey and Vitale. "My taxi will be here any minute. I hope to see you both soon."

"I promise I'll come to Hardup one of these days, sweetheart. Just promise me you'll sort out that mop!" Humphrey tugged on the now floppy silver tress of hair that was once a unicorn horn.

"Now I've got some Fritz—I mean Ultra Gold—my hair is so

manageable." She ran her fingers through it.

"Still, a good haircut can do wonders for a girl's love life," Humphrey said.

"Which has already proved true," she sighed, holding out her ringed finger, letting the rhinestone glitter under the bright lights.

Humphrey and Vitale beamed.

"What a night!"

"Taxi cab for Ms Sylvia Scutlash," a porter called out.

"Taxi cab for Mrs Sylvia Good," Danny said.

Sylvia let out a breath of happiness, sorrow and exhaustion. She leaned into her husband, wishing she could rest there forever. She peeled away and Danny took her hand. With Humphrey and Vitale on her other side, they walked out to the sweeping steps. A cavalcade of white limos made its way around the circular fountain to the front of the Pharaoh's Palace hotel. The windows were darkened, and the number plate KK1 was followed by KK2 and KK3.

"Ah, my client 'as arrived," Vitale declared.

Glamorous bodies slid out of the limos as Danny guided Sylvia to her waiting cab.

"Thanks for saving my life," she whispered as he opened the door.

Danny took her face in his hands and kissed her tenderly. She received it, tasted it and imprinted it in her memory.

"Goodbye, Danny."

"Goodbye, Sylvia."

She got into the car.

"Bye, guys!"

"Au revoir, ma cherie. Au revoir."

"Bye, possum."

The taxi pulled away. Sylvia stuck her head out of the window and waved until they were out of sight.

"You know it's someone special when the windows are darkened," the driver said.

"Mmmm," Sylvia responded as she turned back around to look ahead. She was too busy remembering the soft liquid brown eyes, the smooth black hair, the electric touch of Danny's fingers to worry about who was arriving at the Pharaoh's Palace. Sylvia was too distracted to see the famous despot, Karla Kreeper, haute couture designer and her entourage march into the foyer. She was ready to go home to the Wavy Lady Hair Salon, for now.

The End

EPILOGUE

Sylvia pushed open the familiar door of the Wavy Lady hair salon. She breathed in the scent of freshly laundered towels and shampoo. She wondered why the lights were all off.

"Coooeeee!" she called out.

She flicked the lights on. The place was untidy. The floor unswept, towels dumped over the back of chairs, the trolleys a mess.

"Jez? Are you here?"

One of the chairs squeaked. Jez sat in it, cradling a glass of liquor.

"Jez, dove. What's going on?"

Jez wiped her snotty nose. "He called it off."

"What?"

"Clive. Last night. Said he wanted his independence. Said he couldn't commit after all..."

She gave out a sob.

"Oh, dove!"

"They're all bloody buggers, Sylv. I don't need him." She slammed her glass onto the shelf under the mirror. "I'm sorry. I had to cancel the clients today. The place is a mess. I've let you down."

Sylvia dumped her bag on the desk. Her wedding ring glittered in the light. She slid it off, put it in her bag, and rushed to Jez.

"Oh Jez. I'm so sorry. Don't worry about the salon. It's you I care about. Let's have a cup of tea with that gin and tell me all about it."

In between sobs, Jez told Sylvia about the row they'd had and how she had thrown the ring at him.

"Who needs a man, hey?" Jez said, big fat tears pouring down her cheeks. "Even you can't find a decent bloke, Sylv. We can be single together. You and I."

Sylvia nodded weakly. She couldn't tell Jez that not only was she married, but she had also been promoted to head of UGH, which meant she'd be taking care of a lot more than Jez and the Wavy Lady Hair salon.

DEAR READER

This is me super-stoked that you've read my book!

I hope you enjoyed reading about Sylvia's adventure in the bright lights of Las Vegas as much as I did, especially revisiting the eighties. If you did, it would be flicking brilliant if you could leave me a review. This really helps me get the book into more hands, which makes for happy story lovers (and a very happy author!).

It need only be a sentence or two.

Now, you know there's more to come, don't you? The next time we meet Sylvia, she is ten years older and heading off to the warmth and vibrancy of India.

If you would like to keep up to date with my writing, please join my newsletter email list:

https://www.subscribepage.com/highlights

Until next time, may you have many good hair days,

Karen X

Playlist

It's been so much fun going back to the 1980s, the decade of my teens. Of course, music played a big part of my life back then, so I couldn't resist compiling a playlist of all those daggy, funky and iconic tunes!

Go to Spotify or https://tinyurl.com/nb3ppmcuto listen. Enjoy!

1. Welcome to the Jungle - Gun 'N Roses

2. Where the Streets Have No Name - U2

3. Goldfinger - Shirley Bassey

4. I Could Never Take the Place of Your Man - Prince

5. Who's That Girl - Madonna

6. Walk Like an Egyptian - The Bangles

7. Mony, Mony - Billy Idol

8. A Gamble Either Way - Dolly Parton, I Heard A Rumour - Bananarama

9. China in Your Hands - T'Pau

10. Don't Get Me Wrong - The Pretenders

11. The Devil Inside - INXS

12. Never Gonna Give You Up - Rick Astley

13. Bad - Michael Jackson

14. New Sensation - INXS

15. When Smokey Sings - ABC

16. Shakedown - Bob Seger

17. Paradise City - Guns 'N Roses

18. Alone - Heart

19. Little Lies - Fleetwood Mac

20. Faith - George Michael

21. What's My Scene - Hoodoo Gurus

22. U Got the Look - Prince, Gold - Spandau Ballet

23. True Faith - New Order

24. Lady in Red - Chris Deburgh, I Wanna Dance with Somebody
- Whitney Houston

25. Heat of the Night - Bryan Adams

26. Get Outta my Dreams and into my Car - Billy Ocean

27. Funky Town - Pseudo Echo

28. Eye of the Tiger - Survivor

29. Material World - Madonna

30. Unchain My Heart - Joe Cocker

31. Animal - Def Leppard

32. Wanted Dead or Alive - Bon Jovi, Victory - Kool and the Gang

33. Beds are Burning - Midnight Oil, Don't Dream it's Over -
Crowded House

34. Head to Toe - Lisa Lisa and Cult Jam

35. Skeletons - Stevie Wonder

36. Pet Shop Boys - It's a Sin

37. Golden Years - David Bowie, The Winner Takes it All - Abba

38. I've had the Time of my Life - Bill Medley and Jennifer Warnes

39. 1999 - Prince

40. Big Love - Fleetwood Mac

41. Nothing's Gonna Stop Us Now - Starship

CROSSWORD

Email me at karen@redfeather.com.au for the answers!

Wavy Lady Crossword

ACROSS

4. Has the most fun (5)

5. Sings along in the parlor (5)

6. Is such sweet sorrow (7)

7. Sounds like the end for a change in color (3)

8. Skirting above the eyes (6)

9. Washed out El on the beach (6)

12. Take the edge off shame and leaves a bad smell in the shower (7)

14. Ask the Lord for after fixing what's on your head (9)

17. An upset Pericles has shorn off the pea (8)

19. Duck for this do (3)

21. Hairstyle with a comb in it (7)

22. Who is the fairest of them all (6)

23. Weeps over the broom (5)

24. A poodle's favorite do (4)

DOWN

1. Chook's headdress (4)

2. Tittle tattle (6)

3. Curling _______ (5)

5. Fashion the hair (5)

6. Gee-gee switch ties it back (8)

9. What the wind might do to your washing (7)

10. Sheath worn around the shoulders (4)

11. Used to pass the time under the dryer (8)

13. Sheath surrounding the root of a hair (8)

15. Chop chop (8)

16. This hairstyle smells fishy (6)

18. It's a close one (5)

20. Untangle shrub (5)

About the Author

Karen is originally from the UK but has lived in sunny Perth, Western Australia since 2008, which practically makes her a local. With a writerly father and a lifetime with her head and heart stuck in books, Karen has aspired to be an author for as long as she can remember.

After writing her 'experimental first book', (a fantasy novel) in 2015, she has moved on to the fun genre of cozy mysteries. Still working on becoming an overnight success, she continues to carve out a creative life whilst working as a freelance copyeditor and mothering her two teenagers and a fluffy white cat.

For more information head to:

www.redfeather.com.au

or

www.karenperadonauthor.com

Follow her on socials at:

www.facebook.com/karenperadon
www.instagram.com/redfeatherpublishing

Also by Karen:

Dying Roots – book 1 in the Wavy Lady series
Reviews
"I'd never think you could find such an amazing story set in the world of hairdressers, but here it is."

"Laughed out loud and was at the edge of my seat several times egging the lovable protagonist on. Bravo!"

"I really loved this book! What a treat to get back to the 1970s, and get to know the heroine of this story, Sylvia!"

"A fun book full of twists and turns, as Sylvia is sent on a mission from "Down Under" to London to rescue another hairdresser's salon. I love the constant play on words for the names of the people in the story! Sylvia is also searching for information about her family, and the father that sent her to an Australian convent at a young age. Read along as Sylvia makes new friends and uncovers a few enemies in Britain. An interesting read full of Aussie expressions and London lore!"